A SCANDALOUS BARGAIN

DARCY BURKE

A SCANDALOUS BARGAIN

The Pretenders

Set in the world of The Untouchables, indulge in the saga of a trio of siblings who excel at being something they're not. Can a dauntless Bow Street Runner, a devastated viscount, and a disillusioned Society miss unravel their secrets?

A Scandalous Bargain

Tricked into marriage five years ago, Thomas Devereaux, Lord Rockbourne is suddenly a widower. Rumors abound that his wife's death may not have been an accident and given the troubling secrets Thomas keeps buried, even he isn't entirely sure. But when a woman sees what happened, he agrees to accept her help to disguise the facts in exchange for not divulging her suspicious behavior. Their arrangement grows more complicated under the force of a scorching mutual attraction.

Abandoned by her father—a duke—after the death

of her mother—his beloved mistress—Beatrix Linley has fought to become a daughter he could be proud of, that he would regret leaving. She becomes the toast of the Season until her penchant for pilfering pretty things threatens to expose the illicit past she needs desperately to remain hidden. Soon the scandal and darkness both Beatrix and Thomas fear comes to light, compelling them to finally face their demons—and potentially driving them apart forever.

Want to share your love of my books with like-minded readers? Want to hang with me and get inside scoop? Then don't miss my exclusive Facebook groups!

Darcy's Duchesses for historical readers
Burke's Book Lovers for contemporary readers

PROLOGUE

December 1804
Mrs. Goodwin's Ladies' Seminary

*B*eatrix Linley tried very hard not to cry as another coach left the school, conveying its occupants home for the holiday season. Though the headmistress had told Beatrix that no one was coming for her, she refused to believe it. How could her father ignore her? It was bad enough he hadn't written over the past eight months that she'd been there, let alone brought her home for *any* holiday whatsoever.

"But this is Yuletide."

"What was that?" Selina Blackwell looked up from her book. They were the only two girls left in the dormitory this morning. The last of the others were on their way home until after Epiphany.

"Nothing," Beatrix said as she looked out the window once more. The day was as dark and gloomy as she felt, with gray clouds that threatened rain. It was probably a horrid day to travel. She'd take comfort in that.

"Oh!" Maria stopped abruptly as she entered the dormitory. "I didn't realize there was anyone left here." Her smug tone grated on Beatrix.

Dark curls bobbing, Maria walked in, looking from Beatrix to Selina and back to Beatrix. "I suppose I shouldn't be surprised you two are still here. No one coming to get you?"

Selina, who at fourteen was a year younger than Maria, fixed her with a bored stare. "Don't bother to ask questions you already know the answer to or that you really don't care about."

Maria pursed her lips. "There's no need to be churlish."

Selina's eyes narrowed slightly. "Isn't there?"

Beatrix stifled a laugh and immediately wished she hadn't. Maria wouldn't bother, so why should she?

"Maria!" A familiar singsong voice carried into the dormitory.

Bracing herself, Beatrix turned her back to the door and focused on an oak tree on the other side of the drive.

"Are you ready?" Deborah asked. She and Maria were close friends.

Though Beatrix wasn't facing the door, she could tell Deborah was now in the dormitory.

"Just about," Maria said. "I came back to fetch my third-favorite pair of gloves. I can't believe I forgot them." *Third-favorite.* Beatrix only had three pairs of gloves. Selina only had one. Maria and

Deborah took every opportunity to show how they were superior.

Beatrix pivoted slightly so she could watch them, mostly so she'd know when they were gone.

Maria went to the dresser beside her bed. "Where are they?" she shrieked, opening every drawer and rifling through the contents. When she'd been through every one, she spun about and looked at Deborah, who was standing behind her, hands on her hips. "They're gone."

Deborah turned toward Selina. "I bet she took them."

Selina peered at them over the top of her book, still appearing disinterested. "What would you like to bet?"

"Nothing," Deborah spat. "I didn't mean it like that."

"Then choose your words more carefully." Selina returned her gaze to her book.

Deborah stalked over to Selina's bed where Selina reclined as she read. "I'll say whatever I please."

Selina exhaled, her eyes not leaving the book. "I suppose. Perhaps you could just do it more quietly. *Some* of us like to read." The insult was clear—at least to Beatrix. Deborah did not apply herself to her studies, a trait the teachers never seemed to mind while others were punished for the same transgression. That was because Deborah's father was an earl.

Beatrix distinctly recalled what had happened when she'd been reprimanded for not keeping up with her studies. She'd asked why it mattered since her father was a duke. Miss Everly had said it mattered not at all because of the circumstances of her birth, that no one cared *who* her father was.

"You think you're better than me?" Deborah demanded. Beatrix held her breath as she watched the tall, brown-haired Deborah stand over Selina's bed while Selina continued to read.

"Answer me!" Deborah slapped the book out of Selina's hands and onto her lap.

Selina pushed out a breath as she picked up the book and set it aside. Then she slowly stood from the bed. Deborah was tall, but Selina had her by an inch.

"Yes."

The single word sent Deborah into a fit of rage. She launched herself at Selina, shoving her back onto the bed.

Selina grabbed the other girl's arms and dragged her down too. In a quick motion, Selina rolled on top of Deborah and spit in her face. "Better than you in every way that counts. No one cares about your stupid earl father."

"At least I have a father," Deborah snarled as she tried to wrestle Selina off her.

"At least I have a brain," Selina said. "Someday your father will die, and I'll still be smarter than you."

Deborah sucked in a breath. She brought her hand back and slapped Selina across the face.

Selina's face darkened as her eyes narrowed. Her lip curled, and Beatrix actually felt a tremor of fear.

Grabbing the front of Deborah's dress, Selina stood up and tugged Deborah with her. She pivoted, pulling Deborah toward her until their noses nearly met. "Touch me again and I'll make you hurt in ways you've never imagined. You think I'm some sort of heathen. Don't give me a reason to show you just how right you are." Selina shoved her hard so that she fell to the floor.

"I found them!" Maria's declaration trilled through the dormitory. She stood near Beatrix's dresser.

Too focused on the quarrel between Selina and Deborah, Beatrix hadn't noticed what Maria had been doing. Now, Beatrix saw Maria's third-favorite gloves dangling from her fingertips over the open bottom drawer of Beatrix's dresser.

Panic stole Beatrix's breath. "I...I didn't take them." She didn't *remember* taking them.

"Then why are they in your dresser?" Maria demanded, her dark eyes flashing.

"Because she's a thief," Deborah said, pushing herself up from the floor. She eyed Selina warily as she walked to Maria. "Let's go tell Miss Everly."

"No!" Beatrix ran toward them but stopped short before she reached them. "I swear I didn't take them!"

Maria bared her teeth. "They were in *your* drawer. You're a liar as well as a thief."

"Don't forget bastard," Deborah said with unabashed glee. "And daughter of a whore."

Tears stung Beatrix's eyes. "Take that back," she whispered because it was all she could get past the knot in her throat.

"Why?" Deborah asked, her deep-set eyes blinking in mock-innocence. "It's all true."

"That doesn't make it nice." Selina had come to stand beside Beatrix.

Maria waved her gloves toward Beatrix. "When Miss Everly hears, you'll be punished. You may even be sent away. Where will you go? It's clear your father doesn't want you, and your mother's dead. Perhaps you can go to whatever orphanage *she* came from." Maria pointed at Selina.

"Oh, I didn't come from an orphanage." Selina's lips spread into a slow, rather malevolent smile. "I came from the East End of London. Want to know what's hidden in my bottom drawer?" She leaned toward them, her eyes gleaming with pride. "A *knife.*"

Maria and Deborah gasped in unison.

"Miss Everly!" Maria yelled. "Miss Everly!"

"Bloody hell," Selina swore. "I don't actually have a knife, you dolts."

Beatrix turned her head toward Selina. "Why did you say that?"

"Because for a moment, I was as stupid as them." She clenched her jaw. "I took your ugly gloves," Selina said loudly. "It was a joke."

"A joke on the bastard?" Deborah asked. "Why else would you put them in her dresser?"

"Someone was coming, and I had to stash them somewhere." Selina gave Beatrix an apologetic glance.

Beatrix wasn't angry. How could she be when Selina was covering for her? While Beatrix didn't recall stealing the gloves, she knew she had. It wasn't the first time something had gone missing only for Beatrix to find the item in her dresser. However, Beatrix didn't think anyone else had known.

"Deborah! Maria!" Miss Everly's voice carried into the dormitory. "Your coach is here."

"Coming, Miss Everly!" Deborah called before giving Beatrix and Selina an arrogant smile. "We'll inform the headmistress of your theft before we go. Come, Maria. I'm so excited for you to visit my father's estate for the holidays." As if Beatrix—and everyone else—wasn't completely aware that Deborah had invited Maria to accompany her.

"Do you think they'll still be here when we return?" Maria asked as they turned toward the door.

"If there's any justice at all, they won't. They don't belong here anyway." Deborah sent a vicious look over her shoulder before disappearing from sight.

Beatrix slumped, her body quivering.

Selina's arm came around her shoulders. "Don't worry. They'll probably just make me eat porridge for a week and have me clean the scullery."

"What if they send you away?" The tears Beatrix had fought to keep at bay threatened once more.

Selina shrugged. "Wouldn't be the worst thing that's happened to me."

Beatrix nearly said it *would* be the worst thing that had happened to her, but that wasn't true. She'd lost her beloved mother and been sent here by her father, whom she hadn't even seen since Mama had died. They'd been a happy family, mostly, until Mama had gotten sick. Beatrix knew he had another family just as she knew he loved her and her mother more. How many times had she heard him tell Mama he loved her and that he hated to leave her to go to his other home?

No, Beatrix had lost her family and that was absolutely the worst thing that could happen. She looked askance at Selina. Did she even have a family? Selina didn't like to talk about her past. In fact, today was the most she'd ever shared about it.

"Did you really come from East London?" Beatrix asked. Having grown up in Bath, she didn't know much about London, but she'd heard the East End was less desirable.

Selina withdrew her arm. "I did."

Beatrix recalled the way in which Selina had threatened the horrible Deborah and the confidence she'd exuded. Envy swelled in Beatrix's chest. "I wish I could be as brave as you."

"You will be," Selina said as if there were no question. "Remember, I have a few years on you."

"How will I learn to be brave if you're sent away?" Beatrix asked.

Before Selina could answer, Mrs. Goodwin, the headmistress, came into the dormitory. Both Beatrix and Selina straightened and greeted her as they'd been trained to do since the moment they'd arrived.

It was rare that Mrs. Goodwin came to the dormitory. Miss Everly was typically in charge of them outside of lessons.

Mrs. Goodwin smiled, her kind blue eyes assessing. Beatrix brushed at a speck on her apron.

"Miss Ledbetter informed me you stole her gloves." The headmistress looked at Selina. "Is that true, Miss Blackwell?"

"It is, Mrs. Goodwin." Selina spoke unflinchingly, her chin strong and high. "It was meant to be a prank. I regret that I had to put the gloves in Miss Linley's drawer. She had absolutely nothing to do with any of it."

Mrs. Goodwin appeared skeptical. She looked back and forth between Selina and Beatrix. Finally, her gaze settled on Beatrix. "Is that true?"

Beatrix swallowed. Selina gently nudged her on the back of the hand. "Yes." The lie burned Beatrix's tongue, but it seemed Selina wanted her to give it.

Pressing her lips together, Mrs. Goodwin's gaze turned stern. "I like you girls. Miss Blackwell, you work very hard, and Miss Linley, you have a bright and lovely outlook despite your…troubles. However, you simply must work harder to get along with the other girls. You're…different from them, and as much as I hate to say it, people will hold you to different expectations." Her features softened. "I should know."

Beatrix wanted to ask how, but Mrs. Goodwin inhaled deeply and continued. "Miss Everly will hand down an appropriate punishment, Miss Blackwell."

"Yes, Mrs. Goodwin."

The headmistress looked at them another moment. "Don't fret, girls. I'll see you at dinner." She winked at them before turning and leaving the dormitory.

Beatrix let out the breath she'd been holding and turned to face Selina. "Why did you lie for me?"

"Because I know you steal things and can't help it."

"How—"

"I'm observant." Selina's pale brows pitched over her eyes. "You must try to help it—stealing, I mean. A pair of gloves or a spoon from the dining hall won't bring you too much grief, but should you pinch something more valuable, you will find yourself in a trouble I can't rescue you from."

"I'm not even aware I'm doing it," Beatrix whispered. "And I don't think I did it before. Before I came here, I mean."

Selina gave her an encouraging nod. "It will be all right. You must work on becoming aware. Then you must not do it. I'll try to help you, if I can."

"Why?"

Lifting a shoulder in a light shrug, Selina said, "Because it seems we're both in need of a family."

Tears threatened once more, but Beatrix decided in that moment that she would be brave. And that she had a sister to love.

CHAPTER 1

*B*eatrix's backside was beginning to ache. After perching so long on the tree branch, she adjusted her weight to ease the pain. She exhaled as blood flowed through her hip and thigh. Much better.

She returned her attention to the house next door to the tree in which she perched. More specifically, she looked into the window in the corner of the ground floor where the Duke of Ramsgate sat in a chair near the hearth, one hand clutching a glass of brandy and the other a newspaper.

His brown hair had lightened over the past fifteen years and was now a bit thin on the crown, but his features were the same—the familiar warm brown eyes, slightly hooked nose, and strong, dimpled chin. There were some lines, and he was heavier than he'd been before, but he was still the man she remembered. The father she loved.

Did he think of her at all?

He had to. There was no way he could have adored Beatrix's mother and cared for Beatrix and then simply forgotten his daughter. He'd paid for Beatrix's schooling after all.

He also never wrote or visited, and when you left the school, never made an effort to find you.

Beatrix argued with herself—how could she know if he'd made an effort or not? She and Selina had spent the years since Beatrix had left Mrs. Goodwin's Ladies' Seminary moving around and being generally difficult to find.

But now Beatrix was here in London, and soon *she* would find *him*. He would be shocked at first and then overjoyed when he saw how accomplished and well-regarded she'd become.

She'd mastered the accomplishment portion at the school he'd paid for and in the time since. The regard part was still in progress, and she wouldn't reveal herself to him until there was no question that he'd be proud and thrilled to claim her as his own. Perhaps not publicly—Beatrix didn't really expect that—but privately. She would have her father back.

A shriek followed by a crash from the house in whose tree Beatrix was currently sitting drew her startled attention to the first-story window. The figure of the woman who lived there moved behind the sheer curtains.

A moment later, the man who lived there—her husband—emerged on the small balcony. The railing was quite short, affording Beatrix a clear view of him. Her breath snagged. He wasn't wearing a coat or a cravat, and she could clearly see the triangle of flesh exposed by the opening of his shirt above his waistcoat, which was unbuttoned. His dark hair was mussed, some of it standing up and some falling across his forehead. He was exceptionally handsome, with a square jaw and strong cheekbones. While Beatrix came to Lord Rockbourne's garden to watch her father, seeing the viscount had become a welcome benefit.

He looked troubled tonight, but then he often did. It was apparent his marriage was not a happy one. As far as Beatrix could tell, Lady Rockbourne was a shrew, always screaming at the viscount. Last time Beatrix had been there, Lady Rockbourne had thrown something at him. Despite that, Beatrix rarely heard him raise his voice in response. That was probably just one of the reasons she was infatuated with him.

The others were his good looks, shallow as that was, and the way he sat in his ground-floor library and read, much like her father. It was silly, but it was just an incredibly domestic sight, or so it seemed to Beatrix. And nothing was more appealing to her than a home.

"Where did you go?" Lady Rockbourne's shrill voice carried out to the garden. Beatrix glanced toward her father, but he never seemed to hear what was going on next door. But then, his window was closed.

The viscountess came out onto the balcony. Her pale blonde hair hung in loose waves past her shoulders. She was petite, shorter even than Beatrix's five feet three inches, but she held her shoulders in such a way so as to appear larger, if that were possible.

Lord Rockbourne was much taller, probably

six feet if Beatrix had to guess. He pivoted to face his wife, which put him in profile to Beatrix.

"How dare you threaten me?" she squealed at her husband.

"I didn't threaten you," he said calmly. Beatrix had to lean forward and strain to hear him. "I said your behavior would reflect poorly on you. That is a fact, not a threat."

"No one cares—everyone has affairs. You're angry that others will see you as a cuckold." There was pride in her voice. Beatrix frowned at the woman. Why would she behave so horribly?

"*I* don't have affairs," he said.

"Maybe you should!"

He ran his hand through his hair, tousling it further. "Aye, maybe I should." They stared at each other, and Beatrix found herself holding her breath.

Rockbourne walked slowly toward his wife. There was something dangerous about his movements. They reminded Beatrix of a cat stalking a mouse.

"We are married, madam, and there is no changing that despite all of your transgressions. I suggest you find a way to make peace with that. Lord knows I try every damn day, and I will continue to do so, despite what you just told me, because I don't have any other fucking choice."

Lady Rockbourne's face hardened just before she let out a garbled cry. She said something, but Beatrix couldn't tell what. Then she launched herself at him, raising her hand. He turned to avoid her. She hit the railing, which barely came to her thigh. Her arms flailed, and something fell to the ground. Beatrix would never forget the look of horror etched into the woman's pale features as she followed the object and tumbled to the cobbled stones below.

Too late, Beatrix clapped a hand over her mouth to block her cry of shock. The sound escaped anyway. Her gaze snapped back to the balcony, only to find Lord Rockbourne's dark gaze fixed on her. Then he was gone, stalking quickly into the house.

Beatrix scrambled down from the tree. She should run. Instead, she dashed to the viscountess, sprawled awkwardly on her side, eyes open, her body still. Hands shaking, Beatrix crouched down and held her fingers in front of the woman's nose and mouth. There was no breath.

"Careful, there's blood."

Beatrix whipped her head around and saw black boots shined to a nearly impossible sheen. Lifting her gaze over black breeches to a snow-white shirt cloaked in a burgundy waistcoat, then up to that arresting triangle of flesh, she finally settled on Lord Rockbourne's impassive face.

Beatrix glanced down and saw there was indeed blood, streaming from beneath the viscountess's head and running along the stone straight for her boots. Gasping, she stood so quickly, she lost her balance.

The viscount reached for her, grabbing her arm and keeping her from falling. "All right?" *He* was asking if Beatrix was all right?

Unable to form words, she merely nodded. He released her, then stared down at his wife.

"I don't think she's breathing," Beatrix whispered. She glanced at the woman, but had to look away from the unsettling sight of her. Instead, she focused on the viscount.

Rockbourne lowered himself and held his fingers to the viscountess's neck. "She is not." His face turned a shocking shade of gray. He withdrew his hand to cover his mouth.

Beatrix reached for him with an instinctive need to provide comfort. But how could she? She pulled her hand back before she touched him.

Remaining crouched, Rockbourne slowly lowered his hand. He gently touched the viscountess's brow, and his eyes closed. "I can't believe…" Anguished lines creased his face, tugging at Beatrix's heart.

She again told herself to flee, that she had no business here, but her feet were rooted to the ground while the rest of her began to shake. She couldn't leave him.

Looking toward the house, she wondered about the servants. Surely one of them would come outside any moment.

"I can't believe she's gone." Rockbourne brushed his hand over Lady Rockbourne's eyes and removed his waistcoat to drape it over her upper chest and face. He slowly rose, a ragged breath stuttering from his lungs. "This is my fault."

"No, it wasn't," Beatrix tried to sound calm and firm, but her voice was shaking. "She fell over the railing. It's not as if you pushed her."

Tension and emotion pulsed out from him, clouding the air. "We were arguing."

"That doesn't mean you…" She couldn't bring herself to say *killed her*. For then she'd have to acknowledge the woman was truly dead. But she was, and nothing would change that. Beatrix nearly reached for his hand, but stopped herself again. "It wasn't your fault."

"Thea," he whispered. "Why did it come to this?" He stared down at the viscountess. His eyes closed once more as the muscles of his jaw clenched tightly. "What will I tell my daughter?"

He had a daughter? Horror knotted in Beatrix's throat. The poor child. Beatrix wondered how old she was and immediately thought of her "sister" Selina, who'd lost her parents at such a young age that she didn't remember them at all. In many ways, that seemed far easier than what Beatrix had endured—losing her mother to illness when she was eleven and then losing her father when he'd shipped her off to school and out of his life. She would hope Rockbourne's daughter was young enough to recover better than Beatrix had.

The viscount seemed frozen, his face still ashen. And why wouldn't he be? "Where are the servants?" she asked.

"Hiding, most likely. They always retreat to the nether regions of the house when Lady Rockbourne and I are arguing."

"You think they'll assume you pushed her?"

"No." He shook his head and ran his hand through his hair. "I don't know."

He suddenly turned toward her, his gaze sharp as a bit of color returned to his face. "Who *are* you? And why were you in my tree?"

"I'm Beatrix Lin—" Damn, she'd almost divulged her real name. She hadn't made that mistake in years. "Miss Beatrix Whitford. I was, er, watching the duke next door." She didn't want to discuss that, and he couldn't either, not with what had happened. "You can't possibly be blamed for this. It was an accident. I saw her come after you."

"And you would give evidence as my witness?" Rockbourne sized her up, from her men's boots to the too-large men's suit of clothing to the top hat on her head. "Why would Bow Street listen to you?"

"Because my soon-to-be brother-in-law is a Runner."

His eyes widened briefly in surprise. "That may be, but acting as my witness will damage your reputation beyond repair." He narrowed his focus on her. "Do you *have* a reputation?"

"I suppose so, yes." She was trying to establish herself as a young lady of high regard in order to impress her father. Furthermore, her sister was marrying the son of an earl. He had a point—her reputation was vitally important if she hoped to gain her father's favor. And protect Selina, which was just as critical.

Beatrix could hear Selina's voice in her head: *"Then why are you gallivanting around dark gardens dressed as a man?"*

Beatrix inwardly winced. She'd been very careful, and if not for tonight's unfortunate events, she would not have been found out. For years, she'd crept in and out of places without detection.

"If you are a lady with a reputation, you can't be a witness. You shouldn't even be here." His voice broke, and he looked away, taking a deep breath. It was a long moment before he continued, whispering softly, "But I'm glad you are."

She was glad too. "This is a horrible tragedy, but no one will think it is anything other than an unfortunate accident."

"I am not as confident as you." He stared at her in bemusement. "Why are you still here with me? You should have gone as soon as she fell."

"I know. Forgive me, but I've been listening to the two of you argue—well, mostly her—for some time now."

One of his ink-dark brows rose. "This is not your first visit to my garden? To spy on Ramsgate?"

"No." Beatrix ignored the question in his gaze. Someday, she'd explain. Probably. Or not. "Why do you think you'll be blamed for this?" That wasn't actually the question she wanted answered. "Why do you think it's your fault?"

"Perhaps you are unaware of some critical facts. First, we despised each other. Second, she was having an affair and I knew it. Third, I recently learned, rather publicly, that she tricked me into this marriage." He referred to the manipulation orchestrated by his wife and her brother that had driven Rockbourne to marry her five years ago and that had been made public the prior week. It was no wonder he was angry, nor could Beatrix blame him for feeling that way.

"Fourth, I provoked her tonight because…" He cut himself off, his lips pressing together until they turned white. "I have plenty of reasons to wish her dead, and *many* people know it."

Beatrix desperately wanted to know why he'd provoked her, but it was apparent he did not want to share that part. So she wouldn't press. It didn't matter anyway. "Provocation or not, this wasn't your fault." She cocked her head to the side, studying this man she didn't know at all but felt a need to protect. "Did you hope she would fall?"

His brow furrowed, forming vertical lines that made the number eleven. "That was not my intent."

She sensed there would be more, but he was silent. "Well, if she despised you and was having an affair, I'd argue she'd hoped *you* would fall. Perhaps *she* was trying to kill you so she could marry her lover."

"No." He said the word with cold finality. The ice in his eyes made her shiver.

Rockbourne took a step toward her. "She wouldn't ever do that, and you won't suggest it. Is that clear?"

"If you can prove she wanted to kill you—and I think you probably could—why not do so to vindicate yourself?"

"Because I won't, and that's the end of it." His voice was soft, but dark with warning.

Beatrix wanted to debate him, but realized that would be pointless. He was absolutely set in his decision. Rather dauntingly so, in fact. "None of that signifies since it was an accident."

Wasn't it? Having watched what happened, she'd been completely sure. Still, his behavior was odd.

"What will you do now?" she asked.

Rockbourne stared at his wife a moment, then briefly clasped his hand over his mouth and chin. Lowering it, he said, "I'll summon the household. Except for my daughter." His face turned ashen.

"What am I going to tell her? She's only three. Almost four."

"Tell her you love her and that you'll always be there for her." Beatrix was surprised to feel a tightness in her throat.

His gaze connected with hers, their gray depths simmering with anguish. "You never answered my question. What are you doing here, with me?"

"Helping, I hope." She gave him a tentative smile.

"You were spying on Ramsgate, and your brother-in-law is a Bow Street Runner. Why are you doing the former, and who is your sister?"

"My sister is Lady Gresham, and I'm not spying on Ramsgate. I'm just…watching him."

"I don't know that he's in the market for a new duchess. His son, however, is in search of a wife. You'd do better to set your sights on him. He's at least near your age. Ramsgate could be your father."

Beatrix couldn't hold in the sharp laugh that leapt from her mouth.

A sound from the house drew them both to turn.

Rockbourne looked to Beatrix. "That could be my butler or someone else. You have to go."

"Yes." Beatrix started to turn toward the back corner of the garden where she'd stolen in through the gate. Impulsively, she spun about. Standing on her toes, she brushed a kiss against his jaw—it was as high as she could reach. "Good luck."

She rushed through the garden and out the

gate. Bringing the hat down lower on her head, she hurried toward home.

$\sim$

*T*homas Devereaux, Viscount Rockbourne, had endured many sleepless nights in his five-year marriage, largely due to his wife's anger, but last night had been the worst. Followed by the hardest morning of his life as he'd explained to his daughter that her mother was gone. At her young age, she didn't really understand, as evidenced when she'd asked where Mama was just a few hours later.

The servants had been shocked to see their mistress sprawled on the cobblestones in the back garden, particularly her maid. Spicer had fallen into a fit of sobbing, and had required brandy to calm herself. She was currently sleeping, which was for the best.

Thomas was sure the woman must be concerned for her future employment since she was no longer needed as a lady's maid. He'd do what he could to see that she found a new situation.

The funeral furnisher had just left, and Thomas was in grave need of his own brandy. He went to his library study and had just poured the drink when his butler, Baines, appeared in the doorway.

"Mrs. Chamberlain is here, my lord. She is in the sitting room."

Thomas's mother-in-law. The brandy was needed more than ever. He drank it down in one swallow. "How is she?" He set the empty glass on the sideboard.

"As you might expect," Baines said delicately. Of average height and with a slight frame, the butler possessed kind, dark eyes, a sharp, long nose, and a balding pate. He was a force of calm and organization in the household, an excellent foil for Thea's penchant for agitation.

Mrs. Chamberlain was a slightly less frenzied version of her daughter. Still, she was bound to be bordering on hysterical, and Thomas couldn't blame her.

With a deep, fortifying breath, he went to the front sitting room and strode inside. Mrs. Chamberlain was perched on the settee, her face pinched and her eyes red.

"Where is she?" Mrs. Chamberlain asked before Thomas could greet her.

"In the morning room." Or was it now the mourning room, Thomas wondered absurdly. Two footmen had carried her inside last night. She currently lay atop a rectangular table.

Mrs. Chamberlain rose. "Take me to her."

Thomas hesitated. "Are you certain you wish—"

"She's my *daughter*." The woman's voice rose, taking on a shrill quality that was so like Thea's that Thomas flinched.

Wordlessly, he turned and led her to the morning room at the back of the house. Mrs. Chamberlain let out a sob as she entered behind him. Rushing to the table, she threw her arms over Thea's abdomen and wailed.

Thomas gritted his teeth. He wanted to ask her to be a little quieter so as not to upset Regan, but he also didn't want to interrupt the woman's grief. Hopefully, Regan couldn't hear her since she was two stories up with her nurse. He moved to the other side of the table and leaned against the doorway that led out to the garden, crossing his arms over his chest.

Mrs. Chamberlain abruptly straightened, her gaze locking on him. "Your note said she fell from the balcony. How did that happen?"

"Presumably, she lost her balance."

"*Presumably?* You didn't see what happened?"

"I did not." After Miss Whitford left, he'd gone inside and run into Baines. Thomas hadn't intended to lie, but as he told the butler what happened, the story had simply come out that way: Thomas had been in the sitting room when he'd heard Thea make a sound, followed by glass breaking and a thud. He rushed outside to see her lying on the stones below.

"That doesn't make sense. How could she have fallen?"

"As you know, the balcony does not have a very high railing. It's barely two feet tall."

"Yes, but Thea is short, like me." Mrs. Chamberlain was about the same height as Thea and she had the same blonde hair. Unlike Thea, she was rather round, with full cheeks and small, brown eyes which reminded Thomas of her son. Gilbert Chamberlain had been arrested for extortion just prior to his wedding five days ago. As much as Thomas didn't care for Mrs. Chamberlain, she'd been through a great deal of late, and Thomas couldn't help but feel sorry for her.

"I don't understand how she would lose her balance." Mrs. Chamberlain narrowed her eyes at Thomas. "This is very strange."

It was impossible to miss the distrust in her expression and tone. Thomas's sympathy for her began to wane. Thea had filled the woman's head with stories of Thomas's inadequacies—as Thea saw them—and Mrs. Chamberlain had some time ago ceased disguising her dislike for him.

"She was drunk," he said flatly, not caring if saying so was indelicate. "You know how she can be when she imbibes." Even worse than when she was sober, and Thea could be an absolute virago. His wife had turned out to be nothing like the young woman he'd courted. Thomas had learned firsthand how his own mother had been wooed into marriage by someone only to learn they were not who they'd seemed.

"Of course you would say that," Mrs. Chamberlain spat. "You're always criticizing my dear Thea."

In truth, it was the opposite—her dear Thea was always criticizing Thomas, but he didn't correct her. Nothing he said would change the woman's mind about him or, more importantly, her daughter.

"You asked what happened, and I'm telling you. She'd had more glasses of port than I can count." That much was true. He'd long ago stopped paying attention to much of anything Thea did, except where it pertained to their daughter. And when it came to Regan, Thea didn't do much.

Mrs. Chamberlain stroked Thea's pale face. "My poor, sweet girl." She looked back to Thomas, her features drawn with anguish and fury. "You could have pushed her."

He stared at her, his temper simmering. "I could have, but I didn't."

A flash of shock passed through her eyes. "I should notify Bow Street and have them investigate."

Bloody hell. "It would be a waste of their time, but I'm sure you'll do what you must." He pushed away from the doorway and unfolded his arms. "The funeral furnisher just left. They are sending women to prepare Thea. The service and burial will be Wednesday."

Thea's mother gaped at him. "You planned all that without me?"

"Thea was my wife, madam. It is my duty to care for her—in death as well as life. I've always taken my marriage vows seriously." He added the last and immediately regretted it. Needling her in this manner was akin to what he'd done to Thea the night before.

Was it really? Thea had pushed him first, revealing truths he'd long suspected but had never wanted to face. He shook the thought away. He was doing the best he could to keep the rage and hurt inside him under tight rein.

Mrs. Chamberlain snorted. "You've done no such thing. Thea has told me about every one of your indiscretions."

Thomas wanted to ask what those could be, but what would be the point? He'd never been unfaithful to his marriage despite ample opportunity and desire. "I'll leave you alone." He started to go, but her voice halted him.

"I will prepare her. Where is her maid?"

"Sleeping. She was hysterical."

Mrs. Chamberlain removed her hat and gloves. "I'll be staying—until Wednesday. Where is Regan? I wish to see my granddaughter."

Thomas turned to face his mother-in-law. "Not today. I won't have her upset. She's lost her mother, and she barely understands."

"You can't keep me from seeing her." She gave him a defiant look.

He stepped toward her, his lip curling. He didn't care if he appeared menacing. "I can and I will. Don't push me. This is my house, and I allow you to remain out of deference to my late wife. I will not, however, permit you to upset my daughter. You may stay. For now. Don't make me regret my decision."

After glowering at her a moment, Thomas turned on his heel and stalked from the room. He nearly ran into Baines, who was lurking in the hall.

"Mrs. Chamberlain will be staying until the funeral on Wednesday. Please have the guest room prepared."

Baines inclined his head. "Of course."

"Alert everyone that she is *not* to see Regan today. And when she does see her tomorrow, I will be present."

"I'll take care of that at once."

"She wants to see Spicer when she awakens. Will you take care of that also?"

Baines nodded. "Is there anything else?"

"Not at the moment. I'm going upstairs."

Thomas went up to the sitting room between

his bedchamber and Thea's. He looked toward the door leading to her room and longed to burn everything inside it. Perhaps not everything. He should probably save some things for Regan. She would want to remember her mother. If she could —it was likely she would grow up not recalling the woman who'd given her life.

While that made him sad, he was also grateful. There was nothing good for her *to* remember. He'd save a few mementoes and fabricate stories to go along with them so that Regan would believe her mother had loved her. It was the best he could do.

Thinking of mementoes, he realized he'd never found the penknife Thea had been clutching last night when she'd come at him on the balcony. She'd aimed the blade at the hollow of his throat. It was why he'd stepped to the side and she'd launched forward over the balcony.

If he hadn't moved, she would have sunk the blade into him. He probably wouldn't have died. But perhaps she wouldn't have either.

Was he really telling himself he should have let her stab him? After all the other abuse he'd allowed her to heap upon him the past several years? He picked up a figurine from the writing desk and threw it across the room.

The second the sheepdog shattered, he regretted the rash action. Self-loathing and fear rose in his throat. He worked so bloody hard to contain his anger.

He took deep breaths to calm his racing pulse. Turning, he went out to the balcony. The early afternoon was warm, with a few high clouds, one of which was currently blocking the sun. Though he'd looked last night and again this morning, he searched the balcony once more for the penknife. It still wasn't there.

He went to the low railing and gazed down at the garden. He'd also searched the cobblestones and the surrounding area, to no avail. It was as if the penknife had disappeared. Perhaps he'd imagined the damn thing.

Going back inside, he searched the writing desk, which was where she typically kept it and where she'd grabbed it from last night. The knife wasn't there either.

He should look in her chamber too, he supposed, but he couldn't bring himself to go in there. Not today.

Sadness and weariness settled into his bones. This wasn't what he'd wanted. He'd married Thea hoping they would have a happy life together, a family full of love. At least he had Regan.

Clinging to the only beacon of happiness he had—the one that had kept him going the past several years—he went in search of his daughter. She was his joy and love, and he would do anything to keep her safe.

CHAPTER 2

The night was clear, with a nearly-full moon shining down into the garden. Thomas looked into the tree, but Miss Whitford wasn't there. He couldn't imagine she'd come again tonight, or any night, after what had happened.

Still, he couldn't help searching for her. He realized he wanted her to return.

From the tree, she'd had the perfect position to witness everything that had happened the night before. *Nearly* everything. She couldn't have heard what was said before he and Thea had gone out onto the balcony. And she didn't seem to know that Thea had been holding the penknife.

Miss Whitford firmly believed he was not to blame.

She was, of course, wrong. Thomas might not have pushed Thea over the railing, but he'd provoked her rage. Her tragic fall, even if it was accidental, was why it was so important he never lose control, not even for a moment as he'd done earlier when he'd thrown the figurine.

But you pulled yourself together.

Nevertheless, look at what had happened to Thea. Thomas felt sick.

It didn't help that her mother and maid had spent the afternoon and evening closeted with Thea and were likely commiserating about Thomas's depravity as well as his responsibility for Thea's demise. Countless arrangements of flowers had been delivered, all of which had been crammed into the morning room to help stave off the scent of death.

Baines had told him a short while ago that both women had retired and that Spicer had informed him she would be going to work for Mrs. Chamberlain. Thomas was grateful he wouldn't have to worry about the maid's employment.

He'd be glad when they were both out of his house. That meant Thea would be gone too. The idea of consistent peace was a dream he hadn't dared. Now, his entire being yearned for it with everything he had.

A movement in the back corner of the garden drew his attention. A small, black-clad figure strode toward the balcony. Her head tipped up, and their eyes met.

Wordlessly, she went to the trellis and ascended with the same speed and agility she had the night before. As she climbed over the railing, he noted the curve of her backside and the slope of her hip. When she stepped into the light coming from the windows of the sitting room, he fixed on the dramatic arch of her pale brows, the searing intensity of her hazel eyes, the saucy manner in which her nose turned up at the tip, the enticing bow of her dark pink lips, and the strong jut of her chin. She was a cat, and he briefly wondered if he was her prey.

"You came back," he said simply.

"I had to."

"For Ramsgate."

She put a hand on her hip. "Did I so much as look toward his house?"

He nearly smiled, which in itself was a marvel given the past day. "You didn't appear to. How is it you climb so well?"

"Dressing like a man helps." She flashed a quick smile, which revealed dimples in her cheeks. There was joy in this woman, and the glimpse of it nearly drove Thomas to his knees.

"You didn't answer my question. While you're doing that, tell me why you're dressed like a man."

"I can't very well steal into gardens late at night and watch the Duke of Ramsgate dressed like a woman, particularly since I have to climb a tree to see him."

"Thank you. You also didn't answer *why* you are spying on him. And don't tell me you aren't spying. What you are doing is most definitely spying."

She narrowed one eye at him. "You are full of questions this evening. Are you distracting yourself?"

"Definitely."

She exhaled. "I can't blame you." She stepped toward him, her features creasing with concern. "How are you?"

"Horrid. My mother-in-law is here."

"Oh dear. You don't get along?"

"That's a nice way of putting it." He ran his hand through his hair. "I'm being uncharitable. The woman has endured much in recent days."

"You're referring to the arrest of her son in addition to her daughter's death."

"You keep up on gossip."

She lifted a shoulder. "My sister's betrothed is the one who arrested Chamberlain."

"Your sister is marrying Harry Sheffield?" He was brother to Lord Northwood, with whom Thomas was well acquainted.

"You are *not* keeping up on gossip. Which is to be expected."

"I rarely do."

"You're better off," Miss Whitford said. She hesitated before asking, "How is your daughter?"

"She scarcely understands, which is for the best. Thea wasn't a particularly, ah, devoted parent." Indeed, entire days went by when Thea never even visited Regan in the nursery. That disregard was perhaps the primary reason Thomas had grown to loathe her.

"I'm certain your daughter is quite lucky to have you for a father," Miss Whitford said with grave confidence—and perhaps just a touch of wistfulness.

"I'm still not at all certain why you chose to help me instead of fleeing the garden." Thomas crossed his arms over his chest and leaned against the outer wall of the house. "Are you going to tell me, or will you avoid that question too?"

"I like to be helpful, and you clearly needed help. As you said, your daughter needs a father."

He'd had the sense Miss Whitford hadn't been

aware of Regan, but why would she? Miss Whitford had been visiting his garden to survey the duke next door, not him. "How long have you been coming to my garden?"

"A few weeks." A faint blush stained the upper regions of her cheeks.

"I see. The duke must be very important to you." Thomas pushed away from the wall and dropped his arms to his sides. "If there is any way I can return the great favor you extended me last night, I hope you'll advise me." He stepped toward her.

Her lashes fluttered as she tipped her head up to look at him. The difference in their height was great—she was barely taller than Thea. His stomach turned. He refused to compare them.

"Can I help you?" he asked. "With the duke, I mean."

"He's my father." The words tumbled quickly from her mouth. So quickly that he wondered why she'd avoided telling him, for it seemed that was what she'd been doing. Perhaps he'd misunderstood.

"Oh." Thomas was at a bit of a loss for words. Why would a young woman have to resort to spying on her father? He could only think of one explanation. "Does he, ah, know you?"

"He used to." She cast a frustrated glance over her shoulder toward Ramsgate's house. "He knew me quite well when I lived with my mother in Bath. He spent a great deal of time with us. He loved my mother. And me." There was a simple conviction to her words that pierced straight into Thomas's heart. "My mother became ill, and he stopped visiting. She died when I was eleven. That's when I was taken to a boarding school."

Her eyes widened, and she stared at him in horror. "I shouldn't have told you any of that," she whispered. "Not about my father or the school, any of it. Will you please forget I did?"

There was no way he could. "It seems we both know secrets about each other. I promise not to reveal yours."

"I promise the same." She held out her hand. "A bargain, then?"

He took her gloved fingers in his, but she withdrew her hand, surprising him. After removing her glove, she pressed her palm to his and clasped her thumb and fingers around him. The feel of her flesh against his made his breath catch. He tried to recall just how long it had been since he'd touched a woman.

"A bargain." He quickly let go of her hand. "Why are you watching him?"

"Because it's all I have at the moment. I am hopeful he will notice me this season and desire a reconnection."

He remembered what she'd told him last night, about her sister, Lady Gresham. If Miss Whitford was a bastard, was Lady Gresham also born on the wrong side of the blanket? Did Ramsgate have two bastard daughters? He was curious but wouldn't ask Miss Whitford to divulge more secrets. He doubted her name was even Whitford. He'd caught her slip when she'd started to call herself a different name last night.

"Miss Whitford, I hope you won't think me too forward, but I truly meant it when I offered my assistance. I would be happy to help you in any way, and I won't divulge any of your—or your family's—secrets. I also won't judge you." He was the last person who would hold someone to any kind of standard.

"Thank you. You are most kind." She smiled. "Perhaps you can ask me to dance some time." Her smile evaporated into a grimace. "How obtuse of me. Of course you can't. You're in mourning now."

"That's true." He hadn't really thought about it. He hadn't thought past today. "Well, I'm sure there will be a way I can help you. In the meantime, you're welcome to use my tree." He gestured toward the garden.

"You are most accommodating, my lord."

"Please call me Rockbourne." He'd almost said Thomas, but that would have been too forward.

She nodded. "I did just come tonight to check on you. You won't mind if I do so again?"

"I'll look forward to it, actually." When was the last time he'd had something to anticipate that didn't involve reading a story or playing with dolls?

"Excellent." She turned and went to climb over the railing. As she held on to the trellis with one hand, she waved at him with the other. "Until next time!"

"When you explain to me your catlike abilities."

She laughed. "There isn't much to tell. There was a tree in our garden in Bath, and I climbed it almost every day."

He suspected there *was* more to it than that and hoped she would reveal all—someday.

After descending the trellis, she paused beneath the balcony and looked up at him. "I just thought of something. I am in need of a voucher for Almack's. If you can help with that..." She winked at him before taking off through the garden.

He watched her until she disappeared into the dark corner with the gate. He looked forward to her next visit with great anticipation.

~

"*W*hy are you pacing?" Beatrix asked Selina as she watched her cross their small sitting room.

"Rachel will be here shortly," Selina answered without pausing. In fact, it looked as if she sped up. Tall, with long legs, she strode the distance in probably half the strides it would take Beatrix.

"Yes, and it's just Rachel. You like Rachel. It's not as if Lady Aylesbury is coming. Even if she were, there's no call for you to be nervous." Rachel was Selina's betrothed's sister, and Lady Aylesbury was his mother. Both were lovely women.

Selina's honey-brown brows knitted as she continued to pace. "I realize you were reared to believe you might move in such circles, but I was not."

Raised in London's East End and forced to thieve to support herself, Selina was still adjusting to the idea that she was marrying the son of an earl. Never mind that she and Beatrix had spent over a decade masquerading as genteel women. "We're quite accomplished at pretending to be well-bred, if I may say so."

Selina tossed her a look that said she wasn't sure she agreed.

Beatrix rose from her chair. "Besides, they already adore you almost as much as Harry does." She smiled at her sister who wasn't really her sister but was the only family Beatrix had. Beatrix wanted to include her father and hoped very soon she could.

Intercepting Selina, Beatrix clasped her hands. "Truly they do."

"Harry says so," Selina said quietly, her blue gaze dipping. "I still can't believe…" She shook her head.

Beatrix pulled Selina close for a hug. "I know you think you don't deserve him, but you *do*. This is a new chapter in your life—in both our lives. Don't look backward."

Selina nodded, her head grazing Beatrix's as she squeezed her in return. "Thank you."

They separated, and both had tears glistening in their eyes. "You've cried more in the past week than in all the time I've known you!" Beatrix laughed as she blinked the moisture away.

"It's true. I've become a bloody watering pot." Selina wiped at her eyes just as they heard the housekeeper's voice. "Rachel must be here." Straightening, Selina took a deep breath. She brushed her hands over her cheeks and nodded.

"Mrs. Hayes has arrived." Mrs. Vining, their housekeeper, appeared briefly before stepping aside to allow Harry's sister into the sitting room.

With auburn hair and shining brown eyes, Rachel was the middle of Harry's three sisters, all married. She was also the closest to Harry, and she'd taken a particular liking to Selina. "Lady Gresh—" Rachel rolled her eyes. "*Selina.* Bad habit, I'm afraid."

Selina smiled. "Proper address isn't a bad habit."

Beatrix suppressed a giggle. And it wasn't really proper address. Selina was no more Lady Gresham than Beatrix was Miss Whitford. Sir Barnabus Gresham had been one of the many wealthy people they'd sought to swindle. He'd seen through their ruse, something that almost never happened, but had liked Selina so much that he'd given them the money they needed to get to London and said he didn't care if she called herself Lady Gresham. It turned out he was ill and was glad to help someone in need before he died.

"Let us sit," Beatrix said. She took the chair she'd vacated while Selina and Rachel sat together on the settee.

Rachel had apparently divested herself of her hat and gloves in the entry hall. Once seated, she arranged her skirt in an elegant fashion and looked between Selina and Beatrix with an expression of barely contained excitement. "I have wonderful news."

"About the wedding?" Selina asked, for that was the reason for Rachel's visit—to discuss what needed to be done.

Rachel shook her head. "I have vouchers for Almack's for the both of you." She grinned broadly.

Selina turned her head to look at Beatrix, her eyes alight with joy. "That *is* wonderful news."

Beatrix clasped her hands together in her lap

and squeezed. At last, she could claim a crowning achievement for the Season. She'd begun to think it wouldn't be possible—they'd come to the Season late and they hadn't known anyone who could advocate for them to a patroness.

"Thank you," Beatrix said earnestly. She released her hands and flattened her palms on the chair on either side of her.

"Don't thank me. Mama has been working on her friend who is cousin to one of the patronesses, but she wasn't sure it was going to happen. All of a sudden, this morning she received word that you were approved. Your vouchers should arrive later this afternoon. Truthfully, Mama isn't sure what tipped the scale in your favor, but it doesn't matter!"

Selina cast Beatrix a look of veiled distress. "Are the vouchers for tonight?" The balls were every Wednesday evening. Beatrix was going to need a new gown, and there would be no time to procure one for tonight.

"I believe they're for the entire month of June," Rachel said.

Beatrix exchanged relieved glances with Selina. "Oh good, I don't think I could be prepared to go tonight."

"I'm so glad I was able to deliver the news in person." Rachel settled back against the settee. "Now we should discuss the wedding—though not in too much detail. Mama made me promise we would save the majority of the discussion for this Friday when you come for luncheon al fresco. Have you and Harry decided where you'll live?"

"For now, we'll live here, though he has expressed his desire to find a larger house," Selina said. This house was rather small, and they were only leasing it through the Season. Harry's house was no larger, and he'd insisted it was easier for him to move than for Selina to do so. As it was, he stole into Selina's bedchamber most nights, so he almost lived here already.

The conversation turned to Selina's dress and then the preliminary plans for the wedding breakfast that Harry's parents were hosting.

"Mama can't wait to present you to all of her friends," Rachel said. "But I suppose you'll meet many of them at your brother's ball."

Selina's brother, Rafe, who'd also elevated himself from their background of thievery in East London, was now a wealthy gentleman with an opulent house on Upper Brook Street. They'd decided it was easiest to explain that Selina and Rafe were Beatrix's half-siblings and that they shared a mother. It was, if Beatrix were honest, a bloody tangle and she sometimes feared she would spoil the ruse by misspeaking.

Rafe had come to Harry and Selina's engagement dinner for the family at Lord and Lady Aylesbury's the other night and expressed his desire to host an engagement ball. It was to be a masquerade and would be held a week from Friday. The invitations had already gone out. Beatrix wished Rockbourne could come.

"I'm quite looking forward to that," Rachel was saying. "I've long wanted to see the interior of the house your brother recently obtained."

Rafe had purchased one of the grandest houses on the street and was hurriedly completing renovations before the ball. It was to be his introduction to Society as much as it was Selina's and Beatrix's. Most importantly, he'd invited Beatrix's father. Beatrix just hoped the duke came.

It could very well be the night that changed her life. Just thinking of it made her heart speed with anticipation.

They discussed the ball for a few more minutes before they returned to the actual wedding, which would be held at St. George's in Hanover Square. "It's going to be lovely," Rachel said as she looked to Selina. "How does Harry feel about being married where he arrested a groom less than a week ago?"

"A trifle odd," Selina responded.

That groom was, of course, Rockbourne's brother-in-law. Thankfully, the arrest had happened prior to the wedding. Nevertheless, the bride, Miss Anne Pemberton, was still embroiled in the scandal. "It's highly unfair that Miss Pemberton is suffering because of her betrothed's actions," Beatrix said. "*He* was the extortionist."

"Yes, well, some—not *me*—think she should have shown better judgment," Rachel scoffed. "Women are always held to different standards. Take Chamberlain's sister. Her death is an absolute tragedy, but everyone knows she was difficult and perhaps even unfaithful. Does anyone blame Rockbourne for marrying her?"

"They don't?" Beatrix asked. Society fascinated her, but mostly she just wanted to know about Rockbourne.

Rachel shook her head, making a moue of disdain. "Of course not. As I said, different standards."

Beatrix couldn't keep herself from pursuing the topic. "*Should* he have known better?"

"I have no idea, but the point is that if the roles were reversed, Lady Rockbourne would have been to blame while Rockbourne was revered. In fact, who's to say what the truth of the matter was. Rockbourne has always been a bit of an enigma, and while rumors of Lady Rockbourne's infidelity are well known, perhaps they are just that —rumors."

Beatrix knew they weren't. Unless Rockbourne had lied to her, and she didn't think he had.

"Regardless, I feel terrible for him," Selina said softly.

Rachel nodded in agreement. "It's very sad. I daresay he won't have trouble finding a new viscountess. After he mourns, of course. But that's another way in which men and women are held to different standards. Because Rockbourne is a man with a title and no heir, he'll be expected to replace his wife. And since he has a daughter to care for, he can do so in short order. If Rockbourne had died, Lady Rockbourne would have to shut herself away for months. In truth, no one would blink if she never remarried." Rachel smiled. "On second thought, maybe that is an advantage."

"I thought you were happily wed," Selina said.

"Oh, I am!" Rachel rushed to say. "I just mean that in widowhood, a woman can enjoy a freedom other women can't." She looked over at Selina. "But you know that, don't you?"

"Yes," Selina murmured, her gaze dropping to

her lap.

The lie of widowhood had given her and Beatrix the ability to come to London and enter Society in a manner they could not have if they'd both been unmarried.

"Do you think Rockbourne will remarry?" Beatrix asked, drawing a curious stare from Selina.

Rachel shrugged. "I don't know him very well, but I think North does." She referred to Harry's twin brother, who was the Viscount Northwood and whom most of the family called North. "Perhaps I'll ask him. I'm sure he and Lady Rockbourne would have been invited to the wedding breakfast. Before her death, of course."

Beatrix found herself disappointed that Rockbourne wouldn't be there.

They visited a little while longer before Rachel departed.

"That went very well," Beatrix said after Rachel had left the house.

Walking back from the doorway after seeing Rachel off, Selina arched a brow at her. "Why are you so interested in Lord Rockbourne?"

Beatrix had hoped Selina wouldn't ask. She hadn't told her anything about meeting him. As it was, Selina didn't particularly care for Beatrix going to spy on her father. Spy? Rockbourne would be amused at her choice of words.

"You're smiling. Why?" Selina's eyes narrowed. "Tell me."

Beatrix exhaled. "Like you told me everything about Harry when you were falling for him?"

Selina's jaw dropped, and she crossed the room

to stand in front of Beatrix, who lingered near her chair after rising when Rachel had left. "What is going on with Rockbourne?"

"Nothing. I don't even know the man." That was close enough to the truth. She didn't say she hadn't *met* him. And she *didn't* know him, not really.

"I don't know what you're hiding, but it's something." Selina's features softened. "Let's not keep secrets. I am sorry I wasn't completely honest about Harry. I didn't think anything could happen between us. It was like a dream. Talking about it would have made it real, and I...I couldn't bear it." She wiped her hand over her brow. "You're right. We both deserve to be happy."

"Yes, we do, and we're well on our way." Beatrix seized the chance to change the subject. There was no point in discussing Rockbourne anyway. If Harry had been a dream for Selina, Rockbourne was more in the realm of utter impossibility. Not that Beatrix was thinking of him in the same way Selina had about Harry.

"Almack's!" Beatrix exclaimed. "I wonder if my father will be there." She'd heard he made an appearance there once in a while. His son was in the market for a wife and was deemed one of the prime catches of the Season.

"Hopefully, he will be at Rafe's ball," Selina said.

"It's your ball, not Rafe's."

"I suppose, but Rafe is hosting and paying for it." Selina made a face. "Do you know what we could do with the money it costs to throw a Society ball?"

"I can guess. Isn't Rafe giving you money for

the new Spitfire project?"

Beatrix and Selina had joined an association of Society women called The Spitfire Society. They'd started as a small group of independent-minded women who'd flouted Society's rules but had ended up banding together to work to help less fortunate women. Their numbers were growing, and next week they would meet to discuss plans for a new school and home of rehabilitation for poor women and children. Selina was driving the project and had found a surprising supporter in the Duchess of Clare, who was as passionate about the idea as Selina. For Selina, it was personal. She meant to save girls like herself from the streets.

"He is," Selina said. "I don't know how much, but then I'm afraid to ask how wealthy he's actually become."

"I'm not. I'll do that next time I see him." Beatrix laughed, and Selina joined.

Sobering, Selina pressed her hands to her cheeks. "I can scarcely believe how we got here. And you're on the verge of achieving your dream. Your father will see how lovely you are, how welcome in Society, and your relationship will be rekindled."

"I hope so." Her primary goal these past fifteen years had been to get back into her father's good graces. If he rejected her, she didn't know what she'd do. He was the only blood relative she had. Yes, she had Selina, but they weren't actually related. And now Selina had been reunited with her brother after nineteen years apart.

Beatrix wanted a family of her own. She'd *had* one, and she meant to get it back.

CHAPTER 3

"*P*apa!" Regan bounced into his study, her pale blonde curls swinging. "Alice and I came for our hugs." She stopped in front of his chair near the hearth and held up her doll.

She didn't look like a girl whose mother had been buried the day before, and for that, Thomas was exceptionally grateful.

"It must be time for your nap," he said, taking Alice. The doll stared at him with wide blue eyes. "Sleep well, Alice." He hugged the doll, then returned her to Regan.

"My turn!" Regan bounded into his lap, and he held her close. Love for her filled his soul.

Thomas brushed his lips across the crown of her head. She smelled of lavender soap and the energy only a little girl possessed. "Sleep well, my love."

"Yes, Papa." She slipped from his arms and skipped back to the doorway, where her nurse waited with a warm smile.

Inclining his head toward the young woman, Thomas mouthed, *thank you*. A moment later, his butler appeared in the doorway. "Mrs. Holcomb is here, my lord. I've showed her to the front sitting room."

"Thank you." Thomas stood to meet his aunt, glad she'd arrived.

Charity Holcomb stood in front of the windows that faced Grosvenor Square. Though her hair was gray, she appeared nearly a decade younger than her fifty-three years. She also reminded Thomas so much of his mother—her older sister. Thomas was certain this was close to how she would have looked today if she'd survived the birth of her second child.

"You appear as though you slept," she said, walking toward him. "I knew once she was buried, you would feel better."

"I can't say better is the right word," he said mildly. "Are you going to check on me every day?"

"For the foreseeable future. Unless you tell me not to."

In truth, her presence was a comfort. "You should probably just stay here."

"Nonsense. The last thing you need right now is someone intruding on your household. I am quite content at my brother's. How is Regan?"

"Fine. Normal, really. She hasn't asked for her mother at all." That wasn't unusual. She'd grown accustomed to not seeing Thea every day.

"That's just as well." Aunt Charity went to the settee and sat down. "It's good she wasn't attached to her." Aunt Charity rarely referred to Thea by name, preferring pronouns. She made no secret that she'd never liked her, though she'd always been polite. Thea hadn't liked her either. Consequently, Thomas hadn't spent as much time with his beloved aunt, who lived thirty miles away in Wycombe, as he would have liked.

"It is a blessing," Thomas said even as he'd wished it had been different. He'd hated that Thea hadn't been close to their daughter. A child was love in its purest form. How a parent could turn their back on one mystified him. That wasn't true. It enraged him.

"Only think how wonderful it will be when you remarry and Regan has a real mother."

In the process of lowering himself into a chair, Thomas sat down rather hard upon hearing what his aunt said. "Er, yes."

Aunt Charity tipped her head to the side. "You can't tell me you haven't already thought about it. After five years of marriage to...*her?*" She shuddered. "I don't wish to speak ill of the dead, but I am glad you have another chance at happiness."

Did he? Thomas had botched things so badly with his first try that he wasn't certain he trusted himself to make a better choice the second time. "I'm in no rush."

"Tell that to the ton. Speculation is already rampant."

Thomas pressed a finger to his temple. "Why?"

"You're titled, wealthy, handsome as sin, and you *need* a wife to mother your child as well as an heir. There are also wagers, which I'm sure you're aware of."

He wasn't, actually, but he could well imagine. People were ruthless. "Those mean nothing to me."

"Of course they don't. I only mention them to

say that people are expecting you to wed again soon." She shrugged. "If you wanted to, you could."

Thomas saw through her. And, frankly, he was rather shocked. "*You* want me to."

"I want you to be happy," she said firmly. "Wed, don't wed, just do what you must to find comfort. Promise me? You know how much I love you."

He did, but that didn't mean he wanted her input about this part of his life. "Regan and I are just fine, as you well know."

"I can see my counsel is not needed in this area." She lifted her hands in surrender. "You'll let me know if I can help in any way?"

"Yes." Thomas thought of the other woman who'd given him aid. Miss Whitford hadn't returned since Monday evening. And he'd looked for her every night.

"Will you tell me your plans?" Aunt Charity asked.

"As soon as I have some." For now he would do what he'd always done—focus on his daughter and his responsibilities as viscount. Again, he thought of Miss Whitford.

He couldn't imagine how she could be part of his plans.

"Thomas." Aunt Charity exhaled his name, and though she said nothing else, the word was both full of question and rife with concern. "Forgive me, but I worry about you." She always had. "I can't tell how you feel about all this. Are you sad? Relieved? Concealing your joy?" She waved her hand. "Forget I said the last. Of course you aren't happy."

No, but if he were honest with himself, he *was*

relieved. He no longer had to worry about protecting Regan from her mother's rages. And he no longer had to suffer them himself.

"No matter how awful Thea was, she didn't deserve to die," he said softly. "It's…a terrible situation. I honestly don't know how I'm supposed to feel." So he was choosing to feel nothing. It wasn't difficult. Aside from his daughter, he'd learned to bury all emotion over the past five years. Even that hadn't been hard, because he'd first done it at the age of ten when his mother had died.

Perhaps he was meant to direct all his feelings toward Regan. No, not all of them, just the good ones. The rest he buried. When he didn't, bad things happened, such as his wife dying.

"You'll stay for dinner, I hope? Regan will want to see you, and she is napping at present."

"Yes, of course. Is there correspondence I can help with in the meantime?"

"Absolutely." He smiled at her. "Now *that* fills me with relief."

She smiled widely in return. "There's my boy. Just tell me what you need."

"You can use the desk there." He gestured to the writing desk in the corner near the front window. "There are many notes of condolence, but also some social invitations that arrived either before she died or before her death was known. I suppose you should respond to those, unless people will assume I won't be coming."

"I'll respond. As I said, no one will fault you for going out, not when you're seen as needing a wife. They may, in fact, expect you to come."

Thomas rose. "I'll fetch everything and bring it here."

She nodded, and he turned to go. "Oh, I did take care of your request regarding Almack's. And I hope you'll tell me who Miss Whitford and Lady Gresham are to you."

"Thank you." Thomas didn't look back at her before taking off to his study.

As he gathered the correspondence, one of the missives caught his eye. It was an invitation to a ball to celebrate the engagement of Mr. Henry Sheffield and Lady Gresham. Thomas read the details. It was a *masquerade*.

His aunt's words flooded his mind. He *could* go…

He set the invitation aside and took the rest to Aunt Charity.

～

There was a dampness in the air that presaged rain. Beatrix glanced up at the night sky and silently begged it to remain dry. Just for an hour or so. Perhaps a trifle longer.

She probably should not have ventured out, but she hadn't been able to resist. Now that she was in possession of a voucher to Almack's as well as a few prestigious invitations to Society events over the next fortnight, she knew the time when she would come face-to-face with her father was nigh. And then she could stop spying on him from Rockbourne's garden.

Except that would mean she would stop going to Rockbourne's garden. She'd decided she rather liked going there. More accurately, she liked going to see Rockbourne.

But tonight was to see her father. Or so she told herself as she stole through the gate into the garden.

She hurried along the crushed gravel path that bisected the beds in the middle and made her way to the tree. First, she glanced toward the house, as she'd done since the first night she'd come. She had to make sure no one from Rockbourne's house saw her.

Standing on the balcony, his gaze trained directly on her, was Rockbourne. As on the other night, he wasn't wearing a coat. Unlike then, he still wore his cravat. Pity, she'd rather enjoyed ogling that narrow triangle of his chest.

With a giddy rush, Beatrix hastened to the trellis and quickly climbed up to the balcony. He met her at the railing, offering his hand to help her over.

"How gallant," she said, grinning as she put her fingers in his. She stepped on the railing, and he put his other hand on her waist as he helped her onto the balcony. Instinctively, she grasped his shoulder.

He didn't immediately release her. They stood close together, their hands clasped, his palm against her hip, her fingertips on his collarbone.

"It's almost a waltz," she said softly.

He moved his hand to her back and swept her around as if they were in fact waltzing.

"I haven't yet waltzed. But I know how." Selina had hired a woman to give Beatrix dancing and comportment lessons after they'd arrived in London.

He released her then, and she ignored the wave of disappointment. "You're very good."

She laughed—as much at his statement as to cover her reaction. "And you're an excellent liar."

"That's actually true." Before she could ask him what he meant, he gestured to the narrow door leading inside. "Would you care to come in for a glass of madeira? Or whatever you prefer."

Beatrix wished she wasn't wearing the suit of men's clothing. She wanted him to see her in one of the gowns they'd had made for her Season, especially the one she would wear to Selina's engagement ball. Rafe had insisted on paying for her and Selina to be lavishly outfitted for the occasion.

"Madeira would be lovely, thank you." She preceded him into a sitting room. Decorated in bright yellow and rose, it had a distinctly feminine atmosphere. She noted there were three other doors, presumably leading to interior rooms. Two were ajar, while the third, to her right, was closed.

"That was her room," Rockbourne said, handing Beatrix a glass of madeira.

She'd been so focused on studying her surroundings that she hadn't paid attention to him pouring the drinks. "Thank you."

Their fingers touched, but she was still wearing gloves. Probably best if she left them on. She sipped the wine. "Mmm, delicious. Do you mind if I take off my hat?" She didn't need to ask, she realized.

"Not at all."

She removed the black hat and set it on a small writing desk situated next to the door.

In the center of the room, there was a small settee, really only wide enough for two people, and two chairs. Beatrix perched on one of the chairs and took another sip of wine. She glanced toward the closed door, which was to her right.

"You didn't share a bedchamber?" As soon as the question left her mouth, she wished she could take it back. Besides, what did it even mean? Plenty of married couples of his class didn't share a bedchamber. Or so she'd heard. "I beg your pardon. That was most improper."

"You're in the sitting room adjoining my bedchamber after climbing a trellis dressed in men's clothing. Nothing about this is proper. I can't say I mind." He peered at her over his glass of wine as he sat on the settee across from her. He seemed to take it up entirely. Perhaps it wasn't really large enough for two people. Unless one wanted to sit very close to the other person with whom they were sharing it. Beatrix wouldn't have minded that at all if Rockbourne was the person.

"So you did share a bedchamber?" she asked, since they'd agreed propriety wasn't necessary.

He shook his head. "Mine is there." He inclined his head to the other side of the sitting room. "Would you mind terribly if we didn't discuss her? The burial was yesterday, and I'm...weary."

"Of course." Beatrix longed to wipe away that stressful eleven between his brows.

"Tell me about your father. What is your plan once you reenter his life?"

"It isn't complicated. I want my father back."

"I see." He contemplated her as he drank more wine.

"You're wondering what will happen if he doesn't wish to reestablish our relationship. I am not considering that as a possibility. I am hopeful I will impress him so much that he will be ecstatic to have found me." A part of her hoped he'd been looking for her since she'd fled the seminary.

"You only hope to gain his...affection?" He sounded skeptical.

"Regain. We were close once, before my mother died. I realize he won't publicly claim me, nor do I expect him to."

"You're aware of his other children?"

She pursed her lips at him. "I am." A son and two married daughters. "I am optimistic he has room in his life for another daughter."

"I am somewhat of a pessimist, I'm afraid. I need people like you in my life." He stretched his legs out, and if Beatrix had been sitting in the other chair, she could stretch out her own toe and touch him.

His words made her want to smile. "Then it's fortuitous that you live next door to my father, which made our paths intersect."

"For so many reasons," he murmured. "I could just introduce you to Ramsgate."

"How would that go? You and I aren't formally acquainted."

"That is unfortunately true."

"Anyway, I have a good plan. I now have a voucher to Almack's in my possession." She grinned at him.

"Do you? That's wonderful." He lifted his glass. "To you conquering London."

She raised hers in response, and they both drank. "It's rather extraordinary, really. I didn't even meet one of the patronesses." They typically met everyone before offering a voucher.

"Your sister is marrying the son of an earl. I'm sure that was helpful. I assume the voucher includes her?"

"It does." She narrowed one eye at him. "Did you have anything to do with it?"

He shrugged.

"Well, if you did, thank you."

"I take it Lady Gresham isn't also the duke's daughter?" The question seemed innocuous, but it was one of the tenuous threads holding Beatrix's lies together.

"No. Our mother was wed to her father, who died shortly after she was born." She quickly made up the fabrication and silently repeated it so she would remember what she'd said. If her father decided to publicly claim her, she and Selina would explain to Harry's family that they'd lied about being sisters to protect Beatrix. They wouldn't want Harry's family thinking Selina's mother was a former courtesan and the mistress of a duke. The reality was that Selina's mother could be just about anyone.

What a tangle. So much depended on what the duke decided to do once he and Beatrix were reunited. Because of that, she hadn't planned on what to say in this instance because she'd never revealed her parentage to anyone. She was playing a dangerous game with Rockbourne.

A child's head poked in through the opening of the third door—the one that didn't lead to either bedchamber. Blonde curls rioted around a cherubic face. She slipped into the sitting room, a doll clutched in one arm.

Beatrix smiled at her, which drew Rockbourne to turn his head.

He set his wineglass down on a table beside the settee and shot to his feet. "Regan."

The girl's gaze was fixed on Beatrix. "Papa, who's that?"

"Ah, she's…a friend."

Regan came toward Beatrix. "I'm Regan. Can I be your friend too?"

"Please," Beatrix said. She put her glass on a table between the two chairs and leaned forward toward the girl. "Who is your friend?" She inclined her head toward the doll.

"This is Alice. But shh, she's sleeping. I brought her 'cause she doesn't like to be alone."

"You are most kind," Beatrix said with a soft smile. "I don't particularly like being alone either."

Regan tipped her head to the side, her green eyes fixed on Beatrix. "Who keeps you company? Is it my Papa?" She glanced over her shoulder at Rockbourne, who stood in front of the other chair.

Beatrix's gaze met his for a swift, heated moment. "Sometimes," she said. "When I come for a visit. Mostly my sister keeps me company."

"I want a sister."

"You have Alice," Beatrix said. "Can you pretend she's your sister?" The girl nodded. "How old are you, Regan?"

"Three."

"She'll be four this summer," Rockbourne said.

"How old are you?" Regan asked.

Beatrix hated lying to a child, but she always lied about her age. At twenty-six, she was old enough to be on the shelf. "Twenty-two."

Regan yawned. "Papa, are you that old?"

"Older, if you can believe it." He suppressed a smile. "I'm *thirty*. And you, my love, should be in bed." He swept her into his arms.

She laid her head on his shoulder. "All right."

He turned and went into his bedchamber. Beatrix wondered if she should leave. While she dithered, he returned, closing the door behind him with a soft click. "In the morning, I will instruct her that she must not tell anyone about my 'friend.'"

"An excellent plan, thank you," Beatrix said. "Your daughter can count."

"To ten. She gets lost after that." He sat back down on the settee.

"Still, she knew that twenty-two was *old*." Beatrix made a face.

Rockbourne laughed. "This is a new and exciting concept for her. My aunt has been spending time with us the past few days, and her hair is completely gray. Regan asked about it and Aunt Charity explained that some people's hair turns gray when they get older. That sparked a whole conversation about what older means."

Beatrix grinned. "I wish I could have heard it. She's delightful."

"I think so." He looked like a proud father. Beatrix's heart tugged.

"You allow her to sleep in your chamber?"

"It's easier than taking her upstairs, and her nurse knows I don't mind. Regan is to tell her nurse when she comes down here in the middle of the night. That way, Miss Addy won't awaken in a dead panic when her charge isn't in bed. Regan is thrilled to awaken me by poking my forehead and repeating 'Papa' about fifty times."

"That sounds lovely," Beatrix said with a sigh. "You are an excellent father."

"Forgive me for saying so, but I think your father is an ass for abandoning you."

Beatrix stared at him a moment before she could find her words. "Thank you. I used to tell myself he was overcome with grief after losing my mother."

"I would think that would have bonded him to you even more." Rockbourne didn't hide his disdain.

"I have to think he had a good reason." She *wanted* to think that. No, she needed to, or else she had to accept that he might never have loved her. It was far easier to believe that seeing her brought him too much pain after losing her mother.

"You're probably right." Rockbourne picked up his wine and finished it. "Would you like more madeira?"

"No, thank you. I am not quite finished." She still had nearly half left, and she was loath to drink it any more quickly. When it was gone, she'd have to leave. Or, she *could* have more since he didn't seem in any rush for her to depart.

And really, she should. She shouldn't even be here at all.

He stood and went to the small sideboard near the door to his bedchamber. After refilling his glass, he returned to the settee. "Your sister's wedding is soon, isn't it?"

"A week from next Tuesday at St. George's in Hanover Square." She grimaced. "My apologies. I realize that's where your brother-in-law was to be married last week."

"He's better off in Newgate. I can't say I'm surprised he was extorting people, and not just because I would believe Lord Colton before I would trust Chamberlain." Lord Colton was the man who'd first accused Chamberlain of extortion. After that, others had come forward. "He is as poison-filled as his sister was."

Rockbourne gripped his wineglass and took a drink. Beatrix noted the taut muscles of his jaw and neck.

She sought to divert the conversation once more. He'd said he didn't wish to speak of her, and Beatrix suspected he didn't even care to think of her just now. She drank more of her wine.

Rockbourne gazed at her intently. "Are you going to keep visiting me?"

"That depends. Are you going to keep inviting me in for madeira?"

"If that's what it takes, then yes."

"So you like my company?"

"I do. Right now, it's…difficult to be alone with my thoughts."

Beatrix wished she could squeeze herself next to him on the settee, but she didn't dare. "Why?"

Blowing out a breath, he set his wineglass down on the table. "Guilt?"

She leaned forward. "I've told you it wasn't your fault."

"But I should feel sad, shouldn't I?"

"You must feel however you feel." She nearly told him that her sister sometimes struggled with allowing herself to feel, but to reveal that would encourage a great many questions she couldn't answer. It was bad enough he knew she was Ramsgate's daughter. No one knew that save Selina, Harry, and Rafe.

"I don't know if I can," he whispered. His gaze dropped to the floor, where he stared for a moment before shaking his head briskly and reaching for his wine once more. "Do you know when you'll come next?"

It was an abrupt change of topic, but Beatrix could understand why. He may not be grieving his wife in the normal sense, but his life had changed.

"I don't," Beatrix responded. "There are a great many events between now and Selina's wedding."

"I want to hear how things go at Almack's." The edge of his mouth ticked up. "I can't ask you to visit after the ball—it will be far too late. In fact, I should see you home tonight. I can't believe I haven't before." He looked aghast.

"You do not have to see me home. I'm quite capable of looking after myself."

"What if you're set upon by a footpad?"

She waggled her brows at him. "What if *I'm* a footpad?"

There was a beat before he laughed. "I'd feel better if you'd let me see you home."

"No. You need to take care of Regan." She finished the rest of her wine. It was time to go. "I really am very capable." She rose.

He quickly stood and closed most of the gap between them. "Of protecting yourself from footpads? How can that be?"

"There's a great deal you don't know about me, Rockbourne." Such as the fact that she *had* been a footpad when needs had become dire.

"Perhaps someday I'll learn," he said softly.

A shiver danced across Beatrix's shoulders. She wanted to tell him she kept a small pistol in her pocket and that she knew how to use it. She longed to show him how she could outrun nearly any man.

Instead, she turned and went to the desk. Sweeping up her hat, she smashed it over her hair, which she'd piled tightly to the top of her head.

He beat her to the door and held it open for her. She went out onto the balcony and was slightly disappointed to find it hadn't started raining. If it had, she could have allowed him to see her home.

On the balcony, she abruptly turned to face him. "I shouldn't visit again. We've established it isn't proper."

"But we seem to enjoy it anyway. What's more, you are now friends with my daughter."

Damn, he was right. "I suppose that's true. I wouldn't want to disappoint her."

"And what of me?"

"My lord?" A distressed female voice carried out to the balcony to the sitting room.

Rockbourne's eyes widened. "That's Miss Addy."

Beatrix raced for the trellis and descended quickly. Five or so feet from the ground, she jumped and hurried through the garden, taking care to stay in the shadows. When she reached the corner, she looked back at the house. The balcony was empty.

She let herself out through the gate and made her way to Duke Street. In the light of a lantern, she shook her wrist until the stick of wax slid into her palm.

It was a silly thing to have taken, but she hadn't thought twice. In truth, she hadn't thought at all. The stick had been there, next to her hat, and when she'd picked up the accessory, the wax had simply come along for the ride.

Being an inconsequential object, he likely wouldn't even miss it, which was so much the better. Still, she should probably return it. On her next visit. That she really shouldn't make.

The first raindrop hit her sleeve. Tucking the wax into her pocket, she dashed into the night.

CHAPTER 4

*L*aughing, Thomas swept Regan up into the air the following afternoon on the lawn in the middle of Grosvenor Square. She giggled, and her bonnet went toppling to the ground.

"Oh no," he said, grinning as he lowered her to the ground.

Regan touched her now bare head. "My hat."

Her nurse picked up the accessory and smiled at Regan. "Let's put this back on. We don't want you to get freckles."

Thomas actually liked freckles. Miss Whitford had a few on her face, and they only added to her charm.

"Afternoon, Rockbourne."

Thomas turned to see his neighbor, the Duke of Ramsgate, walking toward him. Of average height with dull brown hair and a round paunch, the duke bore almost no resemblance to his beautiful daughter. Except for the eyes—the shape was the same as Miss Whitford's, though hers were a sparkling mix of light brown and green while the duke's were just brown.

"Afternoon, Ramsgate."

The duke eyed him speculatively. "You look well given the circumstances. Allow me to offer my condolences."

"Thank you." Thomas worked to hide his dislike, which was how he now felt toward the duke after having met his abandoned daughter. How a man could ignore his own flesh and blood was not only beyond Thomas, it made him furious.

"I lost my wife five years ago, so I understand what you're going through."

Thomas doubted that. For so many reasons.

"It's a bit different, of course," Ramsgate continued. "You don't yet have an heir, so you'll want to find a new wife. I didn't need to worry about that."

That's what he meant about understanding Thomas's position? "How did you manage your grief, particularly with regard to your children?" Thomas wasn't sure why he bothered asking, but he wanted to know. Mostly because he wondered if the duke truly ever thought of his other daughter, Miss Whitford.

Ramsgate waved his hand and scoffed. "Bah, grieving is for milksops. My children were fine. Both my daughters were already wed, so I was fortunate there. Managing unmarried daughters can be so troublesome!" He laughed, seemingly unaware that Thomas not only had a young daughter, but that she was standing just a few feet away with her nurse.

Thomas stared at him but said nothing.

"It's good that you're carrying on," Ramsgate said. "That's the way to go about things."

The duke's nonchalance was infuriating. Thomas couldn't seem to let it go, particularly where Miss Whitford was concerned. She'd said her father had loved her mother. Had she been wrong? "So you don't let death or loss concern you?"

"Why should I? The duchess lived a good life. I suppose our daughters were sad, but we didn't discuss it."

"Papa!" Regan wrapped her arms around Thomas's legs. "Fly again!"

Thomas swung her into the air and twirled her around. She shrieked with glee, and he hugged her to his side. "Now it's time to go inside for something to eat." He looked over at the duke, who was gaping at them as if Thomas had stripped off his clothes and run around the square nude.

"Ramsgate." Thomas inclined his head at the man before turning with Regan toward his house.

The moment Thomas stepped into his entry hall, he realized something was amiss. The butler, Baines, was not at his post. Instead, one of the footmen opened the door. And the young man appeared nervous, his gaze furtive and his shoulder twitching.

"What is it, Preston?" Thomas asked.

The footman glanced at Regan in Thomas's arms. Thomas handed her to the nurse. "I'll join you in a moment."

The nurse clasped Regan to her side and nodded before going upstairs.

Thomas turned his attention back to the footman. "Is something wrong?"

"No, my lord. I mean, I don't think so. There is

a Bow Street Runner, er, constable, waiting in the sitting room. And another one is downstairs speaking with Baines." His cheeks flushed, but he didn't look away.

"That troubles you." Thomas gave him an encouraging nod. "Don't let it."

It seemed Mrs. Chamberlain had gone to Bow Street after all. Thomas entered the sitting room and immediately recognized the constable. "Mr. Sheffield."

Harry Sheffield, brother to Thomas's friend North, the Viscount Northwood, inclined his head. "Good afternoon, my lord."

"Please, call me Rockbourne. Your brother is a friend of mine."

Sheffield was a rather imposing figure, with broad shoulders and an inch or two on Thomas. His dark auburn hair was brushed back from his forehead, which was lightly creased. "That's why I'm here. My colleague is leading an investigation into your wife's death, and I asked to accompany him."

Even from the grave, Thea would torment him. "May I ask why? Not why you're here, but why is there an investigation? Thea fell from the balcony. It was a tragedy. She is already interred."

"Her mother, Mrs. Chamberlain, is concerned it may not have been an accident. She asked Bow Street to conduct an inquiry. It's a formality, Rockbourne."

Thomas supposed he understood that. "What will this investigation entail?"

"We'll interview everyone in the household and look at where she fell."

Everyone? "You won't speak with my daughter. She barely understands what happened."

Sheffield shifted, his features displaying a slight discomfort. "That won't be necessary. My apologies. I wish we weren't bothering you at all."

Thomas exhaled. "I understand. Can I get you anything?"

"No, thank you. Shall we sit?"

Gesturing to the settee, Thomas took a chair opposite. He waited for the constable to pose his first question.

Sheffield withdrew a small bound book and a pencil. He opened it and scratched something on the parchment. "Can you tell me what happened prior to Lady Rockbourne's fall on Sunday night?"

Tension spun through Thomas's frame as he tried to find a comfortable position. He hadn't wanted to think about this again, let alone speak of it. "We were in the sitting room, as was sometimes the case at that hour." In truth, Thomas tried to avoid her, but occasionally that was impossible. "She'd imbibed in a great deal of port, which was not unusual."

"Her maid, Miss Emily Spicer, said you and she were arguing and that you often became angry with her."

Spicer had provided testimony? He'd rarely spoke to the woman. She was—or had been—Thea's maid and kept entirely to her mistress.

Thomas flexed his hands, then flattened them on his knees. "Is that what she said?"

Sheffield's gaze was unflinching. "It was."

Unfortunately, the maid wasn't entirely wrong. They *had* been arguing, and Thomas *sometimes* grew angry with Thea. To her, his anger justified her outrage. She hated when he failed to rise to her bait, which he tried to do as much as possible.

"I would rather not discuss the specifics of our conversation. The woman is dead, and I'd prefer to let her rest in peace." Thomas wanted peace too.

"Why would her mother think you'd pushed her? Many married couples argue."

"Do they?" Thomas had hoped his own parents were an aberration. "I understand you are shortly to be wed. Do you expect to argue with your wife?"

A quick smile flashed across Sheffield's mouth. "In fact, I do. I also expect to make up in a thoroughly enjoyable fashion."

Thomas wanted to laugh, but the truth was that he couldn't imagine such a relationship. Envy burned within him. "To answer your question, I can only guess at why my mother-in-law would think I pushed my wife from the balcony. Lady Rockbourne despised me. She likely told her mother any number of untruths about me, such as that I was unfaithful. Which I was not." Thomas saw no harm in telling him something Thea's mother had likely already reported to him or another constable.

"Your wife despised you? How did you feel about her?"

Exhaling, Thomas glanced toward the portrait of them that hung in the corner. It had been painted shortly after they'd wed. He made a mental note to remove it immediately. "I suppose I felt the same way about her." He met Sheffield's gaze and didn't flinch.

"You won't tell me what you were arguing about?"

No, he wouldn't, not entirely. "I confronted her about her infidelity—I doubt her mother mentioned that. The countess grew angry. She went out onto the balcony and the next I knew, she'd fallen. As I said, she was quite intoxicated."

"And this was a common occurrence? Her intoxication, I mean."

"Yes. I would say a night never went by when she didn't have multiple glasses of port. I have the receipts for the quantity I am required to purchase on a regular basis."

Sheffield scribbled some notes in his book before looking up at Thomas once more. "How did you become aware of her infidelity?"

"It's not uncommon knowledge." Distaste curled through Thomas. "I don't wish to soil her reputation now that she is gone. She is still my daughter's mother."

Sympathy creased Sheffield's features. "Yes, I understand. Was she having an affair with a specific gentleman?"

"I believe so, yes. But don't ask me who, because I don't know for certain." However, he had his suspicions. "I can't imagine his identity matters."

"Just so I may make a record, you deny pushing her?"

"I do. Emphatically."

After writing more onto his parchment, Sheffield snapped the book closed and returned it and the pencil to his coat pocket. "You weren't even on the balcony."

"That's correct."

"Well, I thank you for your time. I'd like to speak with whomever else was home that evening. I can wait here."

"You really want to talk with everyone in the household, even the scullery maids?" Thomas knew the answer, but hoped the man had perhaps changed his mind.

"If it's not too much trouble. My colleague, Mr. Dearborn, is downstairs speaking with your butler and whomever else, so I can speak with anyone who hasn't talked with him yet."

"I'll find out." Thomas rose. "May I offer my congratulations on your upcoming marriage?"

Sheffield stood. "Thank you. I'd hoped you would be able to attend the breakfast, but I understand that isn't possible."

"My aunt tells me it is, that the ton is already wagering when I will wed again."

"Is that your intent?" Sheffield's eyes narrowed as he asked.

"No. My intent is to focus on my daughter, who is now without a mother. And despite what anyone says, she doesn't *need* one." Thomas winced inwardly. In his effort to assure Sheffield that he wasn't interested in marrying—and thus might have had a motive in wanting his wife dead —he'd indicated his daughter didn't need a mother. Hopefully, the constable wouldn't interpret that as a motive either.

"I'll go and fetch someone." Thomas took himself from the room and found the housekeeper. As soon as he told her she was to be interviewed by the constable, the poor woman had gone white with fear. Thomas had tried to reassure her that everything would be fine.

However, the truth was he didn't know. There was no telling what his mother-in-law or Thea's maid had said to them.

He could only hope this was exactly what Sheffield had described it to be—a formality—and that it would soon pass. He really just wanted peace. And another visit from Miss Whitford.

~

*A*lmack's was a glittering palace with gilded columns and a plethora of mirrors that reflected the sparkling cut-glass gaslights. For such a beautiful setting, the food and drink was atrocious. Day-old bread, dry, tasteless biscuits, and the most pitiful lemonade Beatrix had ever tasted.

"This fare is worse than what we eat at home," Beatrix said to Selina. Their housekeeper also cooked for them and had no kitchen skills whatsoever. Selina had hired her because of her trustworthiness, which had been the most important trait given the fact that Selina had been conducting business as a fortune-teller under an alternate identity and Beatrix was stealing jewelry to pay for her season. Selina had since terminated her fortune-telling scheme, and they'd returned all the items Beatrix had stolen.

Selina's shoulders twitched. "I didn't think anything could be, but you're right. I admit I'm looking forward to moving to Cavendish Square and having a new cook."

Just that afternoon, Harry had shared the good news that he had leased the house in Cavendish Square that was owned by their friend the Marchioness of Ripley. It had become known as the Spitfire Society headquarters, which Selina didn't mind at all since she was quite involved with the group now. She and Beatrix planned to take up residence there on Friday, and Harry would move in after the wedding.

"I am too," Beatrix said with enthusiasm. "I'm glad Mrs. Vining is able to return to her former position at the inn." Their housekeeper-cook hadn't been at all disappointed to leave their employ. In fact, she'd been relieved to go back to her less demanding job.

"Put down the biscuit," Selina said. "There's another gentleman coming this way."

Beatrix had danced with several gentlemen already. She'd been amazed at how well they comported themselves, but then it had come to her attention that vouchers were often awarded to men based on their dancing ability.

The gentleman who approached was accompanied by Harry's sister, Lady Imogen. She smiled broadly as she greeted Selina and Beatrix. "Allow me to present Lord Worth."

Beatrix was glad she'd managed to swallow her last bite of terrible biscuit because she likely would have choked. The man was a trifle shorter than Rockbourne, with brown hair and somewhat familiar hazel eyes. He was also her half brother.

She dropped into a curtsey. "My lord."

"Lord Worth, this is Lady Gresham, who is to marry my brother Harry very soon, and this is her sister, Miss Beatrix Whitford."

The earl took Beatrix's hand and pressed a light kiss to the back. "It is my pleasure to make your acquaintance. I should be honored if you would dance the next set with me."

Beatrix shot a look of distress toward Selina, who knew that he was Beatrix's half brother. Selina widened her eyes almost imperceptibly in silent communication. Owing to Society's stupid rules, Beatrix couldn't refuse him.

"That would be lovely," she said, trying not to grit her teeth.

Maybe this would be fine. She could get to know him. Hopefully he wasn't interested in her romantically. But why else would he ask to be introduced to her?

He offered his arm, and Beatrix went with him to the dance floor. "I understand this is your first time at Almack's."

"Yes. This is my first Season in London."

"You are most fortunate. Many people are never awarded a voucher."

"So I've heard. And you must be an exceptional dancer, for I've heard that is the easiest way for a gentleman to get one."

He barked out a laugh. "You're a saucy one! I think you just suggested I couldn't get one on my own merits."

Oh dear, she rather had. Wasn't that a good thing? If he thought her rude, he wouldn't be interested in her. "It's my understanding that merit has nothing to do with who's invited." She lowered her voice. "Whether one of the patronesses likes you is far more important." She glanced toward the dais where the patronesses held court and lorded over the attendees. "Which one likes you?"

He laughed again. "I'm not entirely certain, but right now, I only care if *you* like me. What a captivating woman you are."

Damn, she hadn't meant to be captivating. Not to him, anyway. The music began, and she did her best throughout the set to step on his toes and be a generally bad dancer. Fleetingly, she wondered if her voucher could be revoked. Did she even care? Almack's might be *the* place to be and be seen, but so far, she wasn't impressed.

When the set was finished, he guided her from the dance floor. "My, but you're an…exuberant dancer," he said.

Beatrix nearly smiled. She was beginning to like him, and with that realization came a desire to forge an actual sibling relationship.

"Thank you, I do try. Do you come to Almack's every week?" she asked.

"Not every week, no. My father hopes I will wed this Season."

"Your father is the Duke of Ramsgate?"

He nodded.

"Is he here this evening?" Beatrix hadn't seen him, but perhaps he'd been hiding in an alcove.

"No, Father has no need to come. Though, he has threatened to attend and ensure I am making good use of my time." Worth rolled his eyes.

"Why is he so eager for you to wed?" Beatrix wanted to know all she could about her father.

"By my age, he was married with an heir."

"And what age is that?"

"Twenty-nine." He looked at her askance. "You are full of questions."

She lifted a shoulder. "How else can we get to know each other?" As soon as she said it, she wished she hadn't. There was a distinct gleam of satisfaction in his gaze.

Worth was twenty-nine? That was about the age her father had taken Beatrix's mother as his mistress. Beatrix wondered if Worth was aware of that.

"My turn for a question," he said, stopping and turning toward her. "How many suitors do you have?"

"Er, none."

He smiled. "How fortunate for me."

Bloody hell. "I'm not certain I'm ready for marriage this Season."

His brow pleated. "Then why bother with any of this?"

"Because it's entertaining and...educational? How can one determine if they are ready for marriage if they don't get out and meet people?"

"I suppose that's true. Be careful, however. Young ladies who aren't successfully wed within a Season or two are often judged a failure."

She pursed her lips at him. "And how many Seasons have you participated in without becoming betrothed?"

He laughed again. "You are utterly delightful!"

He continued taking her back toward Selina. "May I call on you?"

Beatrix swore to herself again. "Yes, I suppose you may. I can't imagine your father would approve, however. I'm not from a titled family like you." Hopefully, that would deter him.

"But your sister is Lady Gresham, and she is marrying the son of the Earl of Aylesbury. And you did get a voucher to Almack's. You would almost certainly pass his inspection."

A laugh gathered in Beatrix's throat, but she coughed instead. Perhaps she should just tell him the truth.

Thankfully, they arrived at Selina. Beatrix withdrew her hand from his arm. "Thank you for the dance, my lord."

"Please, call me Worth."

The name brought to mind the word worthy and the fact that *he* was worthy and Beatrix was not. She gave him a tight smile. "Thank you, Worth."

He bowed to her and to Selina, then took his leave.

"Can we go yet?" Beatrix asked, turning toward Selina.

"It's scarcely one o'clock," Selina said, blinking. "That's early, from what I understand. But we can certainly go. Goodness knows I'm bored."

Beatrix finally let out the laugh that she'd kept trapped inside. "Then let us depart."

They'd borrowed a coach from Rafe for the evening, and once they were settled inside, Selina kicked off her slippers. "I've decided it's nice to have a wealthy brother."

"I'm so glad."

When Selina had been reunited with him a few weeks ago, Rafe had offered support, but she'd declined. After so many years on their own, it was difficult for Selina to accept help. Especially when she'd felt abandoned by her brother. He'd taken her to the boarding school when she was eleven and had stopped writing to her after a while. Like Beatrix, she'd felt utterly forgotten. In Rafe's case, however, he'd been trying to keep her safe. He didn't want her returning to her old life in London or to him. But now that he had reinvented himself as a prosperous gentleman away from crime, they had reestablished their sibling relationship. Beatrix hoped for the same with her father.

"That doesn't mean it's easy allowing him to pay for things," Selina said. "I hate that, actually."

"I know," Beatrix said softly. "But there's no reason not to. Our lives have completely changed. You're getting married. You're in love. You're secure."

Selina turned her head toward Beatrix beside her and reached for her hand. "You're secure too. Always and forever. I will never abandon you."

Beatrix gave Selina's fingers a quick squeeze before letting her go and putting her hand down at her side. There was something in the pocket of her dress, she realized. A flash of alarm sparked through her. Had she taken something? She couldn't investigate it now.

"So how was your dance with your half brother?" Selina asked. "It looked as if you were struggling."

"On purpose. I was trying to deter his interest."

"Did it work?"

Beatrix exhaled with disappointment. "I don't think so. He asked if he could call on me." She shot Selina a disgruntled look. "Can you imagine anything worse than being courted by your half brother?"

Selina laughed. Eyes dancing, she clapped her hand over her mouth. After a moment, she lowered her hand to her lap. "I *can* think of worse things, actually, but that would still be rather unpleasant. What do you plan to do?"

"Continue to deter him?" Beatrix lifted her hands and shrugged. "What can I do? Tell him we share a father?"

"Will you? If it comes to that, I mean."

"I don't know. I suppose I'll have to see what happens when I finally meet my father."

"Well, you'll meet him on Friday at the masquerade. Hopefully, you will have a private interview shortly thereafter."

"Yes, then I can determine how I will go on." This entire journey to London to have a Season had been for Beatrix to reconnect with her father and forge a future. She just wasn't sure what that future looked like.

"Did you like any of the other gentlemen you danced with?" Selina asked. "The Earl of Daventry seemed nice."

"He was." Except the only man that came to Beatrix's mind was Rockbourne. She desperately wanted to tell him how tonight had gone. Because he'd asked and was clearly interested. And since he knew who her father was, she could tell him about the awkward interlude with Worth.

When they arrived at home, Beatrix quickly went upstairs to her room to discover what she'd stolen.

Alone in her chamber, she removed her gloves and kicked her slippers off. She reached into her pocket and withdrew a small, oval, silver snuffbox. She ran her thumb over the design on the top—a stamped, diamond-shaped pattern—then turned it over looking for any identifying marks such as initials. There were none. And she had no idea from whom she'd taken it.

Scowling, she closed her hand around the object and stalked to her dresser. Crouching down, she opened the bottom drawer and reached into the back, where she'd put a piece of wood as a false backing. Pulling that out of the way, she located the wooden box and extracted it from the drawer.

She sat on the floor, her skirts billowing around her as she put the simple oak box on her lap. About five inches wide and five inches tall, it provided the perfect place for Beatrix to stash the objects she'd stolen without realizing.

Opening the lid, she gazed at the collection of odds and ends. There was jewelry, writing implements, silverware, and now a snuffbox. The items were familiar to her now, but each one had been a mystery as to where she'd gotten it and to whom it truly belonged.

Not quite all of them were familiar. She put the silver snuffbox inside and picked up the last thing she'd added—an ivory-handled penknife with the initials DC carved into an intricate design.

Beatrix set the knife back into the box and

frowned at the contents. Why was she keeping all this?

A light knock on her door made her slam the box closed and thrust it back into the dresser. She shut the drawer and got to her feet. "Come in."

Selina slipped inside, closing the door behind her. "I thought you might need help with your gown."

Of course. They didn't have a lady's maid. "Yes, thank you." She presented her back to Selina, who unbuttoned the garment.

"Are you all right?" Selina asked. "You came upstairs so quickly."

"I just wanted to change out of this gown." But had apparently forgotten to request assistance.

"Are you disappointed your father wasn't there tonight?"

Beatrix pulled her arms from the sleeves. "A little."

Selina helped pull the gown over Beatrix's head. Turning, Selina took it to the armoire. "Now that I'm to be married, I can imagine you want to map your own future."

Beatrix supposed that was true. "I'm not concerned, if that's what you're wondering. Things will work out."

"You've always been so optimistic." Selina smiled warmly. "It's one of the things I love most about you. And it kept me from becoming too lost."

Beatrix thought of what Rockbourne had said —that he needed people like her in his life. She suddenly wanted Selina to leave.

"I wanted to ask you about Rockbourne," Selina said.

Freezing, Beatrix wondered how Selina had managed to read her mind.

Selina untied the petticoat at the back of Beatrix's waist. "You seemed interested in him the other day."

"I wasn't—not specifically." Beatrix stepped out of the petticoat, and Selina took it in hand. "I suppose I just found his story fascinating."

Selina walked the petticoat to the armoire too. "Harry told me Bow Street is investigating his wife's death."

Beatrix's fingers fumbled as she unlaced her stays. Giving up before she finished, she went to sit at her dressing table. "Why would they investigate?"

"Apparently, his mother-in-law thinks Rockbourne may have pushed his wife from the balcony." Selina's eyes met Beatrix's in the mirror. "You mustn't share this information of course. But then, we aren't gossips."

"Of course not." Beatrix's heart was racing. She had to see him. Tonight. She pretended to yawn. "I'm glad we came home. I'm quite fatigued." She turned on the stool and smiled at Selina. "You don't need to linger. Isn't Harry waiting for you?"

Selina blushed. "No. I told him we'd be late."

"So he's not coming?" Beatrix would prefer if her sister was distracted.

"No, he is." She blushed even harder.

Beatrix laughed softly. "I love seeing you in love."

"Thank you." There was an edge of sisterly sarcasm to her tone. She blew Beatrix a kiss and said good night.

As soon as Selina was gone, Beatrix leapt up and changed her attire. A short while later, she slipped out of the house and made her way to Grosvenor Square.

CHAPTER 5

Half past two. She was probably still dancing.

Thomas set his empty glass on the sideboard. He was tempted to pour another, but he ought to turn in. It wasn't as if she would come. He'd told her it would be too late, and it was.

Still, he could see her in his mind, her blonde locks curling about her face with ribbons and silk flowers entwined in the style atop her head. Her ivory gown was trimmed with lace and dark coral ribbon that matched those in her hair. The costume was simple but elegant, allowing her beauty to shine instead of the garments and accessories.

He'd stood in the shadows nearby and watched her enter the assembly rooms. It was as close as he could get in his current state of mourning, and he was grateful for the glimpse. He'd lingered for a while before returning home. Since then, he'd imagined her laughing and dancing, captivating every gentleman at Almack's. How he envied them.

Blowing out a breath of frustration, he turned

toward his chamber. The soft snick of a door drew his head around.

A black-clad figure stood just inside the sitting room. If he didn't know better, he would have been concerned. Instead, he pivoted, unable to keep from grinning.

She swept her hat off and set it on the writing desk as she'd done on her last visit. "I know you said it would be too late, but I had to come." She cast off her gloves as well, setting them atop her hat.

"It is late, but not as late as I thought it would be. Miss Whitford, you should still be at the ball."

"It was so boring." She waved her hand and strode toward him. "And do call me Beatrix. It's past time. I heard Bow Street is investigating you. You must tell me everything." She took him by the hand and pulled him to the settee.

She sat, and he squeezed in beside her, pleased she'd chosen to sit with him here.

Angling herself toward him, she stared at him expectantly. "Well? Why didn't you tell me Bow Street was conducting an inquiry?"

He stifled the urge to laugh. He adored her enthusiasm. "Do you wish to hear about it, or would you rather I answer that question first?"

"Both." She clasped her hands in her lap. "Tell me about the inquiry."

"The other question is simpler. I didn't mention it because I haven't seen you. Furthermore, there isn't much to share. Two constables came to interview me and the entire household on Friday."

Her hazel eyes rounded. "The *entire* household? You didn't let them speak to Regan?"

That she had the same reaction he'd had and with apparently the same affront made him want to kiss her.

It did?

Many things made him want to kiss her.

"Of course not. They wanted to speak to her nurse, but she was too busy with Regan and I refused to let them speak to her when Regan was present."

Beatrix flattened her palms on her lap and leaned slightly toward him. "What did they ask you?"

Distracted by her spicy floral scent, he had to think about her question. "Ask me? Ah, they asked what happened that night." Dammit, he didn't want to talk about that. He wanted to ask her about Almack's.

She narrowed her eyes at him briefly. "You seem rather unconcerned."

He put his arm along the back of the settee. "Sheffield said it was a formality."

"Harry was one of the constables who came?"

"Yes. He accompanied the lead investigator—a young man called Dearborn."

"I don't know him, but I'll find out what I can."

"There's no need. As I said, the inquiry is a formality. My mother-in-law is causing trouble, that's all." His hand was close to her head. Her hair was still dressed as it had been for the ball, though the ribbon and flowers were gone. He could almost touch her curls. Or her cheek. Or the slope of her neck. His fingers twitched with want.

"Why would she do that?"

Thomas was having a hard time keeping his

focus on the conversation. He didn't want to talk about his mother-in-law—ex-mother-in-law—or his deceased wife. "Because she's upset that her daughter died, and she dislikes me."

"So she wants to blame you for her death? That's awful."

"I've survived worse."

She studied him, her gaze inquisitive. "Such as what?"

Hell. He hadn't meant to open up that line of discussion. "Her daughter. I promise you, living with Thea was much, much worse."

Beatrix's features softened. "I hate hearing that." She reached over and touched the hand that rested on his thigh.

The contact jolted through him—and perhaps through her as well. Her gaze lifted to his and that connection was just as potent.

"She's gone now," he managed to say.

"Yes. It must be a…relief."

He expended great effort to not twine his fingers with hers. "I shouldn't say so, but it is."

"Anything you tell me will be kept secret. We have a bargain, remember?" Her fingers moved across the back of his hand, sending sparks of heat up his arm and into his chest. They spread lower, stoking a long-buried desire. He should get up and put some distance between them. Instead, he let his hand glide a bit lower on the back of the settee toward her neck.

"And anything you tell me will be treated the same," he said. "Why did you find Almack's boring?"

"Haven't you been before?"

"I have, but that was several years ago. There's no need to go after you're wed."

"But some people do."

"Then I suppose they must like being bored. And gossip."

She laughed, her dimples creasing half-moons into her cheeks. Her eyes lit with mirth. "You've already said you don't like gossip, and since you stopped going once it became unnecessary, I must assume you also found it boring."

He cocked his head to the side and nodded slightly. "Just so."

She swatted at his upper arm and put her hand back on his, as if they sat in this intimate fashion all the time. How lovely that sounded. "Why didn't you tell me it was tedious? I could have avoided it entirely."

Now he laughed. "You wanted to go! Who was I to dissuade you? Besides, weren't you hoping to see your father?"

"Yes, but he wasn't there. Instead, I had to suffer the attentions of my half brother." She shuddered in horror.

Attentions? A visceral need to protect—or perhaps claim—her shot through him. "What did he do?"

"He asked me to dance, and I think he was flirting." She made a face. "I wanted to tell him to stop, but I didn't. Instead, I stepped on his feet a number of times and tried to behave in a manner that would deter him from finding me interesting."

"How anyone *couldn't* find you interesting is

impossible, but how I wished I could have seen you try."

She beamed at him. "You truly think that?"

"In case it isn't obvious, Beatrix, I am captivated by you."

"That was the word Worth used. And that was after I all but insulted him."

This was the most fun Thomas had had in years. Captivated didn't come close to how he felt right now. "How did you insult him?"

She scrunched up her face. "I may have implied he only received a voucher because he was a good dancer. And that his merits had nothing to do with whether he was invited, that it was because one of the patronesses must like him. In truth, it's probably because he's the son of a duke."

Thomas wasn't well enough acquainted with Worth to know if he'd been truly insulted. Nor did he care. He'd prefer the man left Beatrix alone. "Not true. I've known dukes who wouldn't be invited. Take the Duke of Romsey. Or the Duke of Clare. Or even the Duke of Kilve. Or the Marquess of Axbridge."

"Goodness, that's a great many untouchables who don't pass muster."

"You've heard their nicknames?"

She looked confused. "What's that?"

"You called them Untouchables—that's how they are often described. You hadn't heard that before?" When she shook her head, he went on, "Clare is perhaps the most infamous—he's the Duke of Desire. Actually, Axbridge is quite notorious too. He's the Duke of Danger."

"I thought you said he was a marquess."

"He is, but all the Untouchables have ducal nicknames. It's rather silly."

"My goodness." Her gaze locked on him. "Are you an Untouchable?"

"I am not. I think I was already married before the nicknames became popular. They are all married now, and the novelty seems to have waned."

"So they are called dukes of something. How do they arrive at those names in particular?"

"In Clare's case, it's because he had a rather, ah, scandalous reputation. And Axbridge had a penchant for dueling. In fact, he killed his wife's former husband in a duel."

Beatrix gasped, and for a moment, her hand clasped his wrist. "You're joking."

He shook his head. "I'm not. And, if you can believe it, he and the marchioness are quite thoroughly and obviously in love."

"How extraordinary. That's something one would expect to read in a novel." She shook her head in disbelief. Musing, she fixed him with a contemplative stare. "You would be the Duke of Delight, I think."

Another laugh burst from him. "Delight? I don't think so."

"Why not?" She sniffed, raising her chin. "*I* think you're delightful."

"You might be the only one."

"Why would you say that?" she asked with a hint of distress. "I'm sure your daughter would agree with me."

"Fair enough. That makes two of you."

She edged closer to him on the settee, and every fiber of his being came fully aware. "Just because your wife was cruel doesn't mean others are."

His wife. His father. The primary people he'd looked to for care and support. For love. He had no expectation for people *not* to be cruel.

"You didn't tell me how things resolved with Worth. Did you send him screaming from the assembly rooms?"

"I wish. He asked if he could call on me." She made another face. "Can you imagine?"

He could, and Thomas found he wanted to punch the man in the face. "What will you do if he does?"

"I don't know. I don't want to tell him who I am, not until I see my father. Hopefully, that will be Friday at the masquerade ball."

"Right. I'd forgotten that was coming up." He hadn't at all, but he wouldn't tell her. If his plans came to fruition, he would surprise her. "You're sure he'll be there?"

"He's expected."

"Will he recognize you, do you think?"

"That is my hope. If not, well, I'll have to pay him a visit, I suppose." She lifted a shoulder.

"I really do wish I could introduce you."

"That is very kind of you. Perhaps you should be the Duke of Kindness. Or Thoughtfulness." She licked her lips, and the sight of her tongue sent a rush of blood straight to Thomas's cock. "Does it have to be the duke of something?"

Thomas fought to speak past the stark lust pulsing through him. "Er, no. The Duke of Kendal is the Forbidden Duke. That was his nickname long before the Untouchables."

"I see. He was the start of it all?" She traced her finger over his wrist. Was she even aware? Thomas was. His entire body sang with want. "You should be the Handsome Duke."

He felt absurdly pleased. "You think I'm handsome?"

"Very." The word came out on a rasp. She abruptly pulled her hand away. He nearly snatched it back. "I should probably go." She started to rise, and Thomas wanted to stop her. He yearned to cup her neck and lean over her, to press his lips to hers and forget every disappointment he'd ever known.

When she was on her feet, she looked down at him. "I really did just want to come and make sure you were all right—with the inquiry. If you think nothing will happen, I won't worry."

"I don't think anything will happen. It's been several days, and I haven't heard another word about it."

"I'm still going to ask Harry next time I see him. I think we're having dinner at his parents' house tomorrow night."

"I'd rather you didn't. I'd just prefer if the entire matter could...fade away." He felt a pang of guilt for wanting that. He ought to mourn Thea, but in some ways, he already had. Years ago, when he'd realized his marriage was never going to be what he'd hoped, that she wasn't the woman he thought. Now he was just eager to put the entire mess behind him, for that's what their union had been—a mess.

Beatrix looked a bit disappointed by his request. Even so, she agreed. "If you change your mind, I hope you'll tell me. As your friend, I want to help."

Thomas stood. "You've already done so. We're friends, then?"

"I think so. Don't you?"

"I hope so." In truth, he could imagine her being much more.

She went to the desk and drew on her gloves. Next, she set her hat over her curls, obstructing them from his view.

"Your hair is lovely tonight," he said.

She touched her face. "Thank you. You should have seen it earlier."

"I did, actually." He hadn't meant to tell her, but found he couldn't help himself. "You looked beautiful."

Her mouth opened as she stared at him. "How…?"

"I was spying on you outside Almack's. Like how you spy on your father." He cracked a smile.

"How naughty of you."

"Then you must be too."

"I suppose so, and not just for spying on my father." She grinned. "Coming here in the middle of the night qualifies as naughty."

"It does indeed. The only thing naughtier would be if you thought you could walk home alone. I'm coming with you."

"That isn't necessary."

"I disagree, and tonight you won't talk me out of it. Let me fetch my coat."

She looked down at his feet. "You might need footwear."

He wasn't wearing boots. Or a cravat. "Promise you won't leave while I get dressed?"

"No. You'd better hurry."

He dashed into his chamber and shoved his feet into his boots, then he grabbed a cravat and threw it around his neck. Plucking up the coat he'd taken off earlier, he hurried back into the sitting room. She had her hand on the door to the balcony.

"You want me to climb down the trellis?"

She arched a taunting, pale brow at him. "Are you saying you can't?"

He narrowed his eyes at her and went to open the door. "I'll wager I can do it faster. After you, Miss Whitford."

"I told you to call me Beatrix," she murmured.

He leaned down and whispered next to her ear, "After you, *Beatrix*." He felt the shiver that raced along her neck as she gently twitched. Her scent filled his nostrils once more, and he briefly closed his eyes, savoring the moment of closeness.

She turned her head as he opened his eyes. Again, she licked her lips. He nearly groaned.

Tossing him a saucy stare, she went out onto the balcony. Before he had the door closed, she was over the railing and on her way down. By the time he reached the trellis, she was staring up at him, her arms crossed with mock impatience.

Smiling, he grabbed the trellis and swung over the side of the balcony. The iron moved in his grasp, urging him to descend quickly even if he hadn't planned to. He took only a few steps down the trellis before letting go and dropping to the ground.

"No fair, you're much taller than me, which makes you able to go faster." She made a tsking sound with her tongue. "It's a good thing I didn't take that bet."

He strode toward her. "That depends on what you would have wagered. Some bets are worth losing."

"I'll remember that." Her eyes danced in the meager light shining from the house as she turned and led him through the garden.

Thomas kept up with her, impressed at how quickly and deftly she moved. "You're quite familiar with my garden. Perhaps more than I am."

She opened the gate and slipped through it before he could hold it open. He closed it after he was through and caught up to her. "You aren't even letting me be a gentleman."

"You have nothing to prove to me. I already know you're a gentleman." She flashed him a smile. "Keep up!"

He chuckled. "Your legs are perhaps half the length of mine."

"I'm not *that* short! When it isn't dark, perhaps I'll challenge you to a footrace. And we'll have a proper wager."

"I look forward to it." He leaned close to her and whispered, "Because I'll win."

She ran ahead and turned, sticking her tongue out at him. Damn, she was quite fast. He picked up his pace, but she rounded the corner of Duke Street before he could catch her.

He reached the intersection and turned, only to nearly collide with her as she jumped into his path.

She made a sound that startled him, which was followed by her joyous laughter.

He clasped her elbows, and she tilted her head book to look up at him. "Don't scare me like that. And I don't mean jumping out, I mean leaving my sight. What if a villain grabbed you?"

"He'd be quite sorry." She grabbed his hand and turned with him toward Oxford Street. Unfortunately, she let go after just a moment.

They walked in silence for several paces. He thought back over their earlier conversation. "Beatrix, what will you do after you settle things with your father?"

"What do you mean?"

"Will you be content to have a relationship with him, or will you look for something…else?"

"Such as marriage?"

"You did go to Almack's and you danced with several gentlemen, did you not?"

"I did."

"You will be seen as desiring marriage, and I can't imagine you'll be on the market long."

She made a choking sound. "You make me sound like a cut of prime beef or produce. Or perhaps a broodmare."

He grimaced. "Forgive me. That was not my intent."

"To answer your question, I *would* like to marry. Eventually. The security and warmth of a family appeals to me."

Security and warmth. He couldn't have chosen two more perfect words. "Yes, exactly."

They'd reached Oxford Street, a wide thoroughfare that was mostly quiet at this late hour.

Still, there was the occasional vehicle. Thomas looked in both directions before taking her hand and guiding her across the street.

They turned to the right, and this time, she didn't take her hand from his. With each step, he was more and more aware of her, of his growing attraction to her, of the absolute bliss of this night.

He was so focused on her that he didn't see the movement to their left. The man was already on her before Thomas knew what was happening. He launched himself toward them, fearing he reacted too late.

CHAPTER 6

*B*eatrix had been so enthralled with Rockbourne that she'd completely missed the criminal dashing out from a narrow street until he was nearly on her. She tried to move, but there wasn't time.

"What have we here?" a second man said as the first, a burly fellow who stank of gin, grabbed Beatrix by the arms and dragged her back toward the shadows of the side street.

Rockbourne collided with them, and they all tumbled to the pavement.

The sound of a pistol hammer cocking clicked in Beatrix's ears. She rolled away from the two men who were now grappling for the upper hand and reached into her boot. Withdrawing the small knife, she freed the blade and pivoted onto her knee so that she was close to the man with the pistol. Without pause, she sank the blade into the back of his thigh. Pulling it out, she used her advantage of surprise—and his injury—and leapt up, hitting her forearm against his wrist to knock the pistol from his hand. The weapon flew and landed a few feet away as the man shrieked.

Standing straight, Beatrix pulled a small pistol from the slim interior pocket of her coat and pointed it in the man's face. "Go."

The man didn't hesitate. He hobbled away as quickly as his wound would allow. Beatrix found the gun she'd forced from his grip and plucked it up.

Then she spun toward the two men who were still wrestling. No, not wrestling. Rockbourne had the upper hand and was currently pummeling the man's face. Except it was more than that. He was attacking the miscreant viciously, mercilessly.

"Tom!" she called, not wanting to use his title. "I've got the gun!"

Rockbourne stopped and looked over at her, his eyes wide, his mouth open as he panted with exertion. The footpad seized the opportunity to shove Rockbourne off him. Scrambling to his feet, the brigand nearly stumbled as he fought to get away. Rockbourne lunged for him, but the man moved just out of reach and managed to start running.

"Let him go," Beatrix said, lowering both pistols. "Are you all right?"

"Am *I* all right?" Rockbourne stood. "Are you? Never mind, I can see you are. How on earth do you have two pistols?"

"One was the footpad's and one is mine." She tucked hers back into her coat.

He gaped at her. "You carry a pistol?"

She nodded. "Seems prudent given I'm out this late."

"Prudent." He shook his head as if he was befuddled. "It's bloody dangerous."

"Not since I carry a pistol. Just look how I was able—"

He strode toward her and took the other pistol from her hand. "See how easy it was for me to disarm you?"

She frowned up at him. "You aren't a threat. If you were, you wouldn't have. I would have shot you before you got too close. I know how to use a gun."

He ran his hand through his hair. "Christ, Beatrix. You scared the hell out of me."

"*I* scared you?"

He exhaled and fixed his gaze on her. "Not you, but what happened. Wait, yes, you. You wandering around London in the middle of the night with a bloody pistol scares the hell out of me."

"It shouldn't. As you can see, I'm quite capable of taking care of myself." She looked around. "Do you see any footpads?"

"There were two of them and two of us. If I hadn't accompanied you tonight—" He snapped his mouth closed and grabbed her elbow. "You can't do this again. No more coming to my house after dark."

Her brows formed an angry V. "You aren't my father. Or my husband."

"You don't have a bloody father. At least not one that's worth a damn. And you don't have a husband. You have me, and you'll listen to me, goddammit."

She drew back, surprised at the vitriol in his tone. Suddenly, she realized he *was* scared. And that fear made him angry. "Rockbourne," she whispered. "Tom." She liked the way that felt on her tongue. Reaching up, she gently touched his cheek. "I'm sorry. Please don't be afraid, not for me. I'm stronger—and more capable—than you think."

He seemed to quiet, the fire in his gaze dimming. "You're not used to anyone looking after you."

She realized he was right. "Not really. Just my sister. And she's even stronger and more capable than I am." Dropping her hand to her side, she smiled, hoping to get back to the joy they'd shared earlier.

He tucked the pistol into the side of his waistband beneath his coat. Pivoting, he found her hat. As he handed it to her, she saw the damage to his hand. Blood smeared his knuckles. She hadn't noticed if the footpad had been wounded, but surmised he had been. There was too much blood for it to be from the abrasions on Rockbourne's flesh alone.

Beatrix took the hat with one hand and clasped his hand with the other. "You're hurt."

"It's nothing."

"It isn't nothing."

"Come on, let's get you home. You're on Queen Anne Street?"

"Yes. For now."

He looked at her in question. "You're moving?"

"To Cavendish Square. Tomorrow, actually. The owner, the Marchioness of Ripley, is leasing the house to Harry. This way, he and Selina will have a larger house. Both ours and his are rather small. I'll show you where. We can walk by on our way to Queen Anne Street."

With a nod, he turned in the direction of Cavendish Square. She joined him, and they continued along Oxford Street at a brisk pace before turning left toward Cavendish Square.

His silence made her anxious. She hoped he wasn't angry anymore. She also wanted to make sure he understood that she did not want to be managed.

"I'm not sure I can promise not to venture out after dark," she said gently. "How else can I visit you?"

"Send a note, and I'll come meet you."

"Truly?" Anticipation tripped up her spine. Though, she'd have to determine how to send a note. But wait! They would have at least one footman at Cavendish Square, perhaps even two! She and her mother had employed a footman in Bath. Rather, Ramsgate had. He'd spared no expense when it came to Beatrix's mother. Except then someone in the household would know her secret—that she was at least sending messages to Rockbourne. This would take some planning.

"Yes, truly." Rockbourne sounded calmer.

They turned into Cavendish Square. "The house is just there on the right." She pointed to the house that had most recently been occupied by her friend Jane Pemberton. "Lady Colton has already moved out. She and Lord Colton were wed, rather by surprise, a week ago. It was incredibly romantic."

"In what way?"

"He arrived at her house with a special license,

a vicar, and her sister as well as their best friends." They paused in front of the house.

"Lady Colton had no idea?" Tom asked.

Beatrix shook her head. "None. Isn't that lovely?"

"So long as she said yes." He chuckled, and she was so glad to hear the sound. "That could have ended badly."

"I suppose it could have. Lord Colton probably knew how she felt, don't you think?"

"I think knowing and understanding others' feelings is extremely complicated. I'm glad things worked out for them. I hope they'll be very happy." He said the last with a mix of wistfulness and darkness, as if he expected his hope to be dashed.

"So the house is empty?" he asked.

"Well, the servants are there. Harry is retaining all of them." She turned to look up at him. "Why do you ask?"

"No particular reason. There are just...opportunities with an unoccupied house."

Desire fluttered in her belly—and lower. All night, she'd been aware of an undercurrent of attraction. There had been a few times in his sitting room when she thought he might kiss her. She'd been shocked to realize she wanted him to. Rather desperately, in fact.

Now he was telling her about opportunities with an unoccupied house. Her imagination took flight and winged its way directly into a fervent longing.

Before she could ask about *specific* opportunities, he skimmed his hand against her lower back, and they continued along the square. He didn't keep touching her as they moved, much to her disappointment.

"You didn't answer why you have a pistol," he said.

"I don't recall you asking." She was sure he hadn't.

He didn't look at her as they walked. "Why do you have a pistol?"

"Because I'm, as you put it, wandering around London in the middle of the night."

His exasperated breath permeated the damp night air. "Where did you get that pistol?"

That wasn't a story she felt comfortable sharing. He was already wondering about what kind of woman she must be since she'd held her own against a footpad. What would he think if she told him she'd stolen it? "It was given to me by a…friend."

"How do you know how to use it? You said you did."

"My sister and I thought it wise to learn how to shoot. Her former husband taught us." She hated making up things that were blatantly untrue. Long ago, Selina had cautioned her against doing so because if you forgot what you'd said, you risked being caught in the lie. It was better to rely on half-truths or, better still, to avoid answering troublesome questions altogether. That was becoming harder and harder with Rockbourne. He already knew far more about her than anyone except Selina.

Why had she let her guard down with him?

Beatrix cast him a sidelong glance as they reached Portland Street. Perhaps she should sever this relationship entirely. What was the point of it anyway? She'd helped him, he'd helped her—she was certain he was behind the voucher to Almack's. Everything else was now just…what? What was it?

Temptation.

He was a father in mourning, and she was the bastard daughter of a duke who was hoping to secure her future. There really wasn't any need for them to continue meeting, much as she wanted to. How sad that made her.

She opened her mouth to say so, but he spoke first.

"Tonight was the most fun I've had in a very, very long time." He paused a beat. "Except for the footpads." He said the last with a humor-filled warmth that made her smile. Not that she needed much prodding after he'd said tonight was the most fun he'd had in a long time.

A *very, very* long time.

"The footpad incident wasn't all bad."

"I suppose that's true." Now he looked at her, and she felt the heat in his gaze *everywhere*. "I liked it when you called me Tom."

"I didn't want to call you by your title. Not then."

"Don't feel as though you ever need to use that again. Tom is fine. Tom is lovely, in fact."

Yes, he was.

Against her better judgment, Beatrix reached for his hand and twined her fingers with his. She wished with every fiber of her being that she wasn't wearing gloves.

"We're nearly to Queen Anne Street," she said.

"I know."

She realized their gait had slowed. He seemed as reluctant as she was for the night to end. Maybe they should have stolen into the house in Cavendish Square. But again, to what end?

Beatrix didn't care. She didn't want to think past the next few moments.

"Will you let me know if Bow Street contacts you again?" she asked.

"No."

She frowned. "Why not?"

"What would you do?"

"I don't know. I'd just like to be aware." She was worried about him. Losing a spouse, the parent of one's child, had to be difficult even in the worst of situations, which it seemed their marriage was. He seemed all right for the most part, but his flash of anger—and the way he pummeled the footpad— gave her pause.

"It's a moot issue since they won't be contacting me. You can put the entire affair from your mind."

"Have you?" she asked softly.

"I'm trying to." His voice was tight, and she was almost sorry she'd asked.

"I'm here if you ever need to talk about it."

"I won't, but I appreciate that."

They reached the corner of Queen Anne Street. Beatrix stopped but didn't let go of his hand. "Thank you for seeing me home. I'm glad you were with me. I would not have wanted to face two footpads alone."

"You might be dead." He squeezed her hand.

"Promise me you won't endanger yourself like that again. I couldn't bear it."

The insistence and desperation in his voice pulled at her heart. She moved closer to him. "I won't." The fact was that he wasn't wrong. She would have been in a great deal of trouble. She could have shot one of them, but then what of the other?

Shoving the dark thoughts away, she summoned a smile. "Good night, then."

"You'll send me a note when you want to visit again?"

She nodded, but she wouldn't. Because there wasn't going to be an again.

They stared at each other, the night dark and cool around them. She shivered. He bent his head. She parted her lips, certain that he would kiss her now. Finally.

But all he did was tip her hat back and brush his lips against her forehead. Replacing the hat, he let go of her hand and stepped back. "I'm going to watch until you're inside. Good night, Beatrix."

"Good night, Tom." Her body thrummed with unsatisfied need. Nevertheless, she turned and went to the house, where she slipped down the stairs to the basement entrance.

She hurried upstairs and held back the curtain to see if he was still there. He stood on the other side of the narrow street, a tall, shadowy figure.

They watched each other for several minutes before he finally turned and walked back toward Portland Street. When he disappeared from sight, she stepped back and let the curtain fall.

Sadness wrapped around her and snaked down

her throat, making it feel scratchy and raw. She wouldn't cry. This wasn't an ending, but a beginning. Tomorrow, she and Selina would move to Cavendish Square, to security. And the following night, she would finally meet her father. Her future was assured.

But was it the future she still wanted?

~

*R*egan had bounded into Thomas's room at an exceptionally early hour. He'd been asleep only a short while since returning from walking Beatrix home. And that was after he'd tossed in his bed for some time before finally dozing off, his mind and body rife with the excitement of his evening with Beatrix.

Evening? It had been the middle of the damn night.

And every moment of it had been positively sublime. Well, not *every* moment. Thinking of the footpad attack still made his heart race as well as sparked his rage. When he'd seen that man grab Beatrix, Thomas had wanted to pound him into oblivion.

He might have too, if not for her intervention. There'd been a note of fear in her voice. Had she seen into the rot inside him? He prayed not. Yet, there had been a finality to their parting last night that made him wonder.

No, that couldn't be the end of their association, even if it should be.

The invitation to the masquerade ball her brother was hosting tomorrow night sat in the middle of Thomas's desk. He'd already responded. Last night was *not* the last time he would see her.

He sat back in his chair and tried, for the dozenth time at least, to reconcile her reaction to the attack. She'd fended off the other assailant quite handily. Thomas had been too focused on beating the man who'd gone after her to see what she'd done to make him run. Or how she'd obtained his pistol.

Thomas thought of the weapon he'd locked in a case in his chamber. Then he thought of Beatrix's pistol. She'd had a gun! And apparently knew how to use it. He was simultaneously shocked and impressed by her capability. He was also not entirely certain he understood her explanation.

That she was allowed to move about freely after dark, armed with a pistol or not, was concerning. He had a half mind to talk with her sister. But that would almost certainly ensure they wouldn't meet anymore.

He blew out a frustrated breath. Yet, that's what *should* happen. He was putting her reputation at risk meeting with her like that. Yes, she'd already risked it herself by coming here to spy on her father, but Thomas was now compounding matters. Furthermore, he'd asked her to notify him of further meetings so he could coordinate them. He was rather formally contributing to her potential ruin.

Leaning forward, he rested his elbows on the desk, then put his head in his hands and closed his eyes.

"My lord?" Baines said softly.

Thomas lifted his head and blinked at the butler. "Yes?"

"Mrs. Holcomb has arrived."

"Thank you, Baines."

"How are your hands?" the butler asked tentatively.

Thomas splayed his hands and held them in front of his face. The abrasions on his knuckles were red and raw. The wounds stung, but less now than when he'd arrived home. "Cook had a poultice that Mrs. Henley insisted I use." His valet had applied it twice already. To a person, no one had asked how he'd sustained the injury. Baines, however, had asked if he was all right.

"You're certain you've no other injuries?" Baines asked.

"Thank you for your concern." Thomas gave him a weak smile. And then, because he would have to tell his aunt a story, he said, "It's been a trying time. I'm afraid I took out my agitation on the tree in the garden."

Baines stared at him a moment. "I see. Did that...help?"

Thomas shrugged. "In the moment, yes. But now I have sore hands to contend with." The smile he generated now was more genuine. Or he hoped it was, anyway.

Baines nodded. "Mrs. Holcomb is in the drawing room. She has a gift for Miss Devereaux."

That would be the third gift Aunt Charity had brought for Regan this week. She wanted to make sure Regan didn't miss her mother, which wasn't really necessary.

"Thank you, Baines." Thomas stood and left the study to make his way upstairs.

Situated at the front of the first floor with a pretty view of Grosvenor Square, the drawing room was where they gathered as a family. Aunt Charity sat in the central seating area, a box tied with a bow on the settee beside her.

"Good afternoon, Aunt." Thomas walked toward the seating area. "Thank you for bringing Regan another gift, but it's not necessary. She is almost entirely unaffected by…what happened."

"You're lucky she's so young. And that her mother was a poor excuse for a parent."

Thomas acknowledged things could be much more difficult, and for that, he was grateful. Not for his sake, but for Regan's. He didn't want her to be sad. Yet sadness and disappointment were part of life. He'd learned that at a very young age. Which was precisely why he didn't want his daughter to experience it. She had plenty of time to feel hurt and despair and loss. His chest stung— how he wished he could protect her from such things forever.

Aunt Charity stood and came toward where he stood near a chaise. "Goodness, what on earth did you do to your hands?" She took them in hers and frowned down at the wounds.

"I expended my energy on a tree. It relieved some tension."

She let go of him and gave him a wry stare. "You can't just drink excessively or gamble or take a mistress like other men?"

"I'm doing my best with the drinking."

"Pffft." She waved her hand. "I don't believe

you. And I know you don't gamble much, and you certainly haven't taken a mistress. God knows you should have."

So many people had encouraged him to do that. His valet. Friends. And now his aunt. At what point would he take the advice?

He knew who he wanted in his bed, but she wasn't someone he could take as a mistress.

Aunt Charity returned to the settee, and he took the armchair with a high back that reached his shoulders. She studied him intently. "You're sure it was a tree?"

Thomas shifted uncomfortably. "Yes. Why would you think otherwise?" He regretted the question as soon as it passed his lips.

"It just seems an odd thing to do. But if it made you feel better, you must do as you need."

Regan skipped into the room, her nurse following more sedately. "Papa! Aunt Charity!" She was on her way to Thomas, but he could see the exact moment her attention caught the wrapped package next to Aunt Charity. She veered to the left and bounded onto the settee. "Is this for me?"

"Yes," Aunt Charity said, smiling. "It's the last one, however. Your papa thinks I'm spoiling you."

This mattered not a whit to Regan as she didn't so much as look at Thomas. He chuckled.

"I never used the word spoiled," he said.

Regan tugged at the ribbon and then removed the lid. She squealed and reached inside. Her small hands clutched a book larger than her lap.

"This has all sorts of animals in it," Aunt Charity said. "I know how much you like animals."

"Especially cats! Papa says I can have one since

Mama is gone," Regan said excitedly. "She wouldn't let me have one."

Aunt Charity looked over at him with a smile. "What a lovely idea."

"Soon," Thomas said. He needed to find one.

Regan opened the book and studied the pictures with grave interest.

"I think she likes it," Thomas said softly. "Thank you."

"Papa, can your friend read it to me?"

Thomas furrowed his brow in confusion. "What friend?"

"That nice lady. With the hair like mine."

Aunt Charity's eyes widened slightly as she turned her gaze to Thomas. "What friend is this?"

Bloody hell. Regan meant Beatrix. So much for her not telling anyone. "I'm not sure," Thomas lied.

"She comes here sometimes at night," Regan said without looking up from the book.

Aunt Charity's still dark brows nearly leapt from the top of her forehead. "It sounds as if you have taken a—" She pressed her lips together. "Never mind."

"A what, Aunt Charity?" Regan asked, proving that children heard everything.

"Nothing, dear." Aunt Charity moved the box to the floor and scooted closer to her great-niece to peruse the book over her head. But only for a moment. She returned her attention to Thomas with a thoroughly curious stare.

Thomas knew his aunt would interrogate him later and decided it was best to get it over with now. He turned to Regan's nurse and asked if she could take her upstairs with the book.

"Of course, my lord," the nurse said.

Regan closed the book and handed it to the nurse. Turning, she threw her arms around Aunt Charity. "Thank you, Aunt Charity!"

Thomas's aunt hugged her tightly, her mouth curving into a warm smile. "You are so welcome, my darling girl."

Sliding from the settee, Regan went to hug Thomas before leaving with the nurse.

"Your daughter is absolutely wonderful. You have more than made up for your former wife's lack of care."

"That has never been my goal, not specifically," he said quietly. "Regan is my entire heart."

"Your *entire* heart? There's nothing left for your mysterious blonde 'friend'?"

Thomas rested his elbows on the arms of the chair and leaned forward. "Listen, I would prefer if you didn't discuss this with anyone. This woman is not my mistress. She is just what Regan said—a friend. I find I have need of one right now." That was the absolute truth. Beatrix had come into his life at precisely the right moment. He honestly didn't know what he would have done without her help that night—just her presence had allowed him to navigate an utterly unbearable event.

Aunt Charity's forehead creased with sympathy. "Of course you do. I would never judge you." She looked as though she wanted to ask him more.

"I won't tell you anything else, so don't ask." He gave her a half smile. "Just know that she's a friend. And nothing more."

"If she's helped you through this time, she is

more than a friend—she's an angel. I'm grateful for whatever comfort she gives you."

"Thank you." He sat back and put his palms against the arms of the chair. "Now, let us talk of something that has nothing to do with me."

She grinned. "Then let me tell you an amusing story of your cousin's son, Peregrine."

"Yes, please do. It's been far too long since he and Regan played together."

"We'll have to rectify that," Aunt Charity said. "Soon." Then she launched into her tale, and for a brief while, Thomas laughed.

CHAPTER 7

*B*eatrix and Selina dressed for the masquerade ball at Rafe's house on Upper Brook Street. Selina was absolutely resplendent in a gown of rose with an overskirt of gold gauze that shimmered in the candlelight. The sleeves were embroidered with a variety of flowers in gold thread, and she wore diamond eardrops and a diamond necklace that perfectly matched the diamond betrothal ring Harry had given her. The jewelry made Beatrix think of the demi-parure her mother had promised her—emeralds set in a pair of earrings, a necklace, and a bracelet. Mama had told her they would belong to her one day. Beatrix looked forward to getting them from her father.

"You look beautiful," Beatrix said, beaming at Selina.

"Thank you." Selina blushed as she looked in the mirror. "I don't even recognize myself."

"I do. You're still the brave girl who rescued me at Mrs. Goodwin's."

Selina turned to her, smiling. "You rescued me too."

"I'm so happy for you and Harry. To find a man you love and who loves you in return…" Beatrix sighed.

"It's astonishing. I don't know if I shall ever believe it."

"Just so long as you remember that you *deserve* it," Beatrix said.

"I can't forget that because you and Harry keep reminding me." She adjusted the necklace at her throat, repositioning the diamond just slightly. "Do you think it's odd we don't have masks?"

They'd discussed this with Harry's family at length and decided Harry and Selina shouldn't wear them. Everyone would want to congratulate them, and they couldn't if Harry and Selina weren't easily recognizable. And since Beatrix was hoping to catch her father's eye, she couldn't very well hide her face.

"Not at all. And who cares anyway? We have very good reasons for not wearing them."

A knock on the door drew them both to turn. Selina went and opened it to reveal Harry.

He was dressed in black save his bright white shirt and rose-gold waistcoat that had been made to match Selina's gown. The love in his eyes glowed as he gazed at Selina. Beatrix couldn't have been happier if she were the one about to be married.

"Beautiful," Harry said. Then he looked past Selina at Beatrix and added, "You too."

Beatrix laughed. "Thank you. I'm going down. You two catch up…whenever. Just don't wrinkle her gown." She waggled her brows at Harry as she walked by them and started toward the stairs.

A short while later, people began to arrive. Beatrix kept looking for Tom, which was silly because he wasn't coming. She was soon swept up in the excitement and splendor of the ball. Rafe's house was magnificent, and the ballroom in particular was lavishly decorated with sparkling chandeliers, mirrors that reflected the light, and a great many flowers. The air quickly grew warm, but doors were opened to allow the evening air to flow inside, and several footmen waved fans.

After dancing a set with Lord Daventry, whom she'd also partnered with at Almack's, Beatrix went to fetch a glass of lemonade.

"Miss Whitford, good evening."

Beatrix turned to see her half brother. At least, she was fairly certain it was him. "Lord Worth?"

He chuckled. "Very good! How is the lemonade?"

"Far superior to Almack's, I'm happy to report."

"That is not a difficult accomplishment. I would expect nothing less. Your brother has spared no expense." Worth looked around the ballroom. "His house is exceptional."

Beatrix didn't know how to respond to that, so she finished her lemonade and then handed her empty glass to a passing footman.

"I must apologize for not calling on you yet," Worth said. "I do plan to."

"Wonderful." She flashed a brief smile and glanced around for an excuse to depart before he could flirt with her. She really didn't think she could endure it.

Then it happened. He was here. The Duke of Ramsgate was walking straight toward them. She knew because he wasn't wearing a mask.

Beatrix's heart cartwheeled, and her pulse raced like a frightened pony. She was already a trifle warm, but an anxious heat flashed over her.

The duke stopped near his son and cast a glance toward Beatrix. She smiled broadly—probably too broadly—and waited for him to recognize her.

He barely inclined his head before looking back at Worth. "Have you been here long?"

"Awhile," Worth said. "You just arrived?"

"Yes, against my better judgment. This Bowles fellow is an upstart. His house is a tad vulgar, don't you think?"

Beatrix froze. She couldn't think of a thing to say. She could barely think. He hadn't recognized her at all. In fact, it was as if she wasn't even standing there. Was he giving her the cut direct? She had no idea. What's more, he was insulting Rafe and his house!

Worth sniffed. "I rather like it. You're being overly staid. May I present Miss Beatrix Whitford? She is Mister Bowles's sister." He said the last with a pointed edge.

Her father at last looked at her—really looked at her. And inclined his head again. "Miss Whitford." He didn't seem the least bit sorry that he'd insulted her "brother." Nor did he recognize her. Or if he did, he was exceptionally good at disguising it.

She sank into a well-rehearsed curtsey. "Good evening, Your Grace. I'm pleased to make your acquaintance." Rising, she waited for him to make some pleasant small talk. Instead, he returned his attention to his son.

"I want to introduce you to someone."

"In a moment," Worth said with a hint of irritation. "I'm speaking with Miss Whitford."

The duke's brows pitched down, and his mouth twisted with disappointment. "Now, if you please."

Worth's eyes sparked, and he opened his mouth to respond.

Beatrix cut him off. "It's all right. You go on," she said, eager to be free of him—or more accurately, any potential flirtation. In truth, she somewhat liked him. Or thought she would if they became friends. Or siblings.

He looked toward her. "Are you certain? We haven't danced yet."

She laughed gaily. "Oh, there's plenty of time for that." Right now, she wanted to get away from everyone before the hurt rising in her throat spilled from her eyes.

"Very well." Worth pivoted and went with the duke, who didn't so much as spare a glance toward Beatrix.

Cheeks burning, she spun around and stalked from the ballroom into an adjoining room where people were playing cards. She wove through the chamber and into another, then another. This house was a bloody maze!

At last, she was in a room without people, and, thankfully, she knew where she was. Turning to the left, she went into the wing of the house where the redecoration hadn't yet been completed.

She found herself in Rafe's large, spectacular library. Though there was no one inside, there were lanterns partially illuminating the room.

It was in a state of disarray, the renovation incomplete. Not all the shelves were in place, and those that were held only a fraction of the books they would eventually support. There would be more than she could ever possibly read. Or not. She would enjoy the challenge.

Yes, think of books. Think of anything but your father.

Too late. He'd barely even looked at her! Even if he hadn't recognized her, he'd still been rude. He hadn't even apologized for insulting Rafe even after learning she was his sister.

Tears burned her eyes, but she refused to shed them. Perhaps there was a reason he'd acted that way. What if he'd recognized her and was simply too surprised to look at or speak to her?

Except if he'd been that shocked, she surely would have seen some sign of it. All that aside, he'd behaved horribly. How dare he speak of Rafe like that?

She stamped her foot and furiously worked to rein in her emotions. A movement caught her eye. A man dressed entirely in black, save his ivory shirt, wearing a mask that covered all of his face except his mouth closed the door behind him.

Beatrix's emotions gathered into one—fear. There was only one reason a man would follow her. And she was without her knife and pistol. Looking about for a weapon, her gaze fell on a candlestick on a table.

She took a few steps and wrapped her hand

around the middle. Raising the brass candlestick, she faced the masked man. "Don't come any closer."

The man stalked toward her.

She waved the candlestick. "I mean it!"

"I know you do." He untied the mask and pulled it from his face. "Beatrix."

She gaped at Tom. "I would have hit you."

"I'm aware," he said wryly. "I've seen you defend yourself, and, as you've pointed out, you're quite capable."

She set the candlestick down and took a deep breath, her pulse calming now that there was no danger. "There's only one reason a man follows a woman into a secluded room during a ball."

He arched a brow at her, and she was struck by how handsome he looked in his crisp evening wear, his dark hair combed into a dashing style. "Just one? Why do you think I'm here?"

"Well, not for *that*." Heat flushed through her. She imagined *that* with *him* and wished that *was* why he'd come.

He closed the distance between them, coming to stand right before her. "How do you know?" His voice was a silken cloak that wrapped itself around her.

"You followed me for an assignation?" The last word came out at a much higher pitch, and her heart had begun to speed up once more. "Wait, why are you even here at all? You're in mourning."

"Yes, well, my aunt has assured me that I'm welcome to go out in Society because I'm in need of a wife."

"You are?"

He lifted a shoulder. "So people think. You see, I'm a father of a young daughter and a viscount without an heir." He rolled his eyes. "Obviously, I am in need of a wife."

"Obviously." It wasn't really. Not to Beatrix, but then what did she know of such things?

"I confess I couldn't resist the chance to come tonight—I received the invitation before... Well, *before*. Anyway, I wanted to see you in a gown and all the trappings."

"Didn't you already do that at Almack's?"

He exhaled. "Yes. I also hoped to dance with you. *That*, I haven't done."

"No, you haven't." She sounded like she'd swallowed a frog. He was so close, so wonderfully imposing, and he smelled divine—like sandalwood and spice.

She'd never understood why a woman would swoon. Until now.

Voices outside the door sounded an alarm. She grabbed his hand and pulled him to the other side of the room where one of the new bookcases hadn't yet been pushed back against the wall. It provided an excellent—and the only—place for them to hide.

She pulled him behind the bookcase and held her finger to her lips. The space was rather close, pinning them between the bookcase and the wall. They faced each other, their chests touching. It might not have been an assignation, but it would certainly look like one if they were discovered.

It also felt a little bit like it *was* one.

All she need do was stand on her toes, twine

her arms around his neck, press her lips to his… Would he mind?

The space was rather dim, but she could just make him out in the shadows. He looked down at her, his gaze dark and enchanting. She nearly lost herself, but then the voices were closer—in the room now—and she knew them.

"What happened?" Selina asked.

"I was speaking with… Hell, I don't remember his name. Lord Dimwit or something." That was Rafe. "I just misspoke, but I think I covered it well."

"What did you say?"

"I said Beatrix was your sister."

Thomas's eyes narrowed very slightly as his head cocked to listen to the conversation.

Beatrix's heart beat so loudly, she feared he could hear it.

"Is that all?" Selina asked, and Beatrix could almost hear her frowning. "What did you say?"

"I laughed, and then I said she was *our* sister."

"*Rafe.* What else?" Selina demanded. "What aren't you telling me?"

"Nothing! That's exactly as it happened. Just…"

There was a noise, as if Rafe had kicked something, and Beatrix startled. Tom put his arms around her and held her steady. His touch was at once comforting and arousing.

"I hate having to remember all this nonsense," Rafe said. "I don't know how you and Beatrix did this for so long."

Selina scoffed. "As if you weren't weaving your own lies as the Vicar. It's not that hard. Beatrix is our half sister. We share a mother who is now dead. Beatrix is twenty-two, not twenty-six, though I can't imagine why her age would ever come up. The rest are things *you* fabricated."

Beatrix's stomach dropped through the floor. Tom stared down at her in disbelief. He released her as the color leached from his face. But only for a moment. It came right back, especially in his cheeks, where red swaths marked his anger.

"Rafe, don't worry." Selina sounded concerned but caring. It did nothing to soothe Beatrix, but then, it wasn't directed at her. "I'm sure it was fine. You've survived so much. You won't be toppled by Lord Dimwit or whatever his name was. And neither will I or Beatrix. Now come on, we need to get back."

Whatever Rafe said next was unintelligible. But a moment later, the distinct sound of the door closing was impossible to miss.

Tom took a step back, which would have made him visible to anyone else in the room. "What the hell just happened? Are you not Lady Gresham's half sister? Or Mr. Bowles's half sister? Who *are* you?"

"I'm your friend."

"I thought so, but apparently, I don't know you at all." His voice trembled with such anguish that her heart nearly tore in two.

～

The most sexually charged moment of Thomas's life had turned to ash in the breadth of a short conversation. One that hadn't even involved him. He was still trying to process what he'd heard.

What had she and her sister—who wasn't her bloody sister—done for so long? Hell, she'd even lied about her age. Why? None of this made sense. Unless she and her "siblings" were imposters.

To what end? So they could infiltrate Society and…marry well?

He shook his head as if he could jar his jumbled thoughts into some kind of clarity. "What lies was she talking about? Is anything about you real?"

"Can we move out from behind the bookcase?" she asked.

Thomas took another step back. Pivoting, he stalked to the middle of the room. His body crackled with outrage.

"Are you going to explain, or should I go?" He should leave. What was the point in listening to her explanations? He wanted to know the truth, but how could he ever know if she lied to him or not?

She'd followed him to the middle of the room, her petite form stiffening so that she seemed slightly taller. "I am entirely real. Selina is not my blood sister, nor is Rafe my brother. They are siblings, however. I *am* the bastard daughter of the Duke of Ramsgate. I met Selina at school when I was eleven. The other girls were horrible to me because I'm a bastard, and Selina was kind. We grew close and vowed never to abandon each other."

She spoke so clearly and with such ferocity that it was impossible not to be moved by the ob-

vious love she had for her faux sister. He also
couldn't ignore the lingering pain in her voice
when she mentioned the other girls. Thomas
longed to learn each of their names and make sure
they suffered for their cruelty. Even after learning
Beatrix had lied, he was apparently still drawn
to her.

He remembered the night he'd seen her in the
tree. "You almost gave me another name when I
met you."

"Linley. It was my mother's name. When I left
the school, I took a different name. Selina and I
reinvented ourselves." She looked at him with anguish in her gaze. "Please don't ask me about
Selina. Her secrets are not mine to share."

He could understand that, and for now, he
would honor her request. "Continue. What other
lies was Lady Gresham referring to?"

"Just that—who we really are. We've been on
our own for more than a decade. It's often been…
difficult." She wrung her hands, her stomach
twisting into knots she feared would never
untangle.

Thomas wanted to understand. "In what way?"
He thought of how she'd fought the footpad, of
her ability to wield a pistol.

She dropped her hands to her side and stuck
out her chin. "We're women. We were unpro-
tected. We had to…fib to navigate our way here. It
was always my hope to come to London, to find
my father, to regain my family. I wanted to show
him that I am an accomplished woman, that he
can be proud of me." Her hands curled into fists,
and her shoulders tensed. "I am *so* close."

The fervent commitment—and hope—in her voice erased the remnants of his anger. He resisted the urge to go to her and take her in his arms. "I suspect there is more to it than what you're telling me. If you ever want to unburden yourself, please know that I will listen. And I won't judge."

She stared at him, her gaze inscrutable. He had no idea if she would ever tell him the truth. He also wasn't sure she needed to. Who was he anyway?

"Thank you," she said tentatively. "What will you do?"

"I'm not sure what you mean."

"Will you expose us?"

Ah, that. "As you so aptly pointed out when we met, we share secrets now. And we made a bargain to keep them. I would honor that. I won't divulge that which you have worked so hard to keep private or that which you have overcome."

"I appreciate that. It was difficult not telling you the truth. You're the only person I've ever told about my father, aside from Selina."

He moved toward her, curious. "Why is that?"

She exhaled, her body relaxing slightly. "I don't know. I suppose I just feel...comfortable with you. Perhaps it's the way we met. You were in need, and I wanted to help."

"It was rather horrible, wasn't it?" He stopped just in front of her. She was close enough for him to touch. If he dared.

"Yes. Not exactly the way one hopes to meet...someone."

"No," he murmured, wondering if "someone" meant the same to her as it did to him. He'd met a friend, certainly, but perhaps more. She had firmly wrapped herself around him and infiltrated his life so that he could scarcely contemplate not having her in it.

"I really am sorry," she said softly. "It wasn't just my secret to keep. Selina and I are bound together, and I will protect her with every fiber of my being for all the days of my life. There is no one I love more in this world."

He could tell, and he understood the emotion. "That is how I feel about my daughter."

The moment lengthened as the space between them grew less, each of them edging forward. It would be so easy to hold her, to comfort her, to kiss her. He did none of those things.

Keeping his hands disappointingly at his sides, he said, "You've been gone an awfully long time. You'll have been missed."

She blinked. "Oh my goodness, yes." She pressed her hands to her cheeks. "Are you coming back to the ball?"

"Probably not. I came to see you, and I have."

She lowered her hands. "What about the dance? Never mind. You don't have to answer that. I…understand." She gave him a small smile. "Goodbye, Tom."

Then she walked past him and departed the library.

Thomas silently swore. He shouldn't have let her go. Not without telling her he would dance with her. Now she thought he'd changed his mind about her after learning that she wasn't who she'd said she was.

And shouldn't he have? He'd already married

a woman who'd turned out to be completely different than he'd thought. He'd hadn't fallen in love with Thea, but he'd believed the potential was there. After the wedding, measure by measure, she'd shown him her true self. A spiteful, selfish harpy who hated motherhood almost as much as she hated being married to Thomas. Her chief complaint was that he was too staid because he didn't give her enough money to gamble, and he frowned on her drinking too much. And he complained that she ignored their daughter.

Was it too much for him to have hoped they would have a happy marriage? Apparently so. The worst part was there was nothing he'd wanted more. Like Beatrix, he'd worked for and anticipated something with passionate dedication. He hoped she would not be as disappointed or damaged as he'd been.

But he wasn't sure he would be there to find out. Now was the perfect time to end their association. There was truly no need to continue it, and she'd already shown him she was capable of misleading him. He didn't need that in his life, not anymore, no matter how drawn to Beatrix he might be.

And he was. Almost desperately. Her humor, her brightness, her care—all of it combined to make her incredibly alluring.

Against his better judgment, he returned to the ball. Mask in place, he entered the ballroom. He looked out to the dance floor, where they danced a quadrille. He found Beatrix, the vivid blue of her gown standing out amidst the other women. It was more than her gown. She had a radiance that other women simply didn't possess.

She was dancing with the Earl of Worth. Thomas narrowed his eyes as he watched them. There was no cause to feel jealous. The man was her half brother. In fact, Thomas ought to pity him, for when he found out, he would be vastly disappointed. Poor chap.

"Rockbourne?"

Thomas turned his head at the familiar voice. North, rather, Jeremy Sheffield, the Viscount Northwood, and brother to the groom for whom this ball was held in honor, moved to stand on Thomas's left.

"How could you tell?" Thomas asked, looking at him askance.

North's mask only covered his eyes and the upper half of his nose. "I wasn't sure, but there was something familiar about you and that was my best guess." His mouth quirked into a wry smile. "It was a risky one, however. Aren't you in mourning?"

"Somewhat." He saw no reason to lie. While he was officially mourning, there was no grieving involved. "I received the invitation…before, and I needed to get out."

"Can't say that I blame you."

Thomas continued to watch Beatrix dancing. He tried not to laugh as she trod all over Worth's toes. Apparently, she was employing the same tactics she'd done the other night.

"Something amusing?" North asked.

"Just watching the dancing."

"Are you watching Miss Whitford? I see she's

positively destroying poor Worth's feet. I've never seen her dance like that before."

"Yes, the woman in the blue dress. That's Miss Whitford?" Thomas pretended he didn't know her.

"She's to be my sister-in-law. Her sister is Lady Gresham, who is marrying Harry."

"I see." Thomas bit his lip as he saw Beatrix completely run into Worth. That had to have been painful for both of them. This couldn't go on—she couldn't keep hurting herself in an effort to dissuade him. "Perhaps it's her partner."

"I've never known Worth to be a bad dancer. In fact, he's quite celebrated for the opposite. It's why the patronesses at Almack's love him so much." North made a distasteful sound in his throat. "I'm so grateful that isn't me."

"I haven't danced in ages," Thomas said.

"Then maybe you should." North leaned toward him and whispered, "I won't tell."

Thomas looked over at him. "I appreciate that. I would prefer to keep my presence quiet."

North pressed his lips together and inclined his head toward Thomas before taking himself off. Thomas watched the dance conclude and took a deep breath.

He'd come here to dance, and he wasn't leaving without doing so.

CHAPTER 8

"*I*'m so sorry," Beatrix said, grimacing and then smiling as Worth offered her his arm at the conclusion of their dance. "I suppose I shall have to accept that I am not the best dancer. In fact, I think I suffer from dancing with someone so accomplished."

Worth chuckled. "I don't know about that, but please don't concern yourself. Perhaps next time, we'll just take a promenade. You're a decent walker, aren't you?"

Beatrix was surprised to find herself laughing. "Yes, I believe so. But let's not curse me." She quickly sobered. Perhaps she was already cursed.

She couldn't stop thinking of what had happened in the library. What a tangle. She was so preoccupied that it hadn't taken much effort to dance poorly.

Scanning the ballroom, she saw Selina standing with Harry. They were speaking with Harry's parents, the earl and countess. Selina looked so happy.

Beatrix should tell her about Thomas, that he

knew they were pretenders. But would it make any difference? Only if Thomas exposed them, and he'd said he wouldn't.

She should alert Selina—and Rafe—to the fact that someone knew their secrets. Or at least some of them. That there were still things Thomas didn't know made Beatrix feel queasy. It was another reason she needed to stop seeing him. And she would. She'd told him goodbye in the library.

That made her feel worse than queasy.

"What say you?"

Beatrix blinked and glanced over at Worth as they made their way off the dance floor. He'd clearly said something before the question, and she had absolutely no idea what it was. More troubling was the way he was looking at her—with unabashed delight and something else…anticipation maybe. She nearly blurted right then that she was his half sister.

Thankfully, however, she was saved by a tall, masked gentleman who stepped in their path. *Tom.*

He bowed to her and inclined his head toward Worth. Addressing Beatrix, Tom asked, "May I have the next dance?"

He was asking her to dance? She'd thought he left. She'd told him goodbye. She also knew that it was impolite to refuse a gentleman when he asked you to dance. And in this case, she didn't want to refuse.

"It would be my pleasure." She withdrew her hand from Worth's sleeve. "Thank you, my lord." Then she put her hand on Tom's proffered arm and felt the connection all the way down to her knees, which turned to water.

As Tom led her back to the dance floor, she cast him a sidelong glance. "You didn't leave."

"I was going to, but then I saw you 'dancing' with Worth."

She heard the sarcasm he infused in the word dancing and giggled. "I must appear the worst dancer here."

"Perhaps, but I admit I wasn't watching anyone else." His confession did nothing to help the liquid state of her bones as he took her into his embrace. "It's a waltz."

"So it is. I haven't waltzed with anyone yet. Unless you count that moment on your balcony."

The connection between them seemed to sizzle, like a spark leaping from a fire to start a new conflagration.

"Do you have permission?" he asked silkily.

"Er, yes?" She looked up at him. "Who would give me permission?"

"Your father, but in the absence of one, perhaps your brother or your sister." He looked over her head, and some of her enthusiasm at dancing with him evaporated.

"Are you still upset with me?"

His gaze snapped to hers. The music started, and he swept her into the dance. The press of his palm on her back and the feel of his hand entwined with hers sizzled through her with a delicious heat. They were the barest of touches, but it was the slightness that was so inviting. She wanted more. So much more.

"No. You explained, and I think I understand. At least, I hope I do."

Yes, she'd explained. Partially. What would he

do if he knew she stole things? And not only when she wasn't aware of doing so. She'd developed a skill for picking pockets—and sometimes not even pockets, for she could remove a bracelet from a lady's wrist without her realizing—and stealing into locked chambers. Sometimes that had been the only way she and Selina had been able to survive. There had been plenty of nights, especially when they were younger, that they went to bed hungry or when they were behind on payments for their lodgings and were forced out into the street. Theft had started as a last resort and then they'd relied on it when their other schemes failed to provide the income they needed.

Their other schemes included Selina working as a fortune-teller, pretending to raise money for a charitable cause, or Beatrix feigning an illness that could be treated with medicine they couldn't afford. How could she ever tell Tom about any of that? She'd seen how devastated Harry had been when he'd learned the truth and how broken Selina had been as she'd tried to explain the life she'd led to the man she loved.

Seeing them now, happy, about to be married, gave Beatrix hope for her own future. Especially if her father was open to rekindling their relationship. However, that seemed unlikely given he hadn't even recognized Beatrix. Between that and the disaster in the library, she realized she wanted this evening to be over.

Except for this part. This wonderful, dazzling, beguiling dance. "You're an excellent dancer," she said, sounding—and feeling—rather breathless.

"And you're, thankfully, better than I expected." The twinkle in his eye made her laugh.

"You flatter me, my lord." She batted her lashes, and he grinned, moving her in time to the music, their bodies gliding together as one.

She gave herself over so completely that she misstepped. "You spoke too soon," she murmured, jerking herself into the proper position. The movement made her feel something against her thigh, something in the pocket of her gown.

Oh, God, she'd done it again.

Frustration and anger tore through her. When would she stop? *Could* she stop? Focusing on the last few hours, she vaguely recalled taking something earlier—a bracelet with a single pearl. Perhaps she could return it. Except she had no idea from whom she'd stolen it. She'd find a place to leave it later so that someone would find it.

She made another error, this time stepping on Tom's foot.

"Does this mean you want to be rid of me too?" he asked with a hint of humor.

She should say yes. More than that, she should *want* to be rid of him. She was going to disappoint him. If not tonight—and it was a miracle she hadn't—then sometime. Perhaps soon. He would learn the truth about her because if she didn't find a way to control her impulses, her shameful behavior would be exposed. Not only would she be cast out from Society and most certainly spurned by him after, she could very well find herself imprisoned.

The risk of stealing on purpose never bothered her. She was confident in her abilities and in her reasons for thieving. But this was different. When she took things without realizing, it was as if she were another person. A person she didn't know.

The music built to a finish, and the dance ended.

Tom looked at her in question, his brow furrowed. "What happened there, at the end?"

"I was just thinking how lovely it was to dance with you. Because I don't know when I'll see you again." Her throat tightened.

"You'll come visit—we'll sort it out."

They could, probably, but she wouldn't. She put her hand on his arm and gently pulled him away from the dance floor. "Tom, you shouldn't trust me. I haven't been completely honest with you...and I can't be. I'm not asking you to understand."

His brows were still knotted in confusion. "Good, because I don't."

She made sure no one was nearby and then spoke in a quiet tone. "I will disappoint you again. Just like I did tonight, only worse." She hated the flash of confusion and dissatisfaction in his gaze, but there was nothing to be done for it. Not here, not now. Not ever.

She needed to get out of there before she completely broke down, something she hadn't done in a very long time. It was far easier for her to be positive and enthusiastic. This sense of failure and dread was much, much harder.

"Goodbye, Tom," she said for the second time that night. Taking her hand from his arm, she hurried away, heedless of where she was going. As she left the ballroom, she ran straight into the one person she really didn't want to see: her half brother.

"There you are, Miss Whitford. I've been waiting for your dance to finish. Might I say you are better at the waltz than the quadrille? I will remember that in future."

"Er, thank you. Now, if you'll excuse me." She continued past him through the adjoining room where ballgoers were gathered with refreshments.

Unfortunately—and irritatingly—he went along with her. "I plan to call on you tomorrow. And I'll be speaking with your brother later."

Beatrix stopped short. She turned to face him, her eyes wide as anger overtook her earlier despair. She gave his sleeve a tug and jerked her head toward a doorway. Spinning about, she stalked into a smaller room.

He followed her, and once they were clear of the threshold, she turned. His lips curved into a pleasant smile. "Should we move somewhere a little more private?"

"What?" The word shot out of Beatrix's mouth like a pistol firing.

He moved close to her, his lids drooping over his too-familiar hazel eyes. "We should find a more secluded location—to kiss."

For a moment, Beatrix couldn't speak. And during that moment, he leaned toward her. She put up her hands and pushed at his chest while taking a step back. "No. I don't want to kiss you."

His features crinkled into a state of utter bewilderment. "You don't?"

She gaped at him. "Has no one told you no before?"

He seemed to ponder her question. "No? Not in this instance, because I've never attempted to kiss someone like you. But I'm generally well-liked by the fairer sex."

Someone like her. She nearly laughed. He had *no* idea what she was like.

Instead, she made a very unladylike sound in her throat. "I do like you, but not in that manner. For heaven's sake, I'm your *sister*."

After blinking once, he swallowed. He blinked again. Then he opened his mouth only to snap it closed again.

"Half sister," she clarified. "I'm sorry, but I couldn't allow you to continue to pursue me. *That's* why I pulled you in here. Not so we could... kiss." She made a face.

Worth stared. And stared. Finally, he recoiled, taking a step back. "How is this possible?"

"I'm sure you know how," she said sardonically. "But allow me to provide you with the pertinent details. Your father had a mistress— my mother. She lived in Bath, and her name was Charlotte Linley. He visited us often and always spent a month at the end of summer with us."

The flash of understanding in his eyes told her he believed her. "He was never around."

"No, because he was with me and his beloved Lottie. You had no inkling?"

Worth shook his head. "I mean, I knew he wasn't faithful to my mother—later, when I was older and paying attention to that sort of thing. You say he loved your mother?"

Beatrix could distinctly hear his voice saying, *"I*

love you, my dearest Lottie." "He told her so often enough, yes."

There was a long moment during which Worth stared at some spot behind Beatrix's head. When he returned his gaze to hers, he frowned. "Why didn't he tell me about you?"

"You'd have to ask him that."

Worth cocked his head to the side, his eyes narrowing slightly. "You're certain he's your father?"

Beatrix wanted to kick him. Instead, she grabbed his forearm and dragged him to the other side of the room, where there was a looking glass above the fireplace. "Take off your mask." When he complied, she said, "Look at my eyes. Now look at your eyes. See anything similar?"

His gaze met hers in the mirror, then moved to his own and slowly widened with recognition. "Holy hell."

Beatrix let go of his arm and turned to face him, crossing her arms over her chest.

"I can't believe I was attracted to you." His expression filled with horror. He pivoted toward her. "I'm so sorry."

"It's not your fault. I felt quite bad for you, actually. I wanted to tell you straightaway, but I haven't even told our father I'm in London yet."

He stroked his hand along his jaw. "He saw you earlier tonight, when we were speaking. He didn't seem to know you."

And now her pain and humiliation were exposed. "No, he didn't. I don't know if he didn't recognize me or chose to ignore me. I haven't seen him in a very long time." She decided to tell him the rest, or part of it, anyway. "My mother died when I was eleven, and our father sent me to a boarding school. I was there for four years, during which time he never once wrote or visited."

"What an utter blackguard." Worth shook his head. "I'm sorry, Miss Whitford."

"Beatrix, if you please." She shrugged. "It seems as though you should call me that."

"I've always been Worth, but my sisters—my other sisters—called me Jamie. You can choose whichever one you prefer."

His other sisters. Did that mean? Warmth spread through Beatrix, and her chest constricted as her throat grew raw. "Jamie, I think," she managed to say, hoping he couldn't hear the croak in her voice.

"I can't believe he just abandoned you at that school. I'll say it again. What an utter *blackguard*." He looked at her in concern. And sympathy. She'd never imagined this reaction. "What did you plan to do?" he asked.

"I'd hoped to impress him. Clearly, that hasn't happened." She put her hand on her waist. "I loved him very much when I was younger. I missed him and hoped there was a reason he didn't visit. Perhaps he just missed my mother so much that he couldn't bring himself to see me."

Jamie snorted. "My apologies. You must not remember him very well. He's not the sort to harbor such tender feelings. The fact that you heard him telling your mother he loved her is astonishing to me. I think I recall him telling me that perhaps once."

Beatrix felt sick. She'd spent years planning for

an impossible fantasy. "Honestly, I don't know what to do."

His features hardened with determination. "You're going to go and see him, and I'm coming with you. Tomorrow, unless you'd prefer to wait."

He wanted to accompany her? "You'd really come along?"

"Of course. Whether he doesn't recognize you or is ignoring you, this is a matter that requires support."

She dropped her hand to her side, blinking at him in disbelief. "I never expected this response. I'm…overcome."

"Well, I'm just glad you told me the truth. When I thought you were merely uninterested, it was a blow." At her laugh, he smiled. "It's far more palatable to my self-confidence to know you're my sister." He winked at her. "Shall I pick you up tomorrow, or would you like to meet at Father's?"

That he referred to Ramsgate as "Father," as if he was their shared parent, which he was, filled her with an indescribable joy. "I'll meet you there."

"Three o'clock?" When she nodded, he continued. "You know where?"

"I do." Oh, how she knew. It would be impossible to go and not think of Tom right next door. In fact, she was desperate to tell him about this development. But would she have the chance?

"Excellent." He held out his hand. "May I?"

She put her hand in his. "Yes."

He gave her hand a squeeze. "I'll see you tomorrow."

Then he turned and left, leaving her to stare after him in wonder.

This had been an abysmal night. Or had it?

She smoothed her hand down her dress and felt the bracelet in her pocket once more. Removing the item, she placed it beneath a chair, as if it had fallen off the woman's wrist. Never mind that she probably hadn't even come into this room. Ah well, it was the best Beatrix could do. She decided to categorize the evening as somewhere between mild disaster and slightly successful.

She'd lost Tom, but had apparently gained a brother. Perhaps tomorrow, she'd gain a father too.

Except Tom had never really been hers to lose. They'd shared some wonderful, exciting moments. She would remember them, and him, always. And in so doing, she would try never, ever to think of what might have been.

$\sim$

Thomas couldn't shake the feeling that Beatrix had meant something permanent when she'd told him goodbye last night. Not once, but twice.

Was it because he knew the truth about her and her "siblings"? Or was it something else?

He'd watched her leave the ballroom with her half brother and desperately wanted to know what had happened. As much as he hoped she might come to his garden later, he doubted she would. And not just because he'd told her not to, that he would help coordinate her visits to keep her safe.

Despite his insistence that she not come to his

garden alone late at night anymore, he didn't necessarily expect her to heed him. Beatrix was an independent and rather self-reliant woman.

Perhaps he should visit her instead. There had
to be a way for him to steal into her new residence
in Cavendish Square.

"My lord?"

Thomas had been so lost in thought that he
hadn't noticed Baines standing in the doorway of
his study. He sat straighter in his chair where he
lounged near the hearth. "Yes?"

"Mr. Dearborn from Bow Street is here."

Surprise—and not the pleasant kind—swirled
in Thomas's gut. He stood. "Is he in the sitting
room?"

Baines nodded. "Just so."

"I'll attend him at once. This must be a per-
functory visit to notify me their investigation has
concluded." Thomas couldn't think of any other
reason for him to come. Actually, he could, but he
preferred not to. The sooner he could put Thea's
death behind him, the sooner he could find some
sense of normality.

Thomas entered the sitting room off the entry
hall to see Dearborn studying the portrait of him
and Thea in the corner. The constable, a young
fellow probably five or so years Thomas's junior,
with wavy brown hair that spilled over his forehead and bright blue eyes, turned from the
painting.

"Good afternoon, Mr. Dearborn," Thomas said.
"How can I help you?" Thomas didn't sit, nor did
he invite the constable to do so.

Dearborn inclined his head. He looked a bit

nervous, his gaze uncertain, before he straightened his spine and squared his shoulders, which seemed to give him a jolt of confidence—at least visually. "Good afternoon, my lord. Thank you for seeing me. I hope you are faring well after your recent tragedy."

"As well as can be expected." Better than expected, actually. Was that because he was finally free of Thea's rage, or was it because he'd found Beatrix?

"That's good to hear. I regret I am not visiting under more agreeable circumstances, however I must beg more of your time to discuss new evidence that has come into my possession."

Evidence? What the hell could he have? "I see, and what is that?"

Dearborn reached into the front of his coat and withdrew a piece of folded parchment. "This is a letter from Lady Rockbourne to her mother written a few months ago. In it, she says she is frightened of your temper. Do you have any idea what she meant by that?"

Damn. He'd always been so careful around her. In fact, he could only think of maybe three times he'd been truly angry—when he'd first learned of her infidelity, when she'd fallen asleep holding Regan and the baby had fallen to the floor when she was just a few days old, and the night Thea had died.

Thomas chose his words carefully. "I rarely knew what my wife meant." That was the truth. Thea had been dishonest and difficult.

Dearborn unfolded the paper and held it out to Thomas. "She wrote that your father was abusive, that he beat you and your mother. She worried you would do the same to her or to your daughter."

Rage spilled through Thomas. He ground his teeth together as his blood pumped hot and furious with the slamming of his heart. Why had he trusted her with his darkest, most agonizing secrets? He'd never revealed his father's cruelty to anyone else or his fear that he might someday behave in a similar manner.

Taking the letter, he scanned the words written in Thea's hand. "This is ridiculous."

"What's ridiculous? That your father beat you and your mother, or that you would do the same thing?"

"I've never hurt anyone, especially not my daughter." The words cut from his mouth with a sharpness he hadn't intended.

Dearborn studied him with concern and perhaps a bit of sympathy. "So your father did beat you?"

Thomas gave the offensive letter back to the constable. "I don't understand how that signifies if I've never exhibited that behavior myself."

"You said you wouldn't hurt your daughter. Does that mean you might have hurt Thea?"

Thomas looked at him coldly, uncaring if that didn't help his cause. "No, it does not."

"Not even because she was unfaithful? You told Sheffield you confronted her that night."

"Verbally, not physically." Thomas clenched his jaw and realized he'd curled his hands into fists as his shoulders bunched up with tension. He forced his muscles to relax, but it was deuced difficult.

Dearborn nodded. "You also indicated that Lady Rockbourne's mother might say that you were also unfaithful. She has indeed said so. You still insist that isn't true?"

"Yes."

Exhaling, Dearborn tucked the letter back into his coat, his gaze darting to the side. When he looked back to Thomas, there was a determination set into the youthful planes of his face. "You seem upset. Is there anything you'd care to tell me that might help with our investigation?"

Bloody hell. Thomas took a deep breath, trying desperately to push his anger away. "Of course I'm upset. My wife died." And while he hadn't directly caused it to happen, he was relieved. What did that make him? "In truth, I don't understand why there is an investigation at all. I told Sheffield what happened. The countess and I argued. She was intoxicated and grew angry. She fell from the balcony."

"Her mother insists you pushed her, and Lady Rockbourne's maid agrees. She says you were often furious with your wife." Dearborn pressed his lips together. "In fact, she said Lady Rockbourne was bruised a few weeks ago, and it was a result of you pushing her."

Thomas's breath tangled in his lungs. "That's a barefaced lie."

"You understand it's my duty to investigate Lady Rockbourne's death?"

"I do, just as I understand it's your duty to let a family grieve a loss and not listen to nonsense."

Dearborn nodded. "Yes, of course. I do apologize for bothering you during this difficult time. I regret that I must ask to speak with the remaining members of your household that we were not able to talk to on our last visit. That would be a footman called Osbert and your daughter's nurse, Miss Addy."

Thomas had known they hadn't spoken to the nurse because she'd been occupied with Regan; however, he hadn't realized Osbert also hadn't been available. "Miss Addy is currently busy with her charge. You may return Monday afternoon to speak with her and Osbert."

"Thank you, my lord. I appreciate your cooperation."

"I am eager for this matter to be put to rest, Mr. Dearborn."

"As is Bow Street. Again, I do apologize for troubling you during this time." He bowed, then took his leave.

Thomas glowered at the portrait of him and Thea. He'd bared himself to her in the early days of their marriage, when he thought he might fall in love with her. When he'd hoped for such emotion.

On leaden feet, he went to the window and watched Dearborn walk to the end of Grosvenor Square and disappear. The fury Thomas worked so hard to suppress rose within him. Whipping around, he strode to the corner and ripped the portrait from the wall.

"Even in death, you torment me." He broke the frame against the hearth. The gilded wood broke in several places. Taking a jagged piece of the frame, he speared it through the center of the painting, right between the two of them. He used the fragment like a knife, tearing the canvas across her face and rending her in two.

Growling low in his throat, he tossed the wreckage onto the hearth, but not into the fireplace itself. Chest heaving, he stared at the mess he'd made and silently cursed himself. He should have preserved that for Regan.

Why? So she could remember the mother who'd found her a nuisance? Besides, there were other portraits, including a miniature that hung in Regan's bedchamber.

What was his mother-in-law trying to accomplish? Did she want Thomas imprisoned—or hanged—so that she could take Regan for herself? It wasn't as if her efforts would return Thea to her. Perhaps having her daughter's daughter would soothe her loss. Thomas could understand that.

Even so, he had no idea if any of this was for Regan's benefit or to ameliorate his mother-in-law's grief. Or perhaps it was simply to punish Thomas. The latter had been Thea's goal. She'd even brought up the idea of divorce. He laughed hollowly at the disaster his life had become—the very thing he'd fought so hard to avoid.

"My lord?"

Thomas turned from the hearth to see Baines, silently lurking yet again. Only this time, the butler's features were lined with concern, his mouth drawn into a deep frown.

Waving at the debris of the portrait, Thomas said, "Have this cleaned up."

Then he strode from the sitting room intent on finding the nearest bottle of brandy.

CHAPTER 9

*T*he ball at Rafe's had lasted well into the early morning hours. Beatrix and Selina had arrived home just as the first rays of dawn were spilling over the city. Still, Beatrix had struggled to find rest as her mind had bounced back and forth from Tom to her half brother and father and back again. Thinking of her half brother and father filled her with anticipation and hope, while thoughts of Tom aroused a lingering sadness that enclosed her chest when she acknowledged their flirtation had come to an end.

And flirtation was the best way to describe it, for their connection went beyond friendship but of course not as far as lovers. Could it have reached that point, however?

You'll never know.

She groaned in frustration as she stood from the settee in the garden room, a lovely chamber at the back of their new Cavendish Square residence that opened onto the back garden. The Marchioness of Ripley, who owned the house, had beautifully refurbished the room after moving in, adding the wide doors that made the outside an extension of the interior space.

"Goodness, Beatrix, are you all right?" Selina swept into the room with a look of concern.

"At last!" Beatrix smiled to distract Selina from pursuing Beatrix's problems. "You slept quite late." It was past two in the afternoon.

Selina blushed. "I'm afraid so. That was the very best night of sleep I've had in...well, maybe forever."

Beatrix felt true gladness. "I'm so pleased. You deserve nothing but those from now on." Selina had spent far too many sleepless nights planning how to save them from financial ruin and to keep them from harm.

"Thank you. I admit I do hope it lasts." Selina glanced down at Beatrix's walking costume. "Are you going somewhere?"

Beatrix had begun to hope she would be able to steal from the house without Selina seeing her. "Er, yes."

Selina cocked her head, her eyes narrowing. "Were you keeping it a secret?"

"No. I just wasn't sure if you would come down before I left. I have an appointment in Grosvenor Square."

Knowing that Beatrix's father lived there, Selina stared at her. "Do you? What's happened? Did you speak to the duke last night?"

"Not him, no. I told Worth who I was." At Selina's gasp, she added, "He wouldn't leave me alone. He was going to talk to Rafe about courting me." She gave Selina a horror-filled look.

Selina grimaced. "I can see why that would

prod you to action. And now you have an appointment with the duke. At least, I assume it's with the duke since he lives in Grosvenor Square. What did Worth say?"

Beatrix went to the table and perched on another of the two chairs set around the circle. "He was actually quite supportive. He is arranging the meeting and asked me to meet him at our father's house at three."

"So soon!" Selina shot to her feet. "I'll change."

Beatrix waved her back down. "That isn't necessary. I can go by myself."

"Just because you can doesn't mean you should. I'll accompany you. Stupid Society rules and all that."

Beatrix arched a brow at her. "Do you really think my father or my half brother is going to stand on stupid ceremony now that their bastard daughter and half sister has reappeared?"

"Perhaps not, but you should still present yourself to your best ability."

Dammit, Selina wasn't wrong. But Beatrix wanted to do this for herself. She needed to. Frankly, if it went poorly, she wasn't sure she could handle Selina being there. Wait, was she actually considering it wouldn't go well?

Anxiety pulsed through her. She forced herself to relax, rolling her shoulders and taking a deep breath. "I appreciate you wanting to support me, but I think I need to go alone. If you accompanied me, my father may not let down his guard."

"And that's what you want?"

"I want my father back," she said softly. The man who'd read her stories and watched her play with warmth and delight, who'd taught her to ride a pony when she was eight, and who'd listened to her strum a harp quite badly when she was nine.

The man who'd sent her to a boarding school and never communicated with her again.

All the old justifications came back: he was too grief-stricken to see Beatrix, he hadn't just turned her out, so he obviously cared about her, he was educating her so that she'd make him proud.

So why did it take you so long to seek him out?

Because she meant to make him proud.

Beatrix looked back to Selina. "I've changed my mind. You should come with me. You're right that it's the expected thing to do. However, I may ask if I can speak with him alone."

"Of course." Selina stood, smiling. She took Beatrix's hand and gave her fingers a squeeze. "I'll be ready as quickly as possible. Did you order the coach?"

"I'd forgotten we have one now." It belonged to Harry and had been moved to the Cavendish Square mews. "I'll do that posthaste."

Selina nodded before dashing from the room.

A short while later, the coach conveyed them into Grosvenor Square. It was strange for Beatrix to arrive in this manner instead of creeping into Tom's garden under cover of darkness.

"I meant to ask you about last night," Selina said. "You disappeared for a while. Was that when you were speaking with Lord Worth?"

Beatrix knew she was referring to her time with Tom, not Worth, because she'd overheard her talking to Rafe. She considered telling Selina about Tom, but what would be the point? There was nothing between them. Her gaze drifted toward his house as the coach came to a stop in front of the Duke of Ramsgate's residence. Was Tom inside? What was he doing?

"Yes, that must have been the case," Beatrix said, answering Selina's question.

The coachman helped Selina and Beatrix down from the coach. Selina glanced over at Beatrix. "You say Worth will be here?"

"Yes."

"And you trust that he arranged this appointment and we aren't walking into some sort of trap?" It was Selina's nature to be skeptical, which was to be expected after a lifetime of having no one but herself—and Beatrix—to rely upon. She didn't trust anyone but Beatrix. Or hadn't until she'd met Harry. And Beatrix supposed she'd probably begun to trust her brother again.

"I do, actually." Beatrix realized that made her sound naïve. "I have a good feeling about him."

"I'll let you know if I feel differently," Selina said with a wry smile.

Despite her anxiety, Beatrix laughed softly. "Of course you will, and I expect nothing less."

They walked up the steps to the door. Beatrix cast another look at Tom's house to her right, as if she could catch a glimpse of him.

The door opened to reveal a stiff, heavy-lidded butler. "You are Miss Whitford?" His lips pressed into a judgmental line as he looked between Selina and Beatrix.

"I am Lady Gresham," Selina said with a chilly air. "This is Miss Whitford. We are here to see the duke."

"Yes." The butler opened the door wider and wordlessly invited them inside. At least, Beatrix thought it was an invitation.

The entry hall marble gleamed, and the gilt-framed paintings sparkled. A large bust sat atop a small table against the right wall. Large because the head was bigger than a normal human head, which made the sculpture look rather terrifying.

"This way," the butler said, leading them through the entry hall to another hall in which the staircase was the focal point. The lower half of the stairs was split in two. The butler led them to the right side, which met the left side on a wide landing before continuing up in a single staircase.

On the first floor, he turned to the right and showed them into a large drawing room decorated with several elegant seating areas and enough paintings and sculptures to make it look like a museum. "His Grace will be with you soon."

The butler turned and departed. Beatrix strolled around the room while Selina stood in the center. The windows looked over Grosvenor Square below.

"Good afternoon, Beatrix." Jamie strolled into the drawing room, his gaze settling on Selina while his brow furrowed.

"Good afternoon, Jamie," Beatrix said, moving to stand with Selina. "Allow me to present Lady Gresham."

"Ah yes, your...sister."

"After her father abandoned her, she needed someone to care for her," Selina said coolly.

Jamie inclined his head. "She's lucky to have found you."

"Where is the duke?" Selina asked, looking expectantly toward the door Jamie had just used.

"He'll be along momentarily. He was, ah, he would have preferred more notice before this interview." Jamie faced Selina. "He wasn't expecting anyone other than Beatrix."

Selina pursed her lips. "Surely he would understand that Beatrix requires a chaperone, even to visit her father. Especially so, since no one is aware the duke is her sire."

Beatrix wanted to cheer Selina's staunch support and utterly aloof demeanor. "Jamie, I asked Selina to accompany me."

"Would you mind if she waited downstairs for you? Father would prefer to conduct this meeting privately."

Selina opened her mouth, certainly to protest, but Beatrix touched her arm. She'd planned to see him alone anyway. "That's fine." She leaned close to Selina. "It will be all right."

"Of course it will, but your father is rude." Selina spoke in a lower tone, but not so quietly that Jamie couldn't hear what she said.

"The butler will show you down," Jamie said.

Turning to Beatrix, Selina looked her in the eye. "This is a demonstration of power. Don't let him maneuver you. You're smarter than that." Her features softened. "I'll be right downstairs if you need me."

Pivoting, Selina started toward the door, pausing as she came abreast of Jamie. "Beatrix trusts you. I hope her faith is not ill-placed." There was an edge to her tone that carried a threat—at least Beatrix recognized it as such. She wondered if Jamie did too. Probably not. He likely saw her as just a harmless a woman. He had no idea of the damage she could inflict.

Selina continued on until she disappeared from the room.

Beatrix was surprised to realize that Selina's presence had provided a calming effect. Without her, Beatrix felt suddenly bare, her apprehension rising.

"I take it he was angry that Selina accompanied me?" she asked.

"Father has certain expectations, and he loathes surprises."

Wonderful. He must have been ecstatic to learn Beatrix was here at all. "I can only imagine what he thinks of my presence," she murmured.

Jamie grimaced, his hazel eyes clouding. "He wasn't pleased."

The duke strode into the drawing room. Even though Beatrix had seen him the night before, this was different, because he looked right at her, something he hadn't done at the ball.

After briefly perusing her, he went to sit in a dark blue chair with a high, rounded back and padded arms. He did not invite his children to join him.

Jamie looked to Beatrix and inclined his head toward the seating area the duke had chosen. Situated near a large statue of what looked to be Apollo, there was a settee, a chaise, and another chair. Beatrix sat on the very edge of the settee, poised to flee if necessary. Jamie took the other chair.

"Good afternoon," she said tentatively. "Father."

His lips pursed, then frowned as he regarded her with his flat brown eyes. "I have not given you leave to call me that."

Beatrix couldn't help but feel defensive. "I always called you that." Too late, she realized she should censor herself. It was evident he didn't want her here. This was not going at all as she'd hoped. "Don't you remember?" she asked softly.

"That was a very long time ago. How old are you now? You must be approaching thirty." He said the number distastefully, as if her age were a mark against her.

That he didn't know it was another strike to her long-held dream. "Just twenty-six."

"And here you are having a Season. You're much too old for that, but then you can't possibly understand how these things work."

"I do, actually. Which is why when asked, I say I'm twenty-two. I have no trouble passing for that." She raised her chin, daring him to disagree.

"So you lie."

"I've had to be less than truthful about a great many things in order to get to this point. Do you tell anyone about me?" The look of horror in his eyes was all the answer she needed. "Then you lie too."

Jamie sat forward. "Father, you can't deny Beatrix is your child."

"Of course I can, and I will."

It was what Beatrix had expected—she'd never truly thought he'd publicly claim her—but hearing the words, and spoken with such vehemence, was crushing.

"One has only to look at her eyes and mine to

see that we are related," Jamie said, taking the sting from Beatrix's devastation. At least someone was on her side.

The duke set his elbows on the arms of the chair and steepled his hands. Looking over the tops of his fingers at them, his frown deepened. "That she is my offspring changes nothing. I do not plan to claim her. Were you expecting that, Beatrix?"

"No."

"Then why are you here?"

"I'd hoped we could have some sort of...relationship. I miss having a family." She stopped short of saying, *I miss my father.*

"And how would that look?" He raised a sardonic brow. "If we had a...relationship, people would assume you were my mistress or my daughter. You are definitely not the former and you won't be the latter. I have two daughters already."

Legitimate daughters.

"I don't wish to cause you pain, girl, which is why I sent you to that school. That you left early and went gallivanting about England with Miss Blackwell was your unfortunate decision."

Beatrix's stomach lurched. Of course he would know Selina's name from the school, but how would he know what they'd done after leaving?

Jamie gripped one of the arms on his chair. "You can't mean to just ignore her?"

"Why not? Does she look like she's suffering? Her supposed sister—another lie—is about to marry the son of an earl and her supposed brother —yet another lie—is apparently one of the wealthiest men in London all of a sudden." His eyes narrowed, and the suspicion and haughtiness came off him in waves. He didn't have to ask how Rafe had earned his money or where he came from. It was clear he thought less of Selina's brother simply because he'd come out of nowhere.

So because Beatrix didn't appear to need anything from him, her father would give her nothing. Perhaps she should have shown up here ten years ago when she'd had just two gowns to her name, neither of which fit properly.

"I had hoped that I would make you proud," Beatrix said quietly, shaking inside as she fought to display a collected exterior.

"Father, why not acknowledge her?" Jamie asked earnestly. "Many men do it, and it's not as if Mother is here."

The duke—Beatrix wasn't sure she could think of the man as her father anymore—turned his frosty stare on his son. "You've been fooled by this young woman. She is not what you think. She is a swindler and has spent the last decade leading a life of fraud." The duke transferred his gaze to Beatrix.

The room around her froze in horrifying detail before dissolving into a blur. She wanted to wilt beneath the harsh judgment of his words, but she sat even straighter.

"Shall I detail everything for Jamie?" the duke asked blithely. "I'm certain he would be particularly interested in your thievery."

Beatrix's insides turned to mush. At school, Beatrix had twice been caught stealing. The first time, she'd been young and relatively new to the school. Mrs. Goodwin had been kind and understanding when Beatrix had explained that she hadn't realized what she'd done. Miss Everly, on the other hand, had threatened to tell the duke. Mrs. Goodwin had assured Beatrix that wouldn't happen, provided she didn't steal again.

Only she *had* stolen again, and Selina had covered for her, just as she'd done that first Christmas. But then Selina had left the school and taken her protection with her. Consequently, Beatrix had been caught once more. That time, much to Miss Everly's glee, Mrs. Goodwin said she had to inform the duke and that if Beatrix was caught stealing again, she'd be expelled.

Since the duke had never reacted to the incident, Beatrix had wondered if Mrs. Goodwin had decided not to tell him after all. Regardless, Miss Everly had harassed Beatrix to such a horrible degree that Beatrix had begged Selina to return and fetch her. A year after leaving, Selina had done just that.

The duke continued, "Shall I tell him all about your activities at Mrs. Goodwin's?"

Jamie had moved his attention to Beatrix. His eyes, so kind and welcoming before, were now shadowed with distrust. "Is that all true? You're a fraud?"

Yes, she'd been a swindler, a fraud, and a thief. She'd pretended as though she belonged in this world, but today, her father had reminded her in the most absolute way that she did not.

"As a young woman alone, I've done what I must to survive." She stared at him unflinchingly. "Just because I look as though I am not suffering does not mean I have not suffered."

The duke cleared his throat. It was as if Beatrix hadn't even spoken. "Worth, you will forget you met this young woman and what you know of her. Be on your way now."

Beatrix could see that he was torn, just as she knew the duke would stop at nothing to ensure Beatrix was ignored. If he knew how she'd spent the last decade, then he knew Selina had been part of that, just as he knew they'd lied about being sisters. He couldn't endanger Selina, not when she was finally happy.

Now she understood why the duke hadn't wanted Selina there. She was the leverage he needed.

Beatrix kept herself from dissolving into defeat. She stared unblinking at Jamie, sad that they would never have a sibling relationship. "You should go. I can see this was a terrible idea."

Jamie slowly stood. He looked over at his father and back to Beatrix before leaving without saying a word.

"It seems I've made the situation quite plain to you," the duke said.

"If I try to claim we share any kind of relationship, you will publicize both my background and that of my sister."

"*Lady* Gresham, yes. She is not your sister."

"She is more my sister than you are my father. Blood means nothing, as you've just demonstrated." She stood, her legs surprisingly sturdy beneath her despite the roiling of her insides. "I do want one thing from you. My mother had a demi-parure of emerald jewels she promised would one day be mine."

"You want me to give you a valuable set of jewelry?" He chuckled. "Absolutely not."

She ground her teeth together. "They belong to me."

"If they did, you would have them." He rose, tugging his waistcoat down over his paunch. "You do look rather like your mother. I was fond of her."

Fond? "You said you loved her. Many times."

He shrugged. "That was a long time ago. As I said, I was fond of her, and of you by extension, I suppose."

Beatrix stared at him. "Then she died and your...affinity just evaporated?"

"Precisely." He yawned. "You should be glad I sent you to school, but then you left before you were finished, so perhaps you were not. I am not inclined to reward those who aren't grateful and who don't apply themselves to finish what they start."

"So if I'd stayed at school and gone on to be a dutiful governess, you would give me my mother's jewels?"

"Perhaps."

She didn't believe him, not that it mattered. After Selina's disastrous experience as a governess that had resulted in her being raped by her employer, *nothing* could have made Beatrix take such a position.

"You're a heartless blackguard," she whispered. "I'm glad my mother didn't live to see you treat me like this."

He looked down his nose at her. "If your mother had lived, everything would have been different. The moment you think this life is fair is the moment you lose, my dear. Don't be defeated. You've survived this long, and you should be proud of what you've been able to accomplish. Just as you should be careful not to ruin your fortune. And if you do, well, your mother was an excellent courtesan. I've no doubt you could do quite well for yourself in that endeavor."

Beatrix stared at him, incredulous at his audacity and crudeness. Before she could formulate a response, he'd stalked from the room. It occurred to her that she could steal from him. There were a great many things in this room that she could easily pocket.

Only he would know she took them. Just as he would know if she stole her mother's jewels.

Nevertheless, she was considering it. How could she not? He was pompous, horrible, rotten, and so many other things. The demi-parure was hers. It was all she would have of her mother. She should have told him that. He'd given her nothing, and she'd never imagined that when the coach had arrived in Bath to take her to Mrs. Goodwin's that she wouldn't return home again.

He owed her those jewels.

Beatrix strode from the room and hurried downstairs. Selina stood near a bench in the staircase hall, her features creased with deep concern.

"Are you all right? Worth left without speaking to me. He looked upset."

"We'll discuss it in the coach," Beatrix said tightly.

Selina came forward and took Beatrix's arm.

They left the house without sparing a glance for the footman who opened the door.

When they were situated in the coach and on their way, Beatrix finally released her pent up emotions. "Bollocks. Bloody hell. Damn *everything*."

Selina frowned deeply. "I knew I shouldn't have left."

"It wouldn't have changed anything." Instead, it would have only made things worse. Selina would have been upset by his threats. Beatrix had one regret—that she hadn't asked him specifically what he knew.

"What happened?" Selina watched her cautiously, her features a mix of warm support and disappointment, not for herself but for Beatrix. She alone understood how badly Beatrix had wanted a happy reunion with her father.

"He doesn't care for me at all. He has no desire for any sort of relationship or connection. As I expected, he would never acknowledge me."

"He wasn't even pleased to see you?"

"On the contrary. He was quite put out. Jamie, bless him, tried to advocate on my behalf, but the duke banished him."

Selina clucked her tongue. "He did not look pleased when he passed me on his way out." She shook her head. "I'm so sorry, Beatrix. Did you even bother asking about your mother's demi-parure?"

"I did, but that was also pointless. He refused to consider it." She thought back over his words, growing angry at how awful he'd been. "He had the nerve to tell me life wasn't fair—as if I don't already understand that—and that I should be proud I'd made it this far." Before going on to suggest she could always be some man's mistress if needs must. She couldn't bring herself to tell Selina what he'd said.

Selina's lip curled. "No thanks to him." She gave Beatrix's leg a firm pat. "He's right that life isn't fair and that you've come a long way. Which is precisely why you don't need him. You will shortly have the backing of the Earl and Countess of Aylesbury."

"I'm just sorry that the duke is now aware of the fact that I've lied about being your sister, and that you—and now Rafe—have gone along with that lie." They'd known they were risking themselves, but Beatrix had never imagined things would go this poorly.

"Does he mean to expose us?"

Beatrix heard the hitch in her voice and hated that she might be worried about this. "I don't think so. He was rather clear that we could just avoid each other and that would make him happy. I don't think he wants to cause trouble—provided I don't cause any for him."

Selina let out a breath. "That's a relief, but I am still very sorry. This wasn't the result you were hoping for."

No, it wasn't. She'd spent so long, her entire life it seemed, looking for a way to get back to the family she'd known and loved as a child. She should have realized that family was long gone, that it had died with her mother.

A sudden wave of sadness engulfed her. When she got home, she wanted to go directly to her chamber and dive under the coverlet of her bed where she'd stay for the next week. Or mayhap a year.

No, she couldn't do that. Selina was getting married on Tuesday, and Beatrix would be standing beside her as witness in the church. They *were* sisters in every way that mattered.

Beatrix looked over at Selina and blinked back the tears in her eyes. "The duke made me realize one thing. I mean, I already knew it, but I will never, ever take it for granted."

"What's that?"

"Family is who we choose. Blood doesn't matter."

Selina smiled. "No, it doesn't. You will never be rid of me."

"Nor you of me."

They hugged each other, which was a bit awkward in the small space of the coach. Laughing, they sat back as they turned into Cavendish Square.

"Grieve. Rage. Wallow. Do whatever you must," Selina said. "But only until Tuesday. From then on, you will strike a new path. Think about what you want that to look like." She gave Beatrix a pointed look of encouragement.

A new path. The future lay before Beatrix. The only thing she knew for certain was that she was going to get her mother's jewels.

CHAPTER 10

*T*homas felt a bit strange to be out in public, particularly at church, which he only went to periodically, but it was the only way he could think to see Beatrix. Today was the last day the banns were read for her sister—who wasn't really her sister—and he'd been hoping Beatrix would be there. He was glad to see that she was and had spent a good portion of the service stealing glances in her direction. She sat several pews in front of him, and as far as he knew, wasn't aware of his presence.

"I'm so glad you invited me to accompany you today," Aunt Charity said as they strolled from the church after the service. "Even if I don't fully understand your motives," she added in a whisper.

His motive was singular: to see Beatrix. And determine if his impression from the other night, that she'd been telling him goodbye, was correct. He needed to know if their…whatever it was had reached its conclusion. Of course, he would reveal none of this to his dear aunt.

"My only motive is that I wished to get out of the house."

"Well, I am happy to accompany you wherever you'd like to go." She exchanged looks and smiles with others as people gathered in the vestibule. "Do you mind if I speak with a few ladies?"

"Not at all." Thomas would take the opportunity to hopefully talk to Beatrix. He tried not to make eye contact with anyone as he lingered near the wall and watched for her.

She came out finally, followed by Lady Gresham and Sheffield, who were arm in arm. Behind them were his parents, the Earl and Countess of Aylesbury. And after them, some of the rest of the family. They'd come en masse, apparently, but then they were a large family.

Thomas caught himself frowning. He doubted he'd be able to get any time alone with Beatrix.

Except something magical happened. Her gaze met his. Surprise flashed in their hazel depths, followed by a question. *Why are you here?*

Thomas gave a tiny shrug and, barely inclining his head, moved toward the corner. She did the same. A few moments later, they met.

"I'm surprised to see you here," Beatrix said.

He surveyed her from head to toe, appreciating her smart sage-green walking gown trimmed in a blue so dark, it was nearly black. She looked elegant, and the ensemble made her appear taller, perhaps because of her high straw hat with its trio of feathers. "I was hoping to see you."

"Oh." A smile teased her lips. "That's nice. This is, er, strange."

"Because it isn't dark and you're wearing a gown?"

"Nor are you in a mask. It's like we're normal people." She laughed softly, and he joined her.

He glanced around, knowing they wouldn't have much time alone. Furthermore, they hadn't been officially introduced, so they oughtn't be talking at all. He got straight to his purpose. "I saw you leaving your father's yesterday afternoon. What happened?"

She blew out a breath, and he could have sworn he heard the barest whisper of a curse. "It was an abysmal failure."

"Tell me." Even before he heard what transpired, Thomas wanted to pummel the man into the ground.

"It's a very long story, beginning with my revealing my identity to my half brother at the masquerade."

"You did?"

"I had to. He was going to speak to Rafe about courting me." She made a slight face, scrunching her mouth.

Thomas wondered if he was going to have to pummel her half brother too. "What did he say?"

"He was remarkably supportive, if you can imagine that. He said he would accompany me to see our father, so we arranged to meet at his house."

Thomas had a hard time imagining it, actually, but was glad. "I saw Lady Gresham was with you as well."

"I was trying to be proper." Beatrix let out an unladylike snort. "Not that it mattered. The duke has no interest in getting to know me or in reestablishing any kind of relationship. He was rather cruel about it."

Yes, definitely a pummeling. Thomas flexed his hands. Not that he would actually commit violence. He could *not*. "I'm so sorry, Beatrix," he said softly, aching to smooth the agitated lines from her forehead.

A weak smile lifted her lips. "It was a dream I should have known would never come true."

Thomas's hand curled into a fist. The man had ruined Beatrix's dreams. Just as Thea had ruined Thomas's.

He was running out of time, and he still needed to ask about the future of their friendship. "I wondered if you planned—"

"Rockbourne!" His aunt's voice reached him just before she did.

Stiffening, Thomas exchanged a charged glance with Beatrix before looking toward his aunt. "Aunt Charity."

Aunt Charity blinked at Thomas expectantly.

"Aunt, this is Miss Beatrix Whitford."

"I'm pleased to make your acquaintance," Aunt Charity said.

Thomas looked to Beatrix. "Allow me to present my Aunt Charity, Mrs. Holcomb."

Beatrix dipped a curtsey. "I'm pleased to meet you." Then her gaze drifted to the right and widened slightly.

Thomas followed her line of sight and saw her sister, Sheffield, and some of his family. Lady Gresham was looking at Beatrix and now she was studying Thomas, her brow creased.

"Please excuse me," Beatrix said. "It was lovely to meet you both." Then she was gone, hurrying to the other side of the vestibule.

"Ready?" Thomas asked, offering Aunt Charity his arm.

She curled her hand around his sleeve. "Yes." She glanced after Beatrix before directing her attention forward as Thomas guided her outside.

"She seemed lovely," Aunt Charity observed.

"Yes," Thomas said as they crossed the street.

"Did you just meet her?"

"Not exactly. I danced with her at the masquerade the other night." The second the words left his mouth, he wished he hadn't said them. He cast a wry look at his aunt. "You possess an uncanny ability to get me to disclose things I would normally not."

She laughed gaily. "I'm delighted to hear it, my dear. I hope you know you can trust me." She squeezed his arm. "Truly."

He did know that, which was probably why he'd told her about the dance. "Thank you."

"I didn't realize you'd gone to the masquerade. That's wonderful! So you met Miss Whitford there."

It wasn't a direct question, so he didn't answer it. "She is Lady Gresham's sister."

"Ah, I see. Well, I shall keep my opinions and hopes to myself—mostly. It's good you came out today, if only because you encountered Miss Whitford. Perhaps there's a reason for that." She tossed him a wide grin.

Thomas rolled his eyes. "I am no closer to desiring a new wife today than I was last week.

Dancing and going to church make me feel normal, and for now, normal is good." Normal was great, peaceful. He hadn't felt that in years.

"Very well," Aunt Charity said, sounding a trifle disappointed. "I'm just pleased you are feeling good. That is all that matters to me in the end."

As they made their way along Grosvenor Street, he wished he'd been able to finish his conversation with Beatrix. Or did he? That could have been the end of things. But now he could make the excuse that he wasn't sure if their friendship would continue or not? Since they'd both seemed pleased to see the other, was it too much to hope that they weren't finished?

"Since you are getting out," Aunt Charity said, "perhaps you'd consider attending Lady Exeby's picnic at Hyde Park."

Thomas didn't know a thing about it. "When is that?"

"Thursday. Perhaps Miss Whitford will be there."

"Aunt Charity. No matchmaking. Please."

She lifted her free hand, palm facing out. "My apologies. I am only looking out for your welfare. I know you don't necessarily want a wife at present, but you do accept that you need one eventually, yes?"

He refused to commit to an answer.

"You need an heir."

He silently grumbled to himself. "There has to be a relative somewhere." He thought his father had a cousin.

"So you don't mean to wed...ever?" Aunt Charity sounded alarmed.

"I haven't made any decisions." While he supposedly needed a wife, he wasn't sure he ever wanted another one. After everything he'd been through with Thea and all he'd witnessed with his parents, he had no hope for the kind of marriage he'd once dreamed of. He wasn't sure he could trust anyone, even Beatrix, whom he admired greatly. And who was also an admitted liar.

He looked askance at his aunt. "I implore you to abandon this topic."

"All right." She pursed her lips as they continued along for a few minutes. "What about taking a mistress?"

He nearly tripped. "Aunt Charity!"

"I'm sorry, but you don't have a parent or a sibling. And you have this dark cloud over you. A mistress might help."

It might. Except the only woman he wanted was Beatrix. And oh, how he wanted her.

Not as his mistress, however. Also not apparently as his wife.

A hollow ache opened up inside him, and he rushed to draw it closed. He was fine. Life was returning to normal, as he'd told his aunt, and normal was good. He had Regan, and she had him. They were a family, and that was enough.

~

*A*fter bidding goodbye to Harry's family, Beatrix and Selina, accompanied by Harry, started toward Hanover Square on their way to Cavendish Square. Beatrix braced herself for the inevitable question.

"Who were you talking to?" Selina asked. She walked between Beatrix and Harry.

"That was Lord Rockbourne," Harry said.

"Oh!" Selina snapped her head toward Beatrix. "You know him?"

Beatrix arched a shoulder. She stuck to her rule of relying on at least partial truths. "I danced with him at the masquerade."

"You didn't mention that." Selina's tone held a dubious edge.

"I think he was trying to keep his presence at the ball a secret." She kept her gaze focused ahead as they entered Hanover Square.

"Because he's in mourning?" Selina asked. "I admit I don't really understand what's expected at his, ah, level. Harry, is it odd that he was at the ball and at church today?"

Harry chuckled. "I am not the right person to ask. My brother is the one who has to pay attention to rules. I'd think attending church is something that would be allowed in any instance, surely."

"Seems like it," Selina murmured. "Is he still under investigation?"

Beatrix held her breath. She'd wanted to ask but didn't dare draw more attention to her interest in Tom.

"Yes. Lady Rockbourne's mother has provided evidence regarding Rockbourne's temper. Apparently Lady Rockbourne was in fear of him."

"That's preposterous." Beatrix hadn't meant to say that out loud. "I mean, I don't know him, but I've heard Lady Rockbourne was the one with a temper."

"Have you?" Harry asked with interest. "Is this a specific rumor we could investigate?"

"Er, no." Beatrix only knew from listening to the shrew herself. But she couldn't admit that, nor could she testify to what she'd heard and seen, not without ruining her reputation.

It was tempting, though. She'd been hoping her reputation would appeal to her father. Not only had it not appealed to him, he knew things about her that most didn't. To him, her reputation was already in tatters.

So what did protecting her reputation even matter?

Because it wasn't just about her. It was also about Selina. She was on the precipice of a marvelous future, and Beatrix wouldn't cause her any trouble or pain. Not for anything.

"Pity," Harry said. "If we had evidence that Lady Rockbourne had a temper, that could justify Rockbourne becoming angry with her."

"Would it justify him pushing her over the balcony?" Selina asked incredulously.

"No, of course not. Honestly, it will be hard to prove what actually happened without an eyewitness. We either believe the viscount's version of events, or we investigate whether he might be lying. So far, there does seem to be motivation for him to have at least been angry with her."

Beatrix suppressed a scowl. "Being angry with someone doesn't mean they pushed them."

"No, but it's our duty to investigate all the evidence."

Selina was studying Beatrix intently. Before

she could ask why Beatrix was defending Tom, Harry thankfully changed the subject.

As soon as they arrived at the house in Cavendish Square—home, Beatrix reminded herself—Beatrix excused herself and went upstairs. Not only did she want to avoid further questions or curious looks from Selina, she had an errand to run.

Going directly to the drawer with the box, Beatrix knelt and removed all the stolen items to a small bag. How to proceed to the receiver shop in Saffron Hill—should she go as a woman or dress in men's clothing? The latter seemed the better choice, so she quickly changed her clothing. The bag had a long strap that she draped across her shoulder so that the bulk of the goods sat against her hip. She donned her coat over the strap and adjusted the bag so it was hidden by the tail of the coat. Finally, she stuck her knife into her boot and tucked her pistol into the specially designed pocket inside her coat.

After making sure every strand of blonde hair was tucked into her hat, she made her way down the back stairs to the lower level. Escaping this house unnoticed was more difficult than it had been when they'd lived on Queen Anne Street, when the house had been smaller and they hadn't had a full complement of servants.

That, and she rarely tried to steal away in the middle of the day.

Navigating the lower level, she made her way to the front of the house where a door led to a small exterior landing at the base of a narrow flight of stairs up to the street. She breathed a sigh of relief as she hurried up the stairs.

And ran directly into the cook at the top.

"Oh! My goodness, pardon me," the older woman said, clutching an armful of parcels that she barely managed to hold on to. Her gaze collided with Beatrix's, and her eyes widened in surprise, followed by recognition. "Miss Whitford?"

"Er, yes. I would be ever so grateful if you would pretend you didn't see me." She gave her an awkward smile. "Thank you!"

Dodging around the woman, Beatrix hurried to Holles Street on her way to Oxford Street. There, she caught a hack heading east to Saffron Hill.

A short while later, she walked into the dim interior of The Golden Lion, the receiver shop that had been, until recently, owned by Rafe. She and Selina had used it to fence some pieces of jewelry Beatrix had stolen a few weeks ago to keep them from losing their house. Selina, with Rafe's assistance, had since recovered and returned all the items—anonymously, of course.

Beatrix had never enjoyed taking things from people, but something about the act of stealing had always given her a surge of accomplishment, of excitement, of *pleasure*. Over the past decade, she'd used her skill when it was necessary. In hindsight, she regretted thinking that having a Season to prove herself to her father was necessary. It had been an utter waste of money and energy.

The shop was tidy, with a counter at the back. Shelves bearing a variety of items lined the walls.

A rough looking lad, perhaps eighteen or so, lounged near the door. He eyed Beatrix cautiously as she made her way toward the counter.

A wiry man in his middle-forties rose from a chair behind the counter. His lined face formed more lines as he smiled at her in welcome. "Afternoon."

"Good afternoon." Beatrix pitched her voice low. "I have some things to sell. The Vicar sent me."

That was the name by which Rafe had been known as owner of the receiver shops and as a moneylender. It never failed to spark a look of surprise, followed by a desire to please. This occasion was no different.

The shopkeeper's eyes rounded, then his lids fluttered. "How may I help you?"

Beatrix opened the bag on her hip and removed the first item, a bracelet she'd stolen a few years before. "This is just one of many items." She wanted to see what he would offer before she showed him the lot.

He picked up the bracelet and held it next to a lantern set on one side of the counter. Reaching under the counter, he pulled out a magnifying glass that he used to study the piece. "These diamonds are real."

"Yes."

Lowering the glass, he blew out a breath and offered her an exceedingly fair price.

Feeling confident, she removed the rest of her items, a few at a time. He bought every single one of them.

After she'd tucked the money away into an interior pocket of her coat, she thanked him. "Do you know of a jeweler whom I could trust to make me a demi-parure of very convincing paste emeralds?"

The man grinned. "I do indeed. My brother-in-law is the very best. No one will know they aren't authentic. His shop is just up the street. Marvin's. Turn right."

"Excellent, thank you." Beatrix turned and left the shop, inclining her head toward the young man near the door as she passed.

Beatrix went to the right up Saffron Hill and came across Marvin's a short distance away. Tucked between a printer and a clothing resale shop, the jeweler's space was narrow with a rickety door that Beatrix worried might fall off its hinges as she stepped inside. If she hadn't been referred to this place, she would have likely turned and left.

Instead, she continued inside. Several lanterns burned inside the shop and cast eerie shadows. There was no one in sight.

"Good afternoon?" Beatrix again lowered her voice in an attempt to sound masculine. She strolled to a glass case that displayed several items of jewelry. A necklace with a large pendant of coral caught her eye. A flower was carved into the coral, which was a deep red.

Her call was answered by the scuff of shuffling feet. Beatrix turned her head to see a tall but slightly stooped man come from behind a curtain hanging in a doorway. He squinted at Beatrix as he moved toward her.

She straightened next to the glass case. "Your

brother-in-law sent me. I would like to commission a demi-parure of paste jewelry."

"Paste?"

She nodded. "To look like emeralds. A necklace, earrings, and a bracelet."

"I have something that will suit." He began to pivot.

Taking two large steps toward him, she held up her hand. "No, I need you to make the set to my specifications."

His brow creased as he studied her a moment. "All right. I'll need you to describe what you want while I draw it." He waved her toward a table on the left side of the shop. Two sconces burned over it, providing the brightest space in the shop.

There were two chairs, and as she sat down, she realized it wasn't a table but a desk. After he took the other chair, he opened a drawer and removed a piece of parchment and a pencil. Licking the end of the implement, he looked at her in expectation.

Beatrix described what she wanted in exacting detail. As she spoke, he sketched the pieces, giving them form before her eyes.

"Like this?"

"Perfect, thank you. How much?"

He gave her a price that was well within what she'd just gotten at the receiver shop.

"When will they be ready?"

"In a week."

She frowned. Reaching into her coat, she took out most of the money from the receiver shop and laid it on the table. "Can you have them for me tomorrow?"

He looked down at the money before nodding at her. "Come after five."

"Half now and half tomorrow." She scooped up half the money and put it back into her coat before rising.

He looked up at her, keen interest gleaming in his gaze. "What do you want them for, miss?"

Beatrix exhaled and wondered if the shop-keeper at The Golden Lion had also seen through her disguise. If not, his brother-in-law would probably reveal her secret. "I just want them. For myself. I would have preferred genuine emeralds, but your brother-in-law assured me your pieces would look authentic."

"Aye, they will."

She glanced toward the glass case that held the coral pendant. "I want the coral flower too. Have that ready with the rest, please."

"Do you want to know how much it costs?"

"No. Do you want me to pay for it today?" She was confident she had enough money.

"Tomorrow is fine. It's for you too?"

She shook her head. "For my sister. It's a wedding gift. I'll see you tomorrow."

Feeling satisfied with her errands, Beatrix hastened to catch a hackney back to Holles Street. As she made her way toward Cavendish Square, she contemplated how to get into the house without drawing notice. And whether the cook had said anything to anyone.

In the end, she went in the way she'd left and picked the same careful path through the lower level. This time, she was lucky enough to make it back to her chamber without encountering anyone. Now, she just had to duplicate that tomorrow when she returned to Marvin's to fetch her set of jewels.

Then she'd have to accomplish an even greater feat when she crept into the duke's house. Over the past several weeks, she'd learned many things about him and his house. In addition to spying on him from Tom's garden, she'd also spoken to one of his stable boys. For a relatively small sum, he'd provided her with the household schedule as well as the house's layout.

She just needed luck on her side, and she was due for a good dose of it.

CHAPTER 11

The house was quiet, a phenomenon that had become more and more noticeable in the fortnight since Thea's death. Baines had noted it earlier. There was a peace the household hadn't known in some time.

Thomas poured a glass of brandy in the sitting room adjoining his chamber before strolling out to the balcony. The events of the night Thea died knocked at his brain, but he refused to answer the call. Hopefully, when the investigation was over, keeping the memory at bay would become easier.

Unfortunately, the inquiry continued. Dearborn had postponed the meeting they'd scheduled today with the nurse and footman. He planned to come by tomorrow afternoon instead.

Thomas couldn't help but look in the tree, but of course Beatrix wasn't there. Not just because he'd told her not to come without notifying him first, but because he suspected she wouldn't come again.

As he sipped his brandy, a movement in the garden behind the tree snagged his attention. No, it couldn't be… A dark figure moved in the shadows. Thomas set his glass on the railing and dashed to the trellis. Swinging himself from the balcony, he descended even more quickly than he had last time.

He'd expected to meet her beneath the balcony, but she wasn't there. He took off into the garden, his eyes working to adjust to the darkness. "Beatrix!" he called, using a loud, urgent whisper.

He heard the gate and ran in that direction, catching up to her just as she moved through it. Extending his arm, he nearly pitched forward as he grasped her elbow. "Beatrix!"

She stopped and turned to face him, her features unreadable beneath the brim of her hat because she kept her head down. "Yes, sorry."

"Why are you leaving?" He didn't let go of her.

"I… I came to see you, but then I was afraid you'd be angry that I'd come without telling you first."

He recoiled, jerking his hand away as if she might burn him. No, as if *he* might hurt *her*.

She was afraid. She'd fled rather than prick his anger.

Thomas fought to keep his heart from pounding out of his chest as his blood rushed loud and fast through his head. "I'm sorry. I just wanted you to be safe. I never meant to frighten you."

She looked up at him then, and he saw the concern in her gaze. "You didn't frighten me—not like that. I didn't want you to think I don't care about your wishes that I not come alone in the dark."

Her words did more than relieve him. They touched a place deep inside him that had never seen the sun. "I never meant to control you," he said quietly.

"I know that." She took his hand and drew it to her chest. He could feel her warmth, even through the layers of her clothing. "I should have told you I was coming. It was a spontaneous decision."

Thomas began to feel lighter. "Was it?" He gave her a half smile.

"Yes."

"I'm glad I caught you. I would have hated for you to come all this way for nothing. Do you want to come up for a nightcap before I see you home?"

She hesitated the barest moment before smiling. "How can I say no?"

Had she wanted to? Thomas shook the thought away. He was being ridiculous. She'd come here to see him. Unless... "Did you come to spy on the duke again?"

"No," she responded quickly, and with a vehemence that clearly conveyed her thoughts on the matter. "I'm finished with him."

"I do think that's for the best. And it's his loss." Thomas turned and opened the gate, gesturing for her to precede him.

She led him to the balcony and up the trellis. When he joined her, she was sipping the brandy he'd left on the railing. "Convenient," she said around the rim of the glass with a saucy curve of her lips.

He couldn't help but stare at her mouth. His body stirred with desire.

Following her into the sitting room, he went to pour another brandy. She removed her hat and her gloves. And her coat.

She'd never removed her coat before.

Thomas froze in the action of raising the glass to his mouth. While she might wear something to flatten her chest beneath the men's clothing, her curves were still visible.

There was something arousing about seeing her in a state of undress in a man's costume. He'd almost certainly think the same thing about her in women's clothing. He just liked seeing her undressed.

She went to the settee and sat in one corner, which left enough room for him to join her. The invitation seemed clear, and Thomas wouldn't ignore it.

He sat down beside her and stretched out his legs. "You took off your coat."

She shrugged. "You aren't wearing one, so it seemed appropriate."

That was true. "I'd wondered if you removed it for another reason."

Her eyes narrowed seductively—or maybe that was just his wishful interpretation. "Did you? Would you care to share that reason?"

The temperature in the room climbed, and he was glad not to be wearing a coat. In truth, he wished he could remove the rest of his clothing—and hers—too. He had to clear his throat to speak. "Not just now."

"Well, let me know if you change your mind." She took another sip of brandy and gave him a coy stare.

"If you keep looking at me like that, I will."

"I see." She sat straighter and sobered. When her gaze met his, he saw a worry that gave him

pause. "Harry told me you are still being investi-
gated regarding your wife's death. He said Bow
Street had evidence that she was afraid of you." A
light flashed in her eyes. "Is that why you thought I
was afraid of you?"

Shit. He didn't want to talk about this. Why
couldn't they go back to flirting? He took a rather
large swig of brandy. He looked toward Thea's
chamber, silently cursing her. "She wasn't afraid of
me. I don't think she was afraid of anything." She'd
certainly never been concerned with hiding her
infidelity from him.

Thomas returned his attention to Beatrix. "I'm
surprised Sheffield mentioned this to you."

"It came up in conversation after church yesterday. And frankly, it was a welcome diversion
from Selina's curiosity about why I was talking to
you." She cocked her head and ran her fingertip
along the rim of her glass. "Harry said your
mother-in-law is the one who provided the evidence about Lady Rockbourne."

"She doesn't care for me. She blames me for
Thea's death, and maybe she's right to do so." He
inwardly winced after saying that last part out
loud.

Beatrix set her glass down on the table next to
the settee and turned toward him. "Why would
you think that?"

"I didn't make Thea happy."

"She didn't make you happy either. I'd argue
she made you miserable."

"We made each other miserable." Finishing his
brandy, he deposited the empty glass on the table

to his left. He angled himself toward her as she had done to him.

"But you tried, didn't you?"

"I did." So damned hard. Until he'd given up. And maybe he shouldn't have.

"You can't blame yourself," she said firmly, shaking her head. "I saw what happened. It was an accident. She fell. There was nothing nefarious about it. Maybe I should tell them that."

He gently cupped her face. "No. You can't do that. That would ruin you."

"I wouldn't care if it was just me, but you're right that it would be ruinous—to Selina. She's about to become the daughter-in-law of an earl. I won't jeopardize her standing."

"You are the very best pretend sister."

She laughed. "Thank you."

He reluctantly moved his hand to the back of the settee—close to her, but not touching. "The wedding is in the morning?"

"Yes."

"I was invited to the breakfast. That was before."

"Are you coming?" she asked hopefully.

"I shouldn't. It's one thing to steal into a masquerade or go to church with my aunt. It's something else to show up at a wedding celebration."

She made a sound with her lips and tongue that reminded him of something Regan would do. Except that seeing her tongue drove all thought of his daughter from his mind.

She brought her leg up onto the settee, bending her knee as she fully faced him. "You should come."

He let his hand drift back to her shoulder. "You tempt me." He trailed his fingertips along her collarbone. "In so many ways," he murmured.

"Is that bad?" She leaned forward and licked her upper lip.

Was that an invitation? "Did you do that on purpose?"

"I don't know. It was unconscious." She leaned toward him more and brushed her lips across his. "*That* was on purpose."

She didn't retreat. Thomas clasped the back of her head and kissed her. It was a quick connection, but dazzled him all the way to his toes. He looked at her to make sure this was what she wanted.

Her hazel eyes glinted with desire. She put her hand on his shoulder and tipped her head slightly to the left, bringing her lips nearly to his.

"Beatrix," he breathed before claiming her mouth once more. This time was not quick. Nor was it gentle. Their tongues clashed, stoking the fire that had been smoldering inside him practically since they'd met. He gripped her waist with his other hand and squeezed.

She cradled his neck and clutched at his side. The kiss was electric. Her touch fed his soul. Her hand skimmed up over his chest and tugged at his cravat.

Yes.

He guided her back against the settee, coming over her as he deepened the kiss.

"Papa, what are you doing?"

Thomas and Beatrix jerked apart. Christ, he

hadn't even heard Regan come in. She stood in front of the settee. How long had she been there?

"Well, I'm, ah…visiting with my friend." Thomas moved to the opposite end of the settee from Beatrix and perched on the edge. "You remember her."

"Yes. She's pretty."

Straightening her spine and scooting as far to her edge of the settee as possible, Beatrix blushed. Rather, she blushed more since her cheeks were already quite pink. "Thank you."

Regan continued to stare at Beatrix. "Why do you always dress like a boy?"

"It's comfortable."

Regan transferred her stare to Thomas. "Papa, can I dress like a boy?"

"We'll discuss that another time. Why are you awake?"

"Alice woke me." She held up her doll.

Beatrix seemed to have composed herself. The color in her face had returned to normal. She leaned forward, lowering her head to Regan's level. "Why is that?"

"She wanted a story. Papa tells good stories."

"Does he?" Beatrix's kiss-swollen mouth curved into a heart-stopping smile as she looked over at him.

"Will you tell me a story?" Regan asked Beatrix. "Then it will be new."

"Yes." Beatrix didn't hesitate before answering, and Thomas didn't think his heart could swell any more.

Smiling, Regan turned and padded toward his chamber.

"Where are you going?" Beatrix asked.

"Papa always tells me a story in bed. That way, I can fall asleep easier." She said the last as if it should be patently obvious. Thomas couldn't help but laugh.

Beatrix grinned. "Your daughter is rather brilliant."

Thomas watched as Regan slipped into his chamber. "I think so." He stood and helped Beatrix up. "You don't really have to stay. I can say you needed to leave."

"Absolutely not. I said I would tell her a story, and I won't disappoint her. What kind of friend would that make me?" She tsked, her eyes narrowing briefly.

Thomas caught her hand before she could move toward his bedchamber. "You are wonderful." He kissed her wrist and looked into her eyes. "But know this is not the way I imagined you in my bed."

Her brows climbed her forehead. "You imagined that?"

"*Often.*"

He felt her shiver.

"Well, this is still quite lovely—for other reasons. Come, I'm going to tell a story about two sisters."

"Is it autobiographical?"

She lifted a shoulder. "You'll have to stay awake to find out."

"Oh, I intend to. After all, I have to take you home."

The exhalation that passed her lips was tinged with regret. "Yes. But first, the story." She grinned at him before turning and going into his room.

Thomas hesitated before following her. He couldn't quite believe how much his life had changed in such a short time—and for the better. Entering the chamber, he stopped short, his breath hitching completely.

Beatrix lay on top of the coverlet next to Regan, who was burrowed beneath it. Both were propped against pillows. As he watched them, emotion curling in his chest, Regan snuggled into Beatrix's side. Beatrix's mouth pulled up, and she put her arm around his daughter.

"Once upon a time, there were two sisters, both with fair hair, one tall and one short." Autobiographical, then.

Regan patted the space on her other side. "Aren't you coming, Papa? You'll miss the story."

He had to clear his throat. "Yes, of course." He hastened to the bed and slid over the coverlet until he was next to Regan. "Better?"

She looked up at Beatrix. "Continue, please."

"Now, where was I? Yes, one tall and one short. They were sent away to boarding school by their evil stepfather."

"What's board school?"

"A horrible place," Beatrix said drily.

Thomas made a mental note to ask Beatrix why she'd said that. "It's a school where students go and live."

"Will I go there, Papa?"

He leaned down and kissed her head. "No."

"Because you aren't evil." Regan yawned.

"I hope not."

Beatrix's eyes met his as she whispered, "Not even close."

"What happened at the board school?" Regan asked, yawning again.

"The sisters were taunted by the other girls." Was that true? Thomas wanted to know everything.

Regan looked up at Beatrix. "Why?"

"Because the sisters were smart and pretty, and the other girls were jealous. They did their best to get the sisters in trouble."

"I hope this has a happy ending," Regan said. "Papa's have happy endings."

"How would you know?" he asked with mock incredulousness. "You never stay awake."

Regan giggled. "Because you tell me in the morning. Papa, if I fall asleep, will you tell me the end in the morning?"

"Of course, darling."

"Or she can, if she's still here," Regan said, glancing toward Beatrix.

Thomas looked at Beatrix and glimpsed a future he'd long ago deemed impossible. "You need to let her tell the story," he said softly. He nodded toward Beatrix.

"I promise this story has a very happy ending, and if you fall asleep, I'll make sure your father knows how it ends so he can tell you."

"Thank you."

Settling in, Thomas couldn't wait to hear how it concluded. And for the first time in ages, he wondered if he might find a happy ending of his own.

~

*B*eatrix should have been tired after being out late the night before at Thomas's house, but she was too excited for Selina's wedding. She picked up the small box from her dressing table before leaving her chamber and going downstairs to Selina's room.

After Regan had fallen asleep in Thomas's bed last night, Beatrix had tried to persuade him to let her go home on her own—it was clear he should stay with his daughter. However, he'd insisted on hailing a hackney and accompanying her to Cavendish Square. It was, at least, faster than walking, which meant he was able to return to Regan as quickly as possible.

He'd asked about her time at Mrs. Goodwin's. She hadn't told him quite everything—not the bits about stealing—but sharing the torment of the other girls, her close friendship with Selina, and how she'd left with Selina before her education had been completed had made her feel surprisingly good. Perhaps because he was an exceptional, and sympathetic, listener.

He'd then regaled her with a few stories of Oxford, which involved a great deal of drunkenness and buffoonery. She had a bit of difficulty reconciling the troubled widowed father with the jovial young man and wished she could have known him then.

Although she was quite happy with knowing him now. As well as his daughter. She was charming, and Beatrix was so glad to know she had a loving father.

Situated at the rear of the first floor, Selina's room was the largest bedchamber in the house. When Beatrix stepped inside, she stopped short at seeing Selina in her wedding gown. Made of ivory silk and trimmed in pale pink, the dress looked like a delicious confection.

Her new lady's maid, whom Selina's almost-mother-in-law had insisted she needed, was busy fastening the buttons along Selina's back.

"You look so beautiful," Beatrix said, sighing.

Selina turned her head and smiled. "So do you."

Beatrix glanced down at her new dress. Light green with darker green embroidery, it reminded her of a bright spring day, which today was. "Thank you."

"All finished, miss," the maid said, stepping back.

Selina pivoted and held her arms slightly out from her sides. "Well?"

"Nearly perfect."

Lines furrowed Selina's brow. "Nearly?"

"I have just the thing." Beatrix looked to the maid. "Would you excuse us for a moment?"

The maid dipped a curtsey before taking her leave.

"I shall never get used to that," Selina said.

"I might, but then my mother had a lady's maid." Beatrix held out the small box tied with a blue ribbon. "I have something for you." She placed it in Selina's palm.

"How did you—?" Selina pressed her lips together, her brows drawing together as she untied the ribbon. She opened the lid and gasped. Her free hand shot to her mouth as her gaze lifted to Beatrix's.

Beatrix moved closer and looked down at the coral necklace. "I know it's not the one you remember, but I thought it must be very similar."

"It's lovely. Dammit, you're going to make me cry. I told you I've become a watering pot." Selina blinked several times and laughed. "It's perfect." She ran her fingertip over the flower. "Truly. This is the best thing I've ever received. Except Harry's love." She flashed Beatrix an apologetic smile. "Sorry."

Beatrix grinned. "As it should be."

"Will you put it on me? I want to wear it today."

"I rather hoped you would," Beatrix said softly, happy that Selina loved the gift.

Taking the present, Beatrix removed the necklace and set the box on the dressing table. As she turned to Selina, she hesitated. "I'm going to need a stool. You are, as always, a giant."

"No, you're a sprite." Selina bent her knees. "I'll squat as I usually do."

Smiling, Beatrix went around Selina and fastened the pendant around her neck. The chain holding the flower carved in coral was gold and matched the gold-and-pearl earrings Selina already wore. Her honey-blonde hair had been artfully styled by the maid, incorporating pale pink ribbon and pearls.

Selina looked into the glass at the dressing table and fingered the pendant. "Absolutely perfect. I almost think it's the same kind of flower, but I always thought the one I remembered was a rose and this is clearly a peony."

There was a knock on the door, and they both turned their heads.

"Come in," Selina called.

Stepping inside, Rafe stopped abruptly. His gaze swept Selina from slipper to crown. They were clearly siblings, both tall with golden hair and blue eyes, though Rafe's right one had a peculiar orange spot. He also had a nasty scar that cut through his lip and chin. Beatrix had no idea how he'd gotten it, and she wasn't sure Selina knew either. It hadn't been there when he'd sent her away from London.

"I imagined this day for so long," he said quietly. "You're a beautiful bride."

"You imagined it?" Selina asked.

Rafe came toward them. "I hoped you would wed someday and that I would be there to see it."

"I hope the same for you."

He shook his head. "That isn't the path for me, and I've made my peace with that."

Selina frowned. "This conversation isn't over, but I'm not going to pursue it today." She touched her pendant, her features relaxing. "Look at what Beatrix gave me."

Rafe reached out and she dropped her hand. He slid his fingers beneath the coral and ran his thumb over the flower. His lips parted, and he breathed, "This was hers."

"Our mother's?" Selina asked.

He nodded.

"Not this exact piece, surely," Selina said.

Releasing the pendant, Rafe wiped a hand over his jaw. "I don't know. It's very similar—the coral, the flower. But it may have been a rose."

"That's what I remember."

Rafe looked at her in surprise. "You remember it?"

"Just the coral and the flower and that it hung around someone's neck—I didn't know who. I remember touching it, like you just did."

"I did the same. She would hold me on her lap. Once, we were on a blanket near a small lake. There was a building behind us." His brow creased, and his gaze took on a faraway stare. "It was like a miniature…temple."

"A folly?" Beatrix asked, recalling one she'd visited with her mother once. They'd gone to a country house, but Beatrix didn't remember why or where. She had always recalled the folly, however. She'd wanted to live there with the fairies her mother said inhabited it.

Rafe and Selina looked at her in bafflement.

"It's a fake building. I mean, it's a real building, though I guess some don't have a roof, but it's a replica of something else, like a temple. Some people build them on the grounds of their estate. They might even pay a hermit to live in it." Beatrix remembered one of the girls at Mrs. Goodwin's talking about her uncle's folly with a hermit.

Though they nodded in understanding, Selina and Rafe also exchanged looks of disbelief.

"The bloody rich," Rafe muttered.

"Which is now you," Beatrix said with a laugh.

"You won't see me building a ridiculous folly— it's the perfect name for such a useless thing. And you definitely won't find me *paying* someone to live in it. Jesus."

"But you remember a folly," Selina said insistently, her gaze fixed on Rafe.

"And a lake," Beatrix added.

"Was that where we lived?" Selina sounded incredulous.

"I don't know." Rafe paced to the window. He'd been five when their parents had died and they'd been taken in by a "relative." A decidedly not rich relative who would not have been anywhere near a lake with a folly. The man who hadn't really been their uncle had taken them to East London and used them to swindle people.

"But I can distinctly see the folly and the lake." He inclined his head toward Selina. "And that pendant."

"This exact pendant?" Selina asked, and Beatrix could hear the wonder in her voice.

He turned to Beatrix. "Where did you get that?"

Oh hell. She'd hoped to avoid mentioning the receiver shop. But she could believably explain why she'd bought a gift there. "The Golden Lion."

They both directed surprised looks at her. "Why did you go there of all places?" Rafe asked.

Beatrix shrugged. "I wanted to find something nice, and those are the best places to do so without paying a fortune. And since you recently owned the shop, I thought it the smartest choice."

"Did Tillman help you?"

"If he's the wiry gentleman with an excessively lined face, then yes."

"That's him." Rafe shook his head. "I'll go and speak to him, see where this came from."

"Do you really think this belonged to our mother?" Selina sounded as if she couldn't believe it. Beatrix didn't blame her. It would be beyond astonishing.

"I don't know." Rafe blew out a breath. "It's been an awfully long time. But if it isn't that pendant, it's bloody close. I still want to talk to Tillman about it."

Selina brushed her hand over the coral. "Yes, please. I may hold my breath until you do."

"Don't do that," Rafe said with a smile. "You need to breathe on your wedding day at least."

"Of course." Selina rolled her eyes. "Speaking of that, we should be on our way to church."

"Ready?" Rafe offered her his arm.

"As I'll ever be." She put her hand on her brother's sleeve. "I never envisioned this day. Not once. I still worry something may happen to spoil it."

Rafe put his hand over hers and squeezed. "It won't. I wouldn't let it, but it won't."

Selina nodded. He kissed her forehead before guiding her from the room.

Beatrix lingered a moment, watching them precede her. Unlike Selina, Beatrix had envisioned a wedding day for herself. One where her father would give her away to her groom.

That dream had died when her father had rejected her. Now it was up to her to find a new one.

CHAPTER 12

The wedding ceremony at St. George's had been lovely, with Harry's entire, rather large, family in attendance. He had two parents, a twin brother, three married sisters, and a variety of nieces and nephews. They were the opposite of what Beatrix and Selina—and Rafe—were used to.

Beatrix watched in delight as they all embraced Selina, hovering around her and just generally welcoming her into their fold. She knew the attention was a trifle overwhelming for Selina, just as she knew that Selina had begun to enjoy it.

The breakfast was being held at Lord and Lady Aylesbury's grand house on Mount Street, and the drawing room and adjoining chamber were full of well-wishers. Beatrix was glad to see some familiar faces in the women of the Spitfire Society, which now met at a variety of homes, including those of the Marchioness of Ripley, the Duchess of Clare, and the Duchess of Kendal. Beatrix suddenly realized she'd achieved a rather lofty posi-

tion in Society—at least amongst her friends—
without the aid of her horrible father.

"Ah, Miss Whitford, allow me to introduce
someone to you."

Beatrix had been so busy surveying the room,
she'd missed the approach of Harry's brother, the
Viscount Northwood. Identical to Harry except
that his shoulders were not quite as broad, North,
as he was called, sported the same auburn hair and
tawny eyes.

But it was the man beside him who drew Beatrix's full attention: Tom.

Her breath caught as she schooled her features
not to reflect the fact that she knew him. She
dipped a curtsey. "Of course."

"Rockbourne, may I present Miss Whitford,
my new sister-in-law."

Beatrix hadn't considered that this large, bois-
terous family was now *her* family too. How positively wonderful, for she liked them very much.

Curtseying again, Beatrix tried not to smile at
Tom even though her heart was speeding at a fre-
netic pace. "I'm pleased to make your acquaintance."

"Miss Whitford, this is the Viscount Rockbourne. He's a dear friend of mine."

Beatrix saw the black band encircling Tom's
upper arm. "I heard about the tragedy you suffered. I'm so sorry for your loss."

"Thank you," he said simply, but his gaze,
locked with hers, held a dark, stirring heat.

"I'm glad you decided to come today, Rockbourne," North said, clapping him on the shoulder.
"It's good for you to get out."

"Some would say it's not appropriate," Tom said softly.

"Eh, you're an old friend of the family, and it's not as if you're out frolicking at a gaming hell." North glanced toward Beatrix. "I beg your pardon."

She quirked a smile. "Not at all. Frolicking at a gaming hell sounds rather diverting."

North howled with laughter. "I knew I liked you." His gaze fixed on something across the room and he gave a slight nod. Looking back to Beatrix and Tom, he said, "Please excuse me. My mother is giving me the *eye*." His brows arched in amusement as he took himself off.

"You came," Beatrix said as soon as North was out of earshot.

"It turns out I couldn't resist. Not knowing you would be here." His gaze slid over her like a silken coverlet. "You look magnificent."

She tried not to blush and failed. "Thank you. So do you."

"It's not the same, and you know it. I never get to see you like this."

"Not *never*. You saw me at the masquerade ball." She moved closer to him—as close as she dared. "Are you saying you don't like me in my men's costume?" she whispered.

"I like you in anything. Or nothing, if that's an option."

She sucked in a breath as an electric pulse ran through her.

"Forgive me," he murmured. "That was gauche."

"I am not offended." He was not the first man

she'd flirted with. Or kissed. Or gone to bed with. She'd had precisely one lover, several years ago, whom she'd never told anyone about. Not even Selina. How could she when Selina had endured such a horrible experience at the hands of her employer? "That...*might* be an option."

Tom's breath came out in a hiss. He pivoted toward her. "Beatrix, you are making it difficult for me to stand in a social gathering without drawing undue attention."

Her gaze dipped below his waist. She could just make out the length of his cock. "My apologies. Perhaps we should talk about the weather. Or the price of cockles." She lifted her hand to her mouth and stifled a giggle. "Not *cock*les. How about eel?"

His eyes widened, and he struggled not to laugh. "That's somehow better?"

She pressed her hand harder against her smiling lips. "Not at all." She took a deep breath and lowered her hand. "Turnips. Let us discuss turnips."

"I'd like to discuss turnips in private."

What was happening here? They'd flirted before, a number of times, but now that they'd kissed, their banter had taken on another depth.

She looked up at him and studied the familiar planes of his face—his wide forehead, sculpted cheekbones, and strong, square jaw. Her gaze lingered on his lips, the lower one thicker than the upper, and she recalled how they felt against hers.

They shouldn't keep doing this. And yet when she thought about not... Well, she didn't like thinking about that. "So why did you come today?" she asked softly.

"To see you."

A warmth spread through her, sparking another smile. She hadn't expected him to say so. "I'm glad you did." It was difficult to keep her distance from him. They'd grown so close over the past fortnight, but that had been in a private setting. "This is odd, isn't it? Being here with all these people?"

He grinned, nodding. "Yes. I'm not used to sharing you. Except with Regan."

"I enjoy that, actually."

"I do too." His gaze was fierce. "More than you can know. Thea was not a good mother."

"Oh, well. I couldn't—" She wasn't sure what to say. She wasn't Regan's mother.

"I just meant that it's good for her to see kindness and caring in a woman. She enjoyed the end of your story this morning, by the way."

Beatrix laughed. "Good."

Selina approached them, and Beatrix saw the glint of determination in her gaze. Selina knew there was something between them, and Beatrix wasn't going to be able to deflect her questions any longer—not when Selina kept seeing her with Tom.

"Selina, this is Lord Rockbourne. Lord Rockbourne, this is my sister, Mrs. Sheffield." Beatrix couldn't help but grin. "That's the first time I've called you that. It sounds marvelous, doesn't it?"

"It does indeed," Tom said, taking Selina's hand and bowing. "May I offer my most heartfelt felicitations on your marriage. Sheffield is most fortunate."

"Thank you, Lord Rockbourne."

Turning to Beatrix, Tom inclined his head. "Miss Whitford, it's been a pleasure to speak with you. Please excuse me, ladies." He made his way toward the door. Was he leaving?

"I didn't intend to scare him off," Selina murmured before directing her full attention on Beatrix. "What on earth is going on between you?"

"Nothing is going on." Even Beatrix didn't find that convincing.

"That's hogwash, and you know it. Never mind that you've displayed an interest in and defended him before today and that you spoke with him after the church service on Sunday. Anyone looking at the two of you might think you were courting. Did you really just meet him at the masquerade?"

Beatrix exhaled. "No, it was before that."

"When?" The question was low and clipped.

"You won't approve."

Selina swore quietly. "I don't care. Tell me."

"I don't want to ruin your wedding day."

Eyes widening, Selina gaped at her. "It's that bad?"

Beatrix turned and pulled her to the wall. "Of course not. You know I've gone to Grosvenor Square to spy on my father."

"Yes, but you stopped that." She closed her eyes and took a breath. "Except you didn't."

"Tom—Rockbourne—lives next door to the duke. I climbed the tree in his garden to spy on Ramsgate."

"And that's how you met Rockbourne?"

Beatrix nodded, leaving out *how* she'd met him,

that she'd seen his wife fall over the side of the balcony. "We've become friends."

Selina's brows arched nearly to her hairline. "You looked a bit closer than that. Exactly how often were you visiting him in his garden?"

"You don't want to know."

Selina briefly pressed her hand to her cheek. "Does he want to court you?" She shook her head. "He can't. He's in mourning. Why is he even here? Good gracious, I don't understand Society's rules one whit."

"I don't either. I'm fairly certain if it were you or I who were in mourning, we'd be vilified for coming to a friend's wedding."

"Mmm," Selina murmured in agreement. "It seems like they'll jump on any reason to disparage a young woman." She pinned Beatrix with a dark frown. "You are not helping matters behaving in that way. You can't go to his garden anymore."

"I know." She *did* know.

"Good." Selina touched her arm. "I've been so focused on the wedding, but things will return to normal now. Well, as normal as we can be." She squeezed Beatrix's elbow. "The most normal we've ever been."

"I think that will be nice. Don't you?"

"Exceedingly. I'm looking forward to getting back to work on the orphans' home." This had become Selina's passion—after Harry, of course—and the Spitfire Society had taken up the cause. "I meant to tell you that I met someone whose sister-in-law runs an orphanage in Somerset. Her husband's family has managed it for centuries, apparently. I plan to write to them for advice."

"What a wonderful idea. Perhaps you and Harry should go take a tour. As a wedding trip."

Selina laughed softly. "That would require me to persuade Harry to leave his position at Bow Street for longer than a week, which I am not sure he's willing to do. Things are very busy there lately."

So it seemed. Beatrix was just glad she and Selina were not in any way responsible for that. And they could have been, if things had gone differently. Indeed, Beatrix could still find herself in trouble if she continued to steal.

Instinctively, she smoothed her hands over her gown and then remembered it didn't have pockets. She'd decided all her new dresses, and this was her newest, wouldn't have them. It seemed prudent. Where could she stash a stolen object if she didn't have pockets? Hopefully, it would work.

"What about Rockbourne?" Selina asked with a half smile.

"We are friends."

"Nothing more?"

"He's in mourning."

"He won't be forever."

No, he wouldn't. "If I ever decide to commit myself to someone, as you have to Harry, I want to be sure I'm doing it with my whole heart and that he is doing the same."

"That is very wise. And you deserve nothing less." Selina linked her arm through Beatrix's. "Come, let us pretend we are members of Society for a while."

Beatrix laughed. "We don't have to pretend. Not anymore."

At least not about that.

~

*T*hough Thomas never took naps, he was tempted to lie down with Regan that afternoon. Staying up so late with Beatrix the night before followed by the wedding breakfast had combined to make him exhausted.

It was, however, a good sort of exhausted. For the first time in ages, he felt energized instead of drained.

As she did most days, Aunt Charity arrived in the late afternoon. Thomas met her in the drawing room for tea.

"Good afternoon, Aunt," he said as he sat down with her at the small oval table that overlooked Grosvenor Square.

She poured the tea and added a touch of sugar, just as he liked. "How has your day been, dear?"

"You'll be delighted to know I went to a wedding breakfast this morning."

"Aylesbury's son?" she asked in surprise. A smile brightened her features. "I'm so glad. How was it?"

"Lovely." He was still thinking of the flirtatious conversation he'd had with Beatrix. "I didn't stay very long."

She nodded. "Wise of you. How did people react to your presence?"

He'd noted some looks of surprise, but then he'd mostly ignored everyone but Beatrix. "I only spoke with a handful of people, and they were kind." To a person, they'd asked how he was faring and commented that he'd looked well.

"Brace yourself for the inevitable gossip that you're looking for a new viscountess." She sipped her tea.

"If there is anything you could do to quash such rumors, I'd be most grateful."

"I can try." She set her cup down, her brow pinching in apparent distress. "Speaking of rumors, I'm afraid I must broach a difficult subject. I visited with a friend earlier, and she heard that Bow Street is investigating Thea's death, that it may not have been an accident."

"Goddammit," he breathed, his heart starting to race as his anger stoked. "How in the hell would she know?" His fury reached a boil. "Never mind. It's her bloody mother."

"Agnes Chamberlain?" Aunt Charity's lip curled. "One of her children is to be transported for the crime of extortion and the other was a nasty person—a loathsome wife and mother. Why would anyone believe her?"

"She gave Bow Street 'evidence.'" Thomas vaulted out of the chair and stalked to the hearth and then back again.

Aunt Charity stared at him in alarm. "What sort of evidence?"

"It doesn't matter. It's all horseshit." His voice rose, and he had to suppress the urge to throw something as he'd done the other day. The entire situation was a disaster.

"My lord?" Baines asked from the doorway. "Mr. Dearborn is here for the remaining interviews."

Hell, he'd apparently been too tired, or too distracted, to remember. "Summon Osbert and Miss Addy to the sitting room downstairs. Make sure Mrs. Henley is attending to Regan." The housekeeper often supported the nurse when it was necessary and if she was available. She insisted on doing so because she adored Regan.

"Yes, sir," Baines said.

"Oh, and Baines, I'd like you to sit in on the interviews. If Dearborn objects, I want to know."

"Very good." Baines inclined his head and departed.

"Is Mr. Dearborn from Bow Street?" Aunt Charity asked, her features etched in concern.

"Yes." Thomas gritted his teeth and went to the window. He stared at the lawn in the middle of the square. "He interviewed the entire household except for a footman and the nurse. He's come back today to finish the job."

"Did he talk to Regan?" She lifted her hand to her chest, aghast at the prospect.

"Absolutely not, and he never will."

"You poor boy. That horrid woman is torturing you from beyond."

Thomas massaged his temple and pivoted from the window back toward his aunt. "That was my precise sentiment. I would dearly love to just move on."

"Yes, of course. Can I pour you something stronger than tea?"

"No, thank you. You can talk to me of something other than this investigation or Thea or the mess that is currently my life."

Aunt Charity did just that, and while Thomas

didn't completely relax, he did cease thinking about Dearborn and whatever might be going on during his interviews. But when Baines brought him back to the drawing room, all of Thomas's agitation returned.

"Pardon me, my lord," Dearborn said, holding his hat. "I have concluded my interviews. I would like to ask you a few more questions, if that's acceptable."

"It most certainly is not," Aunt Charity said, her brows pitched in anger.

"Aunt Charity, it's fine," Thomas said softly. He rose from the table and moved to stand near the hearth. He did not invite Dearborn to sit.

Dearborn glanced toward Thomas's aunt in silent question.

Thomas scrubbed his hand across his forehead. "She can stay. I'll tell her everything we discussed anyway."

"That's your choice." Dearborn took a deep breath. "The nurse, Miss Addy, told me there's a woman who visits you late at night—a friend. Who is that?"

Fuck. Thomas stared at the constable. "I'm not telling you her name."

"Were you—are you—having an affair?"

"*No.*"

Aunt Charity stood quickly and joined them near the hearth. "Lady Rockbourne was the one who wasn't faithful." One hand on her hip, she stood close to Thomas and glared at Dearborn as if she might take him down.

"Yes, so we've heard." Dearborn kept his tone even. He looked at Thomas, his gaze probing. "If you aren't having an affair, why does this woman visit you late at night? Was she here the night Lady Rockbourne fell?"

Frustration and fury coiled through Thomas. His hands fisted, and his shoulders bunched with pent-up tension. "The woman is of no concern of yours. It is a tragedy that my wife died, but if you are looking for someone to grieve the loss, you won't find them here. She was a cold, vicious woman—unfaithful and unmotherly. You can't have heard many speak in her favor in this household. Everyone tiptoed around her in fear."

Nodding solemnly, Dearborn said, "Yes, that is the portrait I have drawn of her from the members of your household. Her...disagreeability also provides a motive for wanting her dead."

"Disagreeability?" Thomas gaped at the man. "That's an intensely gross understatement in describing her behavior, Dearborn. As to motive, my relief at her death is not the same as seeking it out."

Dearborn glanced toward the doorway. "Your butler tells me the household is far more peaceful now."

"That is true." Thomas forced his shoulders to relax and shook his hands out.

"Your butler also confirmed something the footman mentioned, that your hand was recently damaged after you hit a tree. Is that what happened?"

"Yes."

"Mrs. Chamberlain has testified that you are a violent man. Do you often hit trees? Or other... things? Or people?"

The rage bubbling inside Thomas boiled over. "For pity's sake, man, do you really want to talk about violence?" He took a step toward the constable. "Let us talk about my wife, who liked to throw things—at me. I could show you the scar on my neck where she raked me with her nails several months ago. It's a shame the bruise from the poker she wielded at my shoulder faded some time ago. Or perhaps I should have let her stab me with the penknife that night instead of side stepping her. Should I have sacrificed myself to her temper to save her from falling?"

Dearborn's eyes narrowed. "You're saying you were on the balcony that night?"

Dammit. There was no help for it now. "I was."

"You lied."

"To protect that faithless shrew." Thomas shook his head once. "Not to protect her, to protect my daughter. I didn't want her to know the cruelty and violence her mother was capable of."

Dearborn exhaled. "Will you tell me precisely what happened? The truth this time?"

Thomas felt Aunt Charity's comforting hand on his arm. Her touch leached away some of his anger and despair. "We were arguing. I went out to the balcony to get away from her raging. She followed me, shrieking about…something." He heard the words quite clearly but wouldn't repeat them. She'd broken his heart in every way possible, and he was supposedly the villain?

"She was always shrieking about something," Aunt Charity said, her hand still on Thomas's arm.

"What happened on the balcony?" Dearborn

asked. He withdrew the little book from his coat along with his pencil.

"She came after me with her penknife, aiming right at my throat. I wasn't wearing a cravat, so she had a straight shot at my bare flesh. Knowing what she was capable of, I moved to avoid the blow. She lost her balance at the railing and fell over." Thomas's vision blurred as he recalled the sight of her body pitching over the side and landing on the stones below. It was as if it had happened in half time, the world slowing to ensure he remembered every awful detail.

He squeezed his eyes shut briefly and shuddered. When he opened them, he blew out a breath. "There was nothing I could do to stop her from falling. I'd moved too far away to reach her." Besides, he'd been too shocked in the moment to act. Shocked? Or had he just not cared enough to do so? If that had been anyone else falling—Regan or...Beatrix—he would have endangered himself to save them.

The blame he'd assigned himself roared through him. Perhaps Bow Street would find him guilty too. If not for his daughter, he might even allow himself to be punished for it. But she needed him, and he would fight for her with every breath he took.

"Oh, Thomas," Aunt Charity breathed. She put her arms around him and gave him a hard, swift hug. Then she turned, eyes blazing, toward the constable. "This poor man has been through enough. Can't you see that?"

"It certainly seems an ordeal," Dearborn said, frowning. He looked at Thomas. "You mentioned a penknife. We didn't find that in our search. Would you mind if I look again?"

"You won't find it. I've searched everywhere."

Dearborn grimaced. He opened his mouth but hesitated before asking, tentatively, "Does this penknife actually exist?"

Aunt Charity drew a sharp breath, and Thomas wiped his hand over his face. "Yes. It was a gift from her father years ago. The handle was ivory with her initials—DC—carved into a design. Her mother knows of its existence, but I can't produce it for you. I've searched everywhere, including her chamber."

The lines crossing Dearborn's brow deepened. "Why would you search her chamber if she attacked you with it?"

"Because I wanted to be sure I wasn't going mad, if you must know. When you live with someone like her for years, you sometimes begin to doubt your own sanity."

Dearborn blanched and tipped his head down as he scribbled a series of notes in his book. Aunt Charity gave Thomas's arm a squeeze before letting him go.

At length, Dearborn closed his little book. His features tight, he replaced the book and the pencil in his coat. "After I conduct my search, I'll be on my way. It may be that we return to search the entire house. I'll send word if that's the case."

"Why are you continuing to pester him?" Aunt Charity demanded. "Can't you see he's been through hell?"

Dearborn turned a frosty stare toward her. "Lord Rockbourne hasn't been truthful, and we've found ample motive for him to have pushed his wife. Her death seems to have been a convenient and welcome happenstance. It is my duty to investigate how it occurred. That it causes unpleasantness is unfortunate, but I'm sure you'll agree that a woman's death is even more so."

Aunt Charity glowered at him but didn't respond.

The constable inclined his head toward Thomas. "Forgive me, my lord. I will be as quick as possible in my search."

"Baines will supervise and provide any assistance you require." Thomas moved to the door and saw the butler lingering just outside. He gave Thomas a look of sympathy. "You heard?" he asked quietly.

"Yes. You continue to have my unfailing support, my lord."

"Thank you, Baines. Please accompany Mr. Dearborn to our private sitting room as well as to Lady Rockbourne's chamber and the balcony. The garden too, I imagine."

Dearborn joined them outside the drawing room. "I'd also like to search your chamber."

"Fine." Thomas waved a hand dismissively. "I've nothing to hide from you."

"Except what you already hid—and the name of the woman who visits you. I wonder, should I reinterview the household to see if any of them recall her name?"

Bloody fucking hell! He tried to remember if Regan knew Beatrix's name. She had to. Had she shared it with her nurse? He wasn't going to ask. It didn't matter. He never should have expected her not to say anything. She was a child. No, the truth was that he shouldn't have exposed her to Beatrix at all. It was unseemly. Even if Beatrix was the kindest, most charming woman he could hope for his daughter to meet, particularly after the horror that was her mother.

"Do what you must," Thomas said through clenched teeth.

Dearborn turned and departed with Baines.

Stalking back into the drawing room, Thomas went straight to the sideboard and poured a glass of brandy. He wished for something more potent —gin would be perfect. His hand shook as he tossed half the contents down his throat.

"I'll take one," Aunt Charity said from behind him.

He set his glass down and poured another for her. Turning, he handed her the brandy, then picked his up to finish it. Now he wanted to go hit another tree.

Aunt Charity sipped her drink. "I'm worried. Who is this woman? You said you didn't have a mistress."

"I don't. It's as I said—she's a friend."

"Who visits you late at night? Why on earth does the nurse know about her?"

Thomas clapped his empty glass down on the sideboard. "Because Regan has met her. Only Regan."

"How long as this been going on?"

"It doesn't matter. It isn't 'going on' anymore." He didn't realize how much that devastated him until that moment. Beatrix had been a beacon, a tether holding him to earth, from the very moment Thea had fallen.

"I'm sorry to hear it. We can use all the friends we can get." She lifted her glass in a silent toast.

Thomas could drink to that. So he poured another glass of brandy and did just that.

CHAPTER 13

$\mathcal{B}$eatrix turned the page, the rustling of the parchment hanging in the air longer than normal because the house felt so very silent. Because Selina and Harry had chosen to spend their wedding night at his house on Rupert Street so they could have privacy.

Not for the first time that night, Beatrix wondered if she should have sent Tom a note. He could have come to visit…

Sighing, she refocused her attention on the page.

"Miss Whitford?" Culpepper, the butler who so capably oversaw the Spitfire house, as Beatrix thought of it, stepped into the garden room.

She looked up from her book, smiling. "Yes?"

"There is a…message for you." His brow furrowed, and he glanced back over his shoulder.

Beatrix set the book on the table beside her chair. "Is this a written message or a verbal one?"

"I'm not certain. There is a…gentleman here to deliver it."

That sounded strange, particularly at this hour.

Beatrix glanced at the clock. It was half ten. "Are you concerned about this gentleman?"

"Not really. He does, in fact, seem like a gentleman. But when I asked for his card, he said he didn't have one."

Beatrix rose quickly, almost certain as to this mystery gentleman's identity. Who else would visit her at this hour and decline to identify himself? "Please show him in." Anticipation heated her blood and quickened the pace of her heart.

Tom strode into the garden room, his hat pulled low over his eyes, his form cloaked in unrelenting black, including a great coat that covered his suit of clothing. He wasn't unrecognizable by any measure, but that was because she knew him. To anyone else, he looked like a man who was trying to escape notice.

Beatrix stood and went to the door, walking close by Tom as she passed. Culpepper lingered outside. She gave him a bright smile. "This gentleman is quite known to me—an old friend of the family. Thank you for showing him in." She closed the door without waiting for the butler to respond.

Turning, she waited for Tom to face her. When he did not, she began to feel alarmed.

"Tom?" she asked tentatively, moving toward him. Upon reaching his side, she touched his arm gently.

He pivoted, sweeping his hat off. His face was drawn and a bit pale, adding to her concern. "Where is your sister?"

"Not here. She and Harry are spending their

wedding night at his house. They wanted privacy. Tell me what's wrong."

"Everything is terrible," he whispered. "I wanted you to come tonight, needed you to. But I knew you wouldn't."

She touched his cheek. "What's happened?"

"Bow Street returned today. They know I lied."

"I don't understand. How did you lie?"

"About the night Thea died."

Beatrix momentarily forgot to breathe. "They know I was there?"

He shook his head. "Not that. I didn't tell them exactly what happened. Nor did I tell you." He looked at her with such darkness, such despair that her heart nearly split in two.

She pushed her hand against his face. "You're cold. And shaking. You need tea."

"No. Just you." He gently cupped the sides of her head. "I only need you."

He could mean a variety of things—that he wanted to just be in her presence, that he wanted to tell her what had happened that night, that he wanted the easy camaraderie they shared. But he'd said *need*. And he'd said it in such a way that led her to believe he meant one thing in particular.

She clasped his gloved hand and turned with him, leading him from the garden room. Instead of taking him to the staircase, she made her way to the back stairs. Up two flights, she didn't let him go. Neither of them said a word.

On the second floor, she opened the door to the corridor and pulled him to her chamber. Unlike Selina, she didn't have a lady's maid. No one would bother them. And Selina wasn't home.

Once he was inside, she untangled her fingers from his and closed the door firmly. Continuing the silence, she took his hat and tossed it onto a chair. Next, she removed his gloves and threw them atop the hat.

She unfastened his greatcoat and moved behind him to take it from his shoulders as he pulled his arms from the sleeves. The garment joined his accessories on the chair. She put her hands on his shoulders again, wordlessly telling him to remove the coat as well. He understood, and it went the same way as the rest of his discarded things.

Beatrix stepped around him and rested her hands on his chest, her fingers burrowing into the snowy folds of his cravat. He looked rather splendid, as if he were going out to his club. Had he meant to come here?

Coals and embers burned in the fireplace, providing a modicum of heat and light. Lanterns on either side of the bed were lit, and they provided enough illumination for her to see the anguish in his eyes.

She tugged at his cravat, unknotting it bit by bit until it was loose. "You'll tell me to stop if you want me to?"

He didn't respond. He just stared at her, his lips pressed together, his nostrils slightly flared. Pulling the silk from his neck, she sent it to the chair with the rest. She then plucked at the buttons of his waistcoat.

"What if it really was my fault?"

He spoke so softly that Beatrix had to strain to hear what he'd said, and it took her a moment to fully comprehend his words. "It wasn't. I was *there*, Tom."

"Not for all of it." He sounded so broken.

She abandoned the waistcoat, though it was now unbuttoned, and put her hands on his jaw. She tilted his face down. "I was *there*. It wasn't your fault. It was an accident, and Bow Street will come to the right conclusion." How could they not?

"There are things…" He swallowed, his gaze straying from hers. "Motive, evidence, the relief we all feel that she's gone." He put his hand over his mouth. When he looked at her again, he radiated a stark distress that made her shiver with cold. "I wanted her out of our lives. I wanted to be free."

"Of course you did. Anyone would have."

"There are things you don't know, Beatrix. There is violence in me."

What was he trying to say? She thought of how he'd beaten the footpad, how merciless he'd been, and wondered if he would have stopped if she hadn't been there. The coldness inside her intensified. A shiver racked her shoulders.

"There is *goodness* in you," she said, gripping his face between her hands. "I see it. Regan sees it. Thea didn't see it, and it was her loss. *Her* loss."

A look of wonder mixed into his anguish. "How did you come into my life? That night of all nights?"

"I don't know, but I'm glad I did."

He clasped her hips and pulled her against him as he lowered his head and claimed her lips in a searing kiss. The ice in her veins melted under the onslaught of his desperate passion as his fingers bit into her, his hands moving to her backside and holding her tight to him.

She felt the hard length of his cock against her lower belly, but that wasn't where she wanted him. It was as if he read her mind, for he lifted her slightly, fitting them together with a better precision. Sensation jolted through her core. She clutched his nape and angled her head as she slid her tongue into his mouth.

Groaning, he met her invasion with heat and hunger. Lips and fingers moved and explored. He tugged her flesh with his teeth. She licked the underside of his jaw.

He picked her up fully, holding her against him, as he moved to the bed. She thrust her fingers into his thick hair, cupping his head and kissing him deeply, claiming every part of him he was willing to give.

Despair may have driven him to her, but now she tasted desire and demand. It was a delicious bliss. He set her down, the bed at her backside, but their kisses continued. Fast and hot, gasping delirium as she pushed his waistcoat from his shoulders.

He found the buttons holding the front of her gown up and quickly flicked them open. The front of the garment fell to her waist. She wasn't wearing a corset—she'd dressed for comfort earlier in the evening, not expecting to see anyone. She was exceptionally glad she had, for he cupped her breasts, and nothing but her chemise stood between his flesh and hers.

He wasn't rough, but he wasn't gentle either.

She cast her head back, moaning, as he pulled at her nipples.

Then his hands were gone. She opened her eyes and straightened to find him staring at her, his eyes round and dark with something akin to horror.

"What's wrong? Why did you stop?"

"I shouldn't be doing this. You're untouched—"

Beatrix held up her hand. "Stop right there. You have no idea what I am. At the risk of sending you running, I am *not* untouched." Shame threatened to turn her face the color of a cherry, but she refused to surrender to that useless emotion. "Apparently, I inherited my mother's brazenness. At least a small amount." She did blush then. "Years ago, when Selina and I were near starving, I never considered whether I would marry. I did, however, worry about having enough money for food and lodging. And I was desperate to reclaim the life—the family—I remembered.

"There was a gentleman who liked me. I was working as a barmaid, and we, Selina and I, wanted to leave that town and find something better."

Tom stilled against her. "What did you do?"

She hated the sorrow in his question, worried she'd ruined this glorious thing between them. "I ensured my future—at least for the short term. I spent a fortnight in his bed. Long enough to earn the money we needed to leave and find our footing somewhere else."

"My God, Beatrix."

She let him go, but she couldn't back away, not

with the bed behind her. "I've disappointed you," she whispered.

"Never." He clasped the back of her neck and pulled her mouth to his. He kissed her with a raw tenderness that turned her knees to water. She clutched at his arms before she melted into the floor.

He put his forehead against hers and put his other hand on her waist. "I'm so sorry you had to do that."

"But that's the worst part," she said, feeling more exposed than she ever had in her entire life. "Did I really have to? I wanted to improve our circumstances. I had an opportunity—he was kind and charming—and I seized it. I've done many things of which I am not proud."

He looked into her eyes. "Would you take them back?"

"I...I don't know."

His fingertips pressed into her. "All those choices and experiences made you the woman you are today. I wouldn't change a single thing."

Beatrix's breath caught and held. "Tom, I want you. If you want me too, will you stay?"

"I want you more than I've ever wanted anything. Yes, I'll stay." He kissed her again, his tongue stroking gently against hers and then more insistently. Passion built between them once more, and Beatrix felt as if every part of her was on fire for him.

She pulled the hem of his shirt from his waistband, and then it became a frenzy of removing clothing—his shirt, her gown, his boots—until she wore only her chemise and he had only his small-clothes.

Tom pulled the pins from her hair, one by one, until it came down around her shoulders and grazed the middle of her back. He ran his fingers through the curls and gently tugged so that she dropped her head back. He kissed along her throat, his tongue licking the hollow at the base as he pulled at the neckline of her chemise until he revealed her breast.

Eyes closed, she felt his lips on her flesh, soft and searching, as he cupped her. His mouth closed around her nipple. Hot, wet sensation drove a gasp from her lips and sent a spark of need straight to her core.

His mouth and hand worked in concert, teasing her and tormenting her until she whimpered. "Tom, please." She wanted him so badly. Needed him to ease her ache.

He laid her back on the bed and lifted the hem of her chemise, baring her thighs and then her sex. She opened her legs, but he pushed them farther apart, exposing her to him. At the first touch of his tongue against her, she bucked up. He curled his hand around her hip and held her fast as he licked along her flesh.

Beatrix clasped her head, an anchor to ground her in the coming storm. This was more than the touch of him against her, the sensations he aroused within her—there was a bone-deep desperation not just to feel, but to share, to open herself to him completely. She abandoned rational thought and surrendered.

His tongue penetrated her, and she moaned, her hips moving beneath him. He put her legs over his shoulders and replaced his tongue with his finger, pumping into her as he licked her clitoris, pushing her to limits she'd never even glimpsed before. It was more than a storm. It was an absolute overtaking of her body and mind. She was coiled and tight, utterly at his command. He owned her in that moment, his mouth and fingers driving her ever higher and hotter until she had no option but to combust.

She cried out as her release shattered her into a million pieces—all his. He was relentless, continuing his onslaught until the waves tossing her body began to slow. Then he withdrew.

Opening her eyes, she watched him strip away his smallclothes. She scrambled to her knees, legs shaking, and drew her chemise over her head, then tossed it to the floor.

He climbed onto the bed, his eyes molten silver, his lips parted, his jaw set in rigid determination. He knelt before her, his sex jutting out and grazing her belly. She reached between them and clasped the base of his shaft. His eyes slitted as he sucked in a sharp gasp.

Eyes fixed on his, she stroked him, slowly at first and then increasing her pace and the firmness of her grip. His lids fell closed, and he moaned. Moisture leaked from him, and she gathered it with her hand, using it to move faster over his velvet flesh.

On the next stroke, she reached lower and cupped his sac, her fingers massaging his balls. *"Beatrix."*

Kissing her, he clasped her waist and lifted her. "Put me inside you," he said raggedly.

She guided his cock into her sex while he held her steady. Slowly, they joined, her body sheathing his. She curled her legs around his hips as he clasped her backside and began to move.

He pierced her completely, sliding in and out of her with ruthless precision. Each stroke made her want to weep.

"Look at me," he whispered.

She did, locking her gaze with his once more. It made the sensation even more intense.

"This is perfection," he breathed. "Nothing will ever be this good."

He kissed her again, his tongue tangling savagely with hers as he swept her back, pushing her to the bed beneath him. She managed to unfold her legs and not lose him. Settling between her thighs, he drove hard into her. She wrapped her legs around him and dug her fingers into his back, crying out as the ecstasy built to an almost impossible height.

He went faster, and she fell apart again, whimpering with each thrust that brought an even greater pleasure. He shouted and let out a soft curse as he pulled himself from her and spilled his seed on her thigh.

"My God, Beatrix. I'm sorry."

She panted, trying to regain her breath. "Why would you be? That was, as you said, perfect."

He rolled to the side and swore again. "I almost forgot to pull myself from you. Jesus." He put his arm over his eyes, his chest heaving.

Beatrix slipped from the bed and found a cloth

to clean herself. Dropping it into an empty basin, she took another cloth to him and tidied him too.

He lowered his arm and peered at her, barely lifting his head from the bed. "What are you doing?"

"Tending to you." She smiled as she finished. "All clean now." Then she went and threw the soiled linen atop the other one.

Returning to the bed, she curled next to him, laying her hand on his chest. "Now. Will you tell me what happened? The night we met, I mean. I think you must."

He glanced at her, the anguish they'd banished for a short time having returned.

"Not because I want you to, but because it will help." She rose upon her elbow and looked down at him, at the torment lining his handsome face. "You have such a burden. Will you share it with me?"

"I don't know if I can." His gaze met hers. "I don't know if I can bear for you to hate me."

She touched his jaw, gently stroking his warm flesh. "I don't think I ever could."

Something in him released—she felt it in the relaxation of his muscles, saw it in the sudden calm illuminating his gaze. "I'll tell you everything."

~

A soul-stirring serenity seeped into Thomas as he gazed up at Beatrix's beautiful face. Her pale hair was a tousled mess, a halo of raucous disarray surrounding her angelic features. Tonight had been a revelation.

He twisted his finger in a lock of her hair. "I haven't taken many women to bed, and it's been years. For me, that was astonishing. I hope it was the same for you."

She laughed softly. "You didn't have to tell me about your experience."

"Why not? You told me about yours."

Sobering, she looked away from him. "That's different."

He supposed it was, but he didn't want her to feel bad about a choice she thought she'd had to make. Curling his hand around her nape, he tugged at her to look at him again. "Don't ever feel embarrassed or ashamed with me. I'm grateful for your openness, your vulnerability."

Her eyes softened, the green in them a warm, vivid hue. "And I am grateful for yours—and for your support. I haven't let many people get this close to me. To know me this well, I mean."

"I understand." He pulled her head down and lifted his to kiss her. Their lips met and briefly molded together.

Thomas sat up and pulled the coverlet back. She moved with him, and they both slid between the bedclothes. He sat against the headboard and put his arm around her as she nestled into his side.

"I probably shouldn't have come here tonight, but I needed to see you." He ran his hand through his hair, scrubbing his scalp. "I didn't think it through. What if Selina and Harry had been here? It's their bloody wedding night."

Beatrix put her hand on his chest. "They

weren't. All is well. Or it will be. You seem like you're feeling better than when you arrived."

He couldn't help but smile. "How can I not?" Truthfully, he felt better than he had in his entire life. He wanted to ignore the anguish pushing at the back of his mind—Bow Street, Thea, all of it.

"I'm glad." She kissed the base of his throat.

He realized if he didn't start talking, he might never get to it. His body was already rousing, eager to explore Beatrix once more.

"I lied to you—and to Bow Street—about what happened the night Thea died. You saw that she followed me onto the balcony and that she fell, but I don't think you saw what really happened. More importantly, you don't know what happened inside."

"No, I didn't. I could tell you were arguing—I could hear raised voices. It wasn't the first time I heard you. Rather, her. I could always hear her voice, yours less so."

"She raged about a multitude of things. Regan's neediness, because she asked her mother to read her a story once in a while." Thomas heard the un-ladylike sound clogging Beatrix's throat and felt her tense.

"What a horrid woman," she muttered. "Sorry, continue."

Thomas brushed a kiss atop her forehead. "Thank you for leaping to my daughter's defense. That means more to me than you could ever know." Regan, as she would soon learn, was the crux of everything—at least to Thomas. "She also raged about needing more money to pay her gambling debts, wanting a phaeton, which I refused to buy for her, and generally bemoaning her lot in life as a bloody viscountess. More specifically, as *my* viscountess."

Beatrix looked up at him. "Do you think she would have been happier with someone else? Some people just can't find satisfaction in any situation."

"Thea was one of those people. I don't know that she could have ever been happy. I honestly don't know if she could even understand or recognize what that felt like." He swallowed, gathering his courage to share what he'd only ever told her and had regretted doing so. "My father was the same way. My mother was wonderful—kind, thoughtful, loving. He never appreciated her. Or me."

"What happened to your mother?"

"She died shortly after giving birth to my younger brother. He died within a few hours, and she perished a few days later. My father insisted she get out of bed and not wallow in grief. He was punishing her for my brother's death. He looked for any reason to torment her. And, to a lesser extent, me."

"Oh my God, Tom. How old were you?"

"Ten. Mama was weak. She'd had another stillborn child and a third one only lived to be about six months old. I learned later that she'd nearly died when I was born and that the physician said she might not survive having another child." The old familiar rage gathered inside him. "That never mattered to my father. His cruelty and inability to care for anyone but himself knew no bounds."

"I'm so sorry." She sat up straighter, and he

dropped his arm behind her. "How did you become such a good man? Such a wonderful father? After everything you've been through…"

"I could ask the same of you. You've endured a great deal—losing your mother, the harassment of the girls at school, your father's abandonment. Twice." Pain flickered in her eyes, and he regretted bringing all that up. "I shouldn't have said any of that. Forgive me."

"Why? It's all true. We're a pair." She kissed his cheek. "Perhaps that's why we found each other."

Thomas loved that idea.

He forced himself to go back to the recounting of what had happened before Thea died. He hadn't gotten to the worst part yet. "Somehow, I managed to marry someone as awful as my father—or nearly as awful." He shook his head. "No, she was every bit as bad, just in different ways. She was especially angry that night. She brought up divorce again, but I explained that would never happen, and even trying would only reflect poorly on her, just as her infidelity did. But she didn't care. She never thought about consequences." A sad smile crossed his lips. "I suppose I should be grateful, because if she had, I wouldn't have Regan."

Beatrix's brow creased. "What do you mean?"

Thomas took a deep breath, his fingers lightly touching the small of Beatrix's back, a comfort for his beleaguered soul. "She told me that night that I am not Regan's father, that I couldn't be. She didn't want to have children yet and took special care to use a sponge to prevent a child, not that we shared a bed terribly often, even in the early months of our marriage."

At the moment he'd said he wasn't Regan's father, Beatrix's hand had shot to her mouth. Her eyes rounded, and as he'd continued, tears had formed. "Oh, Thomas." Her voice broke as she threw her arms around his neck. "But of course you're her father."

Thomas folded her in his embrace and held her tightly. "Of course I am, and I always will be. She doesn't ever need to know the truth."

Beatrix pulled back and cupped his face, her eyes searching his. "Still, you must have been devastated when Thea told you this."

"Primarily because she did it to inflict maximum pain. She had this…pride in telling me that Regan wasn't mine." It was hard not to feel destroyed by her malice all over again. "And I don't know who her father is. I didn't ask, and I don't care." He had wondered if Thea even knew. She certainly hadn't taken care to use her precious sponge with whomever it had been, which told him the act had been spontaneous and rash.

Here is where the telling became difficult, where he felt a burning shame. "I was more than upset. I was seething. That she'd brought our daughter—*my* daughter—into her selfish, malignant behavior enraged me." His pulse was racing. As Beatrix dropped her hands to his shoulders, he wondered if she could feel it pounding beneath his skin.

"I have worked very hard not to be violent like my father. He pushed and hit my mother often, causing bruises and cuts, and even broken bones. He did the same to me until I became bigger than him. My injuries were not so serious, but that's because I tried to evade him and usually succeeded. My mother didn't do that. She took everything he did to her. I think it was to protect me."

Silent tears tracked down Beatrix's face. Thomas forced himself to continue. "I'm afraid I lost my control," he said quietly, as self-loathing stole through him. "When she told me about Regan, I couldn't breathe. I couldn't think. I just reacted. I grabbed her. She taunted me." He recalled her sneer, the shrill vitriol of her voice. "She asked if I was going to hit her like my father hit my mother.

"I regret telling her about that. She's the only person to whom I revealed the truth—until you. And I wasn't going to tell you. Because I was afraid."

Beatrix took his hand and held him tight. "I would never use that against you. *Never.* You are not your father."

"How can you know that? You don't know what happened next."

"I know you didn't hurt her. I think you let her go and went out to the balcony to escape, to regain your sanity."

That's precisely what he'd done. She *did* know. "But I thought about it," he whispered. "I wanted to do it."

"You didn't, though. That's what matters." She wiped her face with her free hand. "Not telling Bow Street about this doesn't mean you lied. You didn't lie to me either."

"I omitted."

She shrugged. "As far as I'm concerned, that's not a lie. You told me when you wanted to." She gave him an encouraging smile. "Thank you." Then she leaned into him and kissed his throat. "Oh, Thomas. You didn't lie."

"I did—to Bow Street. I told them I didn't see her fall, that I remained inside."

Gasping, Beatrix drew back, her brows pitching into a deep V. "Why would you do that?"

"You did a very good job convincing me that it should look like an accident so there could be no doubt. I thought my being on the balcony might cause problems." He exhaled. "That's only a small part of it. She came out to the balcony—you saw that."

"And I heard what she said. I also saw her raise her hand and come toward you."

"She had a penknife in her grip aimed straight for my throat, which, if you recall, was exposed."

"I absolutely remember that. Nearly every time I visited your tree and saw you, your cravat was missing." She traced her fingertip in a triangle at the base of his throat. "This view was my favorite thing about spying on my father."

Thomas was surprised when he laughed. That she could lighten his mood in the midst of this harrowing discussion was wonderful beyond words. He let go of her hand and clasped her head, kissing her hard and fast. "You are a marvel."

"And you have an exceptionally attractive neck." She frowned, her forehead pleating. "I just remembered that something fell from the balcony before she did—that must have been the penknife. I'd forgotten all about that."

He dropped his hands to the bed and angled himself to face her. "You saw it? Dearborn—the constable—he searched my house for it today because I can't find it. He suspects I'm lying about her trying to stab me because I didn't tell him the truth at the start.

"I was only trying to protect Regan. I didn't want her to know her mother had tried to harm her father. No matter how horrid Thea was, I didn't see any point in revealing the truth of her despicable behavior to Regan, not after she was gone."

Beatrix eyes glazed with tears again, but she was smiling. "You are the best man."

"I don't know about that. I'm certainly in a mess until Bow Street finishes their investigation."

"You don't think they would arrest you? They can't possibly have enough evidence. *You didn't push her.*"

"They say I have motive, which, as you can see, I do. Can you imagine what they would do if they discovered I had just learned Regan wasn't my blood?" He shivered at the prospect. He couldn't go to prison—or worse. Regan needed him. "Furthermore, I lied to them initially, so now they aren't inclined to believe me."

"This is ludicrous. You had a perfectly good reason for lying. I'll talk to Harry."

"No, I don't want you to get involved. Even though you aren't trying to impress Ramsgate any longer, you still have a reputation to uphold. I'm not worth ruining yourself over."

Her frown deepened. "You are worth a great deal more than you know."

"I just wish I'd been able to produce the penknife. Perhaps that would have been enough to persuade Dearborn to conclude his inquiry. Doubtful, but it doesn't matter since I can't find it."

She averted her gaze and chewed her lip. "What does the knife look like?"

"It has an ivory handle. Her initials—DC for Dorothea Chamberlain—are carved into the design. It was a gift from her father."

Beatrix scrunched her face up. When she looked at him again, her eyes were clouded with sorrow. "Now it's my turn to confess my...omission. I know what happened to the knife."

He stared at her in surprise. "How can you?"

"Because I stole it."

CHAPTER 14

*B*eatrix saw the befuddlement in his gaze and instinctively pulled away. She started toward the edge of the bed, intent on finding her chemise. The feeling of nakedness went more than skin deep—she felt exposed and vulnerable in a way that made her uncomfortable.

Thomas clasped her wrist, keeping her from moving farther away. "Don't. I won't let you run away. You were here for me. Let me be here for you."

This was more difficult than she'd anticipated. She licked her lower lip and forced herself to speak. "I…steal things."

"I don't understand. You said you stole the penknife, but you also said you only just remembered that something fell from the balcony and that it must have been the knife. Did you forget that you stole it?"

"I don't always know when I steal something." She knew how ridiculous that sounded. "You will think I'm a lunatic."

"No," he said calmly, stroking her wrist with his thumb. "Will you explain it to me?"

"I'll try. It's difficult because I don't always understand it myself. When I went to Mrs. Goodwin's, I began to take things. I had no idea I was doing it. Objects would appear in my dresser or under my bed or in my pocket, and I had no recollection of how they'd gotten there." She recalled the terror she'd felt when it had first happened. "It continued all during my time at the school, but became less of a problem after we left."

"It's become a problem again, I take it?"

Beatrix nodded. "Since we came to London. Selina has a theory that when I'm stressed or agitated, I am prompted to take things. She thinks it soothes me somehow."

"That's not a bad theory. Why didn't you want to tell me?"

"It's embarrassing. But that's not the entire reason. I became rather good at stealing, and Selina was already incredibly accomplished from her time on the streets in East London."

His eyes rounded, and his jaw dropped. "You didn't tell me that."

"No, I said it was her story to tell, so I won't say much more than that. I have to reveal that much if I'm to tell you about the things I've done—and why. Because I had a natural skill for thievery, Selina taught me how to pick pockets without detection."

He stared at her, his hand still against her wrist. "Oh my God, you weren't joking when you said you were a footpad."

"Not really, no."

"And when you fought that footpad." He narrowed his eyes. "How did you provoke that one to flee?"

She felt the heat in her face and the fact that it spread all the way down to her breasts. Hell, she was still naked! "I stabbed him. With the knife in my boot." She didn't think his eyes could grow bigger, but they did.

"How did I miss that completely?"

"You were occupied." She licked her lower lip again, troubled by the uncertainty and astonishment in his shocked expression. "I didn't want you to know that I could hold my own in that way. Selina taught me that too."

"I can't believe your sister is from the streets."

"She isn't *from* there, but she doesn't remember anything else. Rafe said they had parents—he barely recalls them—but they became orphans when they were very young. They had to fight to survive, quite literally."

He shook his head in disbelief. "This is incredible. So, you were a thief?"

"When I had to be. Among other things." She looked away from him, her throat constricting. "I thought I'd left all that behind, but we started to run out of money here in London. Everything is so bloody expensive, and I just *had* to have a Season to impress my father." Anger rose inside her. She jerked her arm from Tom's hand. "I nearly caused Selina to lose everything. And for what? A man who doesn't care about me and who would just as soon tell the world what I've done, how I'm a thief and a bastard. No, not a bastard, for then he'd have to explain how he knew, and he would never want to associate himself with the likes of me." Her blood raced through her veins, pumping so loudly, she wondered if Tom could hear it.

Tom clasped her shoulders and drew her to look at him. "I'm not sure I understood all that, but it doesn't matter. Are you still a thief?"

"Only when I can't help it." She winced inwardly at the lie. Her mother's jewels didn't count. Was it stealing if the item rightfully belonged to you? "As with the penknife. I found it in my pocket, but I didn't remember how it had gotten there. I stashed it with my collection of unknown items, but I sold the lot just the other day. I can probably get the knife back. Would that help you?"

"I can't see how it would. You...sold it?"

"Fenced it is the proper term." Heat flushed her face and neck once more. "I can try to buy it back tomorrow."

He shook his head. "I don't think it matters, and honestly, good riddance to the damn thing. You said your father would tell everyone about your past. He knows?"

She nodded, anger and frustration beating at her chest. "I was caught at the school, and they notified him. He then tracked us after I left Mrs. Goodwin's. He knows that Selina and I are frauds. Swindlers." The heat of her ire cooled and was replaced by a searing cold. "She pretends to be a fortune-teller. I pretend to be sick and in need of money for treatment. We pretend we're starting a charitable organization and collect donations." She looked him in the eye. "I'm not proud of it, but surely you agree it's better than selling myself." It was as if her body had been immersed in ice. She twitched and shivered as her skin turned to gooseflesh.

He still held her shoulders, but now he drew her against him. Wrapping his arms around her, he lifted her until she was on his lap as he settled back against the headboard. He pressed his lips to her temple and massaged her flesh, bringing warmth back, slowly, to her body.

"As you said, we are definitely a pair."

"Yes, but a pair of what?" She rubbed her cheek against his chest.

"Unfortunate souls." He chuckled, and she closed her eyes, grateful for this man and what they shared.

"This has been a very educational night," she said wryly. "However, I must admit that I am feeling rather *fortunate*. Aren't you?"

"Yes. More than I have in years. Perhaps forever. And that is due to you." He cupped her cheek and tipped her head up so he could kiss her, his lips seducing hers with a gentle sweep and press. His tongue entered the fray, and her defenses—of which she had none against him, nor did she want any—were completely lost.

She kissed him back in ardent abandon, twining her arms around his neck. The revelations of the night gave way to a keener understanding, perhaps a more insistent craving. The more she knew of him, mentally, physically, emotionally, the more she wanted.

"What will your father do?" Tom asked softly. "Do I need to call him out?"

Beatrix smoothed her palms over the muscular

planes of his chest as her gaze met his. "You would do that?"

"I think I might. He has no right to expose you, not after the way he's treated you. He's despicable."

"It seems we were both burdened with terrible fathers. How remarkable that you are the complete opposite." She smiled as she continued to explore him, her fingertips gliding along the ridges of his muscles and the small peak of his nipples. He sucked in a breath.

"So long as I leave him alone, he'll leave me alone. I don't trust him, but I've no reason to believe he'll expose my or Selina's secrets. If he does, I will tell everyone he is my father, and *that* he does not want."

"You don't want that either," Tom said, brushing his thumb over her lower lip. "Society is cruel, but then you know that from the girls at the school."

Yes, she did. And no, she didn't want her past or the circumstances of her birth laid bare for all to see.

Bare… She stared at the expanse of his chest before her. She leaned forward and licked across his nipple. His cock, already stirring beneath her, hardened.

"Beatrix, I—"

She scooted down his thighs and moved her hand to stroke his length. "Yes?"

"I should probably go."

"Why? Selina and Harry aren't here. Just leave before dawn."

"There are reasons I shouldn't stay longer."

She kissed his throat. "There are reasons you

should." She tipped her head back and looked up at him. "Tom, it's only tonight. I think we both deserve it."

His expression flickered with uncertainty.

"Will you stay?"

～

There was nothing he wanted more. In the end, he allowed desire to overcome reason.

Clasping her waist, he turned her so that she straddled his hips. He lifted one hand to her temple and brushed her hair back from her face. He tangled his fingers into her curls and pulled her to him for a blistering kiss.

Their mouths slanted together, lips and tongues eagerly devouring. He tugged at her hair, and she dropped her head back, stretching the column of her throat. Thomas licked down her flesh. She rose up, offering herself to him. Greedily, he took her nipple between his lips. He nipped at the hardened tip, pulling a deep, erotic moan from her.

He quivered with need for her, his body taut and hungry, his cock hard and ready. It wasn't just that it had been a long time before tonight, but that he'd gone forever without her. Until now. He suddenly wanted to go back in time, to relive the past five years with her instead.

But that was impossible, and he had no idea what the future held. That left tonight. He would savor every moment.

She released his cock and ran her hands up his

chest, her fingers massaging his flesh. He sucked hard on her, unable to get enough. She ground down against him, her sex wet with desire.

Thomas reached between them and teased her folds. He pressed her clitoris, then speared his fingers into her sheath. She was so tight around him. He released her breast and cupped her nape to kiss her again.

"Please," she begged. "Now." She whimpered and breathed his name, the sounds an aural seduction.

Putting his hand over hers, together they guided his shaft into her sex. He went slowly at first, closing his eyes in ecstasy at the spectacular sensations shooting through him. Eager to claim her, he thrust up, hard and deep, burying himself completely.

He held the back of her head as his other hand stroked her backside. "Look at me, Beatrix."

She opened her eyes, the lush green glowing amidst the warm, chocolate brown. Holding his shoulders, she moved over him, her thighs trembling against his.

He pumped his hips, clutching her body so he could drive into her. Looking into her eyes, he felt an overwhelming sense of joy, of rightness. He kissed her and increased the pace of their joining. Her fingers dug into his flesh.

Before he lost himself, he dragged his hand around her hip and slipped it between them. He flicked his thumb across her clitoris. She gasped into his mouth, and he snagged her lower lip with his teeth. Her muscles clenched around him, drawing a low, shuddering moan from his throat.

He held on as long as he could, filling her as she rode the wave of her release. When she started to ease, her body melting against his, he let go. He pulled her up and turned his hips, his seed spilling to the side.

As his orgasm raced through him, he was shocked to feel her hand curl around his cock, stroking his flesh as he spent himself. He struggled to catch his breath. She was still partially astride him, her legs straddling his lower thigh. He clutched her hip with his right hand, his fingertips splayed across her backside.

"My God, Beatrix. You are a wonder."

"So are you." She leaned down and kissed his cheek, his jaw, the hollow beneath her ear. Moving behind him, she burrowed beneath the covers, pulling them up as she snuggled against his side. He felt her breath on his back as her hand splayed across his rib cage.

Thomas closed his eyes, relishing her warmth and the utter peace of this moment. His body slowly stilled, as did hers. That joy he'd felt earlier coursed through him with even greater strength. He almost didn't recognize what he was experiencing. He was completely overwhelmed, almost robbed of rational thought.

What was happening? Was he in love with Beatrix? He wasn't sure. All he knew was that she made him smile, he thought of her with ever-increasing frequency and intensity, and when he wasn't with her, he strategized ways in which he could be. And for a man who was supposedly mourning his dead wife, this was difficult.

Right now, the fact that he'd had a wife or perhaps just Thea in particular seemed so far away. Another life, perhaps.

Except it *had* been his life. He'd been so desperate to find happiness and love that he'd barreled into a marriage he thought would give him both.

Was he doing the same with Beatrix?

He thought back to when he'd courted Thea. He'd originally been interested in Miss Jane Pemberton. But then his attention had been diverted to Thea. Her brother had told him that Miss Pemberton had already bestowed favors of a physical nature on another gentleman. Thomas had been so intent on finding a pinnacle of honesty and kindness that he'd turned his focus to Thea instead.

Then, just recently, he'd learned that Chamberlain had spread that vicious lie about Miss Pemberton with the singular purpose of driving Thomas to Thea. That revelation had come only a few days before Thea's death, at Chamberlain's aborted wedding to Miss Pemberton's sister of all people.

Thomas had thought it was the final insult, that he ought to consider establishing a separate household from his duplicitous wife. But that had been before the she'd sent that most poisonous arrow into his heart: that Regan wasn't actually his daughter.

If only he'd married Miss Pemberton.

Except then he wouldn't have Regan at all, and he simply couldn't imagine that. Nor did he want to. She might not be his blood, but Beatrix had known the truth—she was his daughter in every way that mattered.

Thomas opened his eyes, suddenly realizing that Miss Pemberton, now she was Lady Colton, was blonde and perhaps an inch taller than Beatrix, who was also blonde, as Thea had been. And he'd estimate Thea was an inch shorter than Beatrix. Did that mean he was drawn to women of a certain appearance?

Could it be that he was also drawn to volatile people? Not that Jane had been volatile. He hadn't come to know her that well, but he recalled her being charming and witty—more like Beatrix than like Thea. Was Beatrix volatile?

He turned and saw that she was asleep, or seemed to be anyway. Her features were relaxed in repose, her lips curved in the barest hint of a smile, as if she was already dreaming of him. That was assuming he made her feel even half as wonderful as she made him feel.

She'd been a fraud and a thief, but he'd never seen evidence of volatility. He wouldn't count their encounter with the footpads. She'd behaved defensively and bravely. Brilliantly was how he'd describe it best.

That she comported herself with such calm and purpose was in itself remarkable. She'd certainly led a life that would push anyone to their limits. Just her father's abandonment and the way he'd treated her recently would be enough.

Thomas kissed her forehead and gently stroked her hair. "You're very brave," he whispered.

She inhaled through her nose but gave no indication that she'd heard him.

He watched her for a while longer. Her blonde lashes fluttered, and occasionally, her pink lips pursed slightly. He wanted her again with a ferocity that scared him.

Easing from the bed, he dressed. When he was finished, he returned to the bed and pulled the coverlet higher, to just beneath her chin. Hopefully, a housemaid wouldn't find it odd that Beatrix was nude. Or maybe Beatrix always slept naked.

He grinned, thinking that with her, it was not an impossibility. She was surprising and singular. He'd never met another woman like her and doubted he ever would again.

But he was a man who'd relied too much on emotion and hope, and he couldn't do that this time. He had to be certain, and the only thing he was sure about right now was that Regan needed him. She must come first, and she would.

Thomas touched Beatrix's hand through the coverlet. Exhaling softly, he turned and went home to his daughter.

CHAPTER 15

*T*he designated area for Lady Exeby's picnic in Hyde Park on Thursday afternoon was just inside Cumberland Gate, situated between two paths amidst trees on a lush expanse of lawn. Selina and Harry were enjoying their time at home as newlyweds, so Beatrix arrived in the company of their friends Jane, who was the Viscountess Colton, and Phoebe, who was the Marchioness of Ripley. Jane's sister, Anne Pemberton, was supposed to have joined them, but had decided to stay home. Though it had been three weeks since her wedding to Gilbert Chamberlain, who was Lady Rockbourne's brother, had been interrupted by Chamberlain's arrest for extortion, she was not yet ready for a Society event.

Both Phoebe and Jane were founding members of the Spitfire Society, and of course Phoebe owned the house where Beatrix currently lived. Their husbands had also come along, but they left to join another group of men almost immediately.

"Is this what happens after you wed?" Beatrix asked, looking at the separate groups of men and the groups of women. There was one area where men and women mingled, and upon recognizing a few of them, Beatrix realized they were unmarried.

"Somewhat." Phoebe said, exchanging a look with Jane and then laughing. "I feel fortunate, however, because after we visit with our friends, we always find our way back to each other as soon as possible."

That sounded so lovely. And romantic. Beatrix perused those gathered in search of Tom. He'd sent her a note yesterday saying how much he'd enjoyed the previous night and asking if she would be at the picnic today. He said he planned to be there.

"I'm sorry Selina couldn't join us," Jane said. "But I do understand how it feels to be recently wed." She sent a rather wistful gaze toward her husband.

Beatrix followed her line of sight and saw the viscount was returning her look, and even from this distance, Beatrix could feel the heat between them. It reminded her of how she felt whenever she looked at Tom. Or touched him. Or was with him.

She searched for him again but still didn't see him.

"Are you watching for someone?" Phoebe asked.

Beatrix shrugged. "Not really. Just taking stock of who's here."

Jane stepped closer to Beatrix's side. "Are there any gentlemen who've caught your fancy?"

"No one in particular." That was as great a lie

as she'd ever told, but of course her relationship, or whatever it was, with Tom was a secret. She wondered if it would remain that way. As much as she'd loved the other night, she didn't think it should happen again. She wouldn't be his mistress, no matter how she felt about him.

And how was that?

She wasn't certain, but she suspected she was in love with him. She'd nearly asked Selina, but she wasn't ready to say it out loud. What if she was alone in her feelings? She wasn't sure she could face another rejection after her father.

"Oh, there are the Spitfires," Phoebe said with a grin. She linked her arm with Jane, who then linked her arm with Beatrix, and they made their way to where four ladies were gathered.

Their small circle opened to welcome the newcomers. Beatrix knew all of them from their meetings. The oldest was Lady Satterfield, a thoroughly wonderful countess who in many ways was the mother of their group. Her daughter-in-law, the Duchess of Kendal, was also present, as were two of her close friends, the Duchess of Clare and the Countess of Sutton.

"Good afternoon," Lady Satterfield said. "Miss Whitford, how is your lovely sister?"

"Quite well, thank you. She would have loved to come today and looks forward to reentering the social whirl after she's acclimated to marriage." In truth, Selina wasn't sure she would ever return to attending the number of events they had in pursuit of establishing Beatrix in Society. She was content to simply be a wife and a member of the Spitfire Society.

Beatrix wasn't sure she wanted to continue with all this either. Today was different—she had the chance to see Tom. But overall, what was the point now that her father had rejected her? Was she hoping to make a marriage?

Only if it's with Tom.

She pushed the thought away. That wasn't an option right now, and it might never be.

She noticed a gentleman walking straight toward her. Not Tom, unfortunately, but someone she didn't know.

Lady Satterfield, however, knew him. She smiled as he approached. "Good afternoon, Lord Sandon. How pleasant to see you. Did you just return to London?"

"In fact, I did. My family's estate in Ireland is lovely, but it does not compare to the land of my birth." He laughed lightly, his gaze drifting to Beatrix.

"Allow me to present Miss Whitford," Lady Satterfield said, moving closer to Beatrix. Tall, with mostly dark hair that was just showing signs of silver at the temples, the countess was regally beautiful with a kindness that matched the warmth in her dove-gray eyes. "Her sister very recently married Mr. Harry Sheffield."

"North's brother?" Sandon asked. "How pleasant."

Lady Satterfield gestured toward Sandon. "Allow me to present the Viscount Sandon."

There was something vaguely familiar about the viscount, but Beatrix couldn't determine what. He was attractive, she supposed, about the same height as Tom and close to her in age, probably.

His eyes were a mix of blue and green with a bit of a sleepy quality about them that made him look... romantic, she thought might be the best word. He possessed a square chin with a cleft. Also romantic. To some. To her, Tom was the romantic ideal.

She remembered to curtsey. "I'm pleased to make your acquaintance, my lord."

"The pleasure is more mine, I assure you." He took her hand and bowed slightly as she straightened.

"You're new to London this Season?"

"Yes."

"Then it is my misfortune to have missed most of it."

Beatrix would have typically said something witty and flirtatious in return, but at that moment, she saw Tom walking along the path toward one of the groups of men. The one with Jane's and Phoebe's husbands, in fact.

Forcing her attention away from him before she was caught, she flashed a smiled at Lord Sandon. "I haven't been here the entire Season, if that helps."

He laughed again. "It does, it does. Perhaps you will save me a promenade later? I believe the picnic is about to be served."

"That would be lovely." On the contrary, it would be torture. The only man she wanted to promenade with was Tom. Oh, this was miserable. She was most definitely in love with him, and every other man paled in contrast. It was even worse now that he was here, and she could so easily compare them.

"I'll look forward to it." Inclining his head toward the rest of the ladies, he walked away with a lightness in his step.

"Well, that was interesting," Lady Satterfield said as she turned back toward their circle.

"That was the Earl of Stone's son?" Lady Kendal asked.

Lady Satterfield nodded. "I didn't think he was looking for a wife yet. Probably because he's been gone most of the Season. Clearly I was mistaken."

Jane leaned toward Beatrix. "He set his sights directly on you. Perhaps you'll find yourself wed like your sister before the Season ends."

"I'm not sure I'm ready for that, actually," Beatrix murmured. She shot another look toward Tom. Had he seen her?

"My goodness, is that Lord Rockbourne?" Lady Satterfield asked.

"Yes." This came from the Countess of Sutton. "I haven't spoken to him since Lady Rockbourne's funeral, but we planned to have dinner next week." She did?

"You know him?" The question leapt from Beatrix's mouth before she could stop it.

Lady Sutton, who was exceptionally cheerful, smiled. "He's my cousin. Our children like to play together. Actually, his daughter likes to take my son by the hand and lead him everywhere. She is nearly two years older and adores playing big sister. It's a shame she doesn't have any siblings of her own. Of course, Peregrine will soon have one and then he can be the big brother." She briefly stroked her round belly.

"He will be no help to you," the Duchess of Clare said wryly. "Not yet, anyway. I keep hoping

Leah will manage her younger brother, but I suppose I could at least wait until she turns two."

"You might," Lady Kendal said with a laugh.

"Children are so delightful," Lady Satterfield
said. She'd told them at a recent Spitfire Society
meeting about losing her daughter to illness when
she was young and then being fortunate to become a mother to her stepson, the Duke of Kendal.
"This is why I am so thrilled we've decided to
open an orphanage."

Beatrix suddenly recalled what Tom had told
her about Kendal. She wanted to ask if he was really called the Forbidden Duke, but realized that
might be rude in front of his wife and stepmother.
She suddenly remembered the Duchess of Clare
was also married to one of those Untouchables.
Beatrix decided to leave that subject alone. Perhaps she'd ask Tom's cousin about it later. Or,
preferably, she'd just ask Lady Sutton about Tom.
Had she known him as a child? Had he been
happy, or had his experience with his father made
him wretched?

He couldn't have been happy. Certainly not
after his mother had died. But somehow she
doubted he'd allowed his father's treatment to affect him completely. He hadn't let Thea's awful-
ness do that either. He still managed to be an
adoring father and a charming gentleman.

She glanced his direction once more. He was
magnificent.

And she was disgustingly lovesick.

It was time to be seated on blankets and par-
take of the fare Lady Exeby had provided. Beatrix
sat with Jane and Phoebe and their husbands while

footmen delivered plates of food containing fruit, cold meat, bread, and cheese. There was also wine and ale aplenty.

"Well, good afternoon!" The Earl of Daventry, with whom Beatrix had danced at Almack's and at the masquerade, arrived at their blanket. "It seems Lady Exeby has arranged for six to a blanket, and you appear to have an open space. May I join you?"

Damn. Beatrix would have much preferred to save it for Tom. She'd lost sight of him when they'd taken to the blankets and deeply regretted it. She looked wildly about in search of him, but it was no use. Lord Daventry was here, and to refuse him would be rude.

Damn again.

Daventry was dazzlingly handsome with wavy blond hair and piercing blue eyes. He also possessed an easy smile and charm to spare. She'd enjoyed dancing with him. But she didn't want to share her picnic blanket with him when Tom was an option.

Except Tom wasn't an option. For all she knew, he'd already left.

Ripley gestured to the open spot next to Beatrix. "Afternoon, Daventry. Please join us."

"Thank you." As soon as the earl was seated, a footman brought a plate and asked if he preferred wine or ale.

"Ale, thank you." Daventry looked to Beatrix. "I am so pleased to see you here, Miss Whitford. And I am particularly grateful for the chance to enjoy your company for such a long period while we dine."

Beatrix forced a smile, then took a drink of wine. This was going to be a *very* long picnic.

~

*D*aventry was sitting too close to Beatrix. Thomas finished his ale and tried not to glower in the direction of Beatrix's blanket. He sat several blankets away with his cousin, Aquilla, the Countess of Sutton, who'd invited him to join her and her husband. The Duke and Duchess of Clare were also seated on the blanket, as was Aunt Charity, who'd made it a point to seek out her niece and nephew and was delighted they were all seated together.

"Do you know Miss Whitford?" Aquilla asked.

Thomas turned his attention to his cousin. Her mother was Thomas's mother's younger sister, and Aunt Charity was the youngest of the three. "We've met."

"I've just noticed you keep looking in her direction."

Bollocks.

Tom said nothing. What could he say? Besides, she hadn't asked a question.

"We're both in the Spitfire Society," Aquilla said, her bright blue eyes shining beneath the rim of her straw bonnet. "I like her and her sister very much. They have so many wonderful ideas about the orphanage we're founding."

"You're founding an orphanage?" Thomas asked.

"How does one gain membership in this Society?" Aunt Charity interjected.

"It's nothing formal. We keep inviting friends and relatives, so we are growing all the time. If you'd like to attend our next meeting, we'd be delighted to have you come."

"Oh, I would, thank you. An orphanage is a marvelous endeavor."

Thomas could imagine that Beatrix, and Selina in particular, might be rather passionate about helping orphans. "Where will this orphanage be located?"

"We haven't decided yet. There is much to do first." Aquilla glanced toward the Duchess of Clare. "Ivy and her sister Fanny, the Countess of St. Ives, have been leading an endeavor to found a workhouse that will teach women skills and help them find employment. They are much further along, and the Ladies' School for Betterment will be opening later this summer. Once that is running, we will focus our full energies on the orphanage."

"My goodness, I had no idea," Thomas said, impressed. "You never asked me for a donation."

Aquilla blushed slightly. "My apologies. If you'd like to donate, we'll happily take your money."

"Yes, happily," Lady Clare said with a grin.

Thomas was glad the conversation had moved from his, apparently obvious, interest in Beatrix. For the remainder of the meal, he worked diligently to keep from looking in her direction.

It was deuced difficult.

Not just because he was eager to speak with her—he'd thought of little but her since the night before last—but because he was aware of Daventry and the man's proximity to Beatrix. And before that, bloody Sandon had made a point of going over to her. If Thomas didn't make a claim, he risked losing her to one of them. Or someone else.

As soon as the footman removed his plate and cup, Thomas excused himself. He meandered to the outer rim of the blankets so as not to blatantly walk straight to Beatrix. After lingering for a few minutes, he walked a path that took him close to her blanket. He moved slowly and, certain she saw him, made eye contact. He half smiled, not wanting to draw attention, and just barely inclined his head toward a copse of trees away from the picnic.

As he strode past the blanket toward the trees, he hoped she understood the silent message. Hiding himself away from view, he waited.

Thankfully, it wasn't even a quarter hour before she found him.

The moment she stepped out of sight from the picnic, Thomas grabbed her by the hand and pulled her fast against him. Her arms wound around his neck just as his lips met hers.

The kiss was ardent, passionate, the perfect expression of everything he was feeling—longing, desire, jealousy, and a thousand other things he wasn't sure he could name. Beatrix had awakened every emotion inside him, things he'd buried and abdicated, never believing he would have cause to experience them again.

She cupped his face and pulled back slightly, her lips curving into an alluring smile. "I've missed you. Seems you've missed me too."

"It feels like it's been a month instead of a day."

"And a half. A day and a half."

Thomas kissed her cheek and jaw, nibbling along her flesh. She shivered against him as her hands slipped to his shoulders.

"I wanted to throw Daventry off your blanket."

"He's not a bad sort."

Thomas pulled back and looked down at her. "Is he courting you?"

"Not yet, but he intimated that he's interested in doing so." She exhaled. "And I'm supposed to promenade with some fellow called Sandon."

Jealousy speared through him again, along with envy and distress. He couldn't lose her.

Before he could speak, she said, "I would have preferred it was *you* on our blanket. I was afraid you'd left."

He relaxed, hugging her to him. "I was trying to keep my distance."

"Why?"

An answer didn't immediately come to him. He held her waist but pulled slightly back. "I don't know. I suppose I didn't want people to gossip."

"They will always gossip." She brought her hands down to his chest. "I don't know how much time I'll spend in Society in the future. There's no reason for me to do so—I'm not trying to make an advantageous marriage, and I'm certainly not trying to impress my father any longer. I'll be focusing my energies on the Spitfire Society."

"My cousin Aquilla was just telling me about your endeavors. I am donating money to your excellent cause. I imagine the orphanage is of particular concern to you and Mrs. Sheffield."

"It is. She is an orphan, and while I'd never

thought of myself as one because I believed I had a father, I now realize that was foolish." She smoothed the lapels of his coat. "Thank you for supporting our cause."

They couldn't stay here much longer without their absences being noted by at least a few people. "Beatrix, I want you to know that I can't stop thinking about the other night, about you—"

A sound to Thomas's right made him freeze. She heard it too, for her head turned in that direction, her lips parted.

"Go," he whispered urgently, taking his hands from her waist.

She turned and fled. He went to one of the trees and peered around it to watch her return to the picnic. He looked about for whoever—or whatever—had made the sound, but saw nothing.

Dammit. He hadn't said what he'd wanted to. And what was that?

That he loved her. That he hoped they could have a future together. Could she promise she was the woman he thought her to be?

Thomas turned and leaned back against the tree, knocking his head against the bark in frustration. Damn Thea for filling him with doubt and fear. He had no reason to think Beatrix was anyone other than the caring, witty, charming, and utterly wonderful woman he'd come to know. That he couldn't trust that—trust *her*—made him furious.

It wasn't that he didn't trust her. He didn't trust himself. He'd chosen so poorly the first time. What if he did so again?

He pushed away from the tree and left the

copse. As he approached the picnic, Aunt Charity intercepted him. Her face was lined with concern, her eyes shaded with agitation. She wrapped her hand around his forearm. "I'm afraid there is a terrible rumor racing through the picnic since the meal concluded."

Thomas braced himself. "I assume this is about me?"

"It's an…exaggeration of the one I mentioned to you before. Now, people are saying you *pushed* Thea to her death and that Bow Street is investigating you for murder."

Bloody fucking hell. "There is only one person who would make that publicly known."

"Thea's mother." Aunt Charity pressed her lips together and made a low, dangerous sound in her throat. "It's too bad that woman isn't here. I might call her out."

Thomas laughed. "That *is* too bad."

She looked up at him in distress. "This isn't amusing!"

"What else can I do but laugh? I can't control a single bit of this. Thea is holding all the power, even from her damned grave."

"She can't possibly. You didn't do what that horrid woman is saying. The truth will come out."

Thomas wished he possessed his aunt's conviction. As Dearborn had plainly stated, without an eyewitness, his version of the event could not be corroborated. Furthermore, Thomas had demonstrated to Bow Street his ability to lie.

"I'm going home." Thomas wanted to hug his daughter and forget about everything for a while.

"All right, dear. Give Regan a kiss from me."

She tried to give him an encouraging smile, but wasn't entirely successful.

"I will." He bussed her cheek before walking toward Cumberland Gate.

He didn't even pause to look for Beatrix. She was probably promenading with Sandon anyway. And, frankly, Thomas had no desire to see that.

CHAPTER 16

As she escaped the copse of trees, Beatrix saw a squirrel dart away. She narrowed her eyes at the wee beast and silently chastised it for cutting short her time with Tom.

Even so, it was probably for the best since her absence was likely due to be missed if she'd been gone much longer. Society and its rules were so annoying.

She didn't particularly want to stay and promenade with Lord Sandon. Making her way back to Jane and Phoebe, who were standing near where their blanket had been, Beatrix wondered if they were ready to leave. The fact that she couldn't just go home by herself was another stupid rule.

"That is not true!"

Beatrix turned to look at who had said this rather loudly. It seemed to have been Lady Sutton —Tom's cousin—who was speaking to an older woman. Lady Sutton looked angry, her cheeks dark pink and her eyes slitted.

Phoebe looped her arm through Beatrix's. "Come, we must leap to Aquilla's defense."

"Do you know what's going on?" Beatrix asked as they strode toward Lady Sutton.

"Not the slightest idea," Jane said.

"I would expect you to defend him," the older woman said. "However, Mrs. Chamberlain would not lie about such a thing. The poor woman has endured unimaginable tragedy of late."

Phoebe gave the unknown—at least to Beatrix —woman an acid-filled smile. "Please excuse us." She let go of Beatrix and took Aquilla's arm. The four of them marched away.

"You're shaking," Phoebe murmured.

"Did you hear what that awful woman said?" Lady Sutton threw a glare back over her shoulder.

"No, we were too far away," Jane replied.

"Apparently, it's all over the picnic. Lady Rockbourne's officious mother is saying my dear cousin actually pushed his wife to her death."

Beatrix stumbled, prompting Jane to reach for her and ask if she was all right. "I'm fine, thank you, just a bump in the lawn."

Lady Sutton stopped and pivoted, her gaze sweeping over the people still milling about. "Where is my aunt? Has Rockbourne left already?"

"I don't see him," Jane said, scanning the area.

Beatrix didn't see him either. Had he left? And if so, had he done so before hearing the rumor, or had he heard it too? This was terrible, and not just because it was completely untrue! It was perhaps time she came forward as the eyewitness he needed to put all this behind him.

Yes, it would ruin her reputation, but what did that matter now? Still, there were Selina and Harry to consider. She would talk to Selina as soon as she got home. How she hated to intrude upon her happy honeymoon with this.

She'd tell Selina everything, including how she'd fallen in love with Tom. Perhaps Selina could help her decide what to do.

"I don't see your aunt either," Phoebe said. "However, there is Lord Sutton." Phoebe gestured several yards away.

Lady Sutton started in his direction, moving as quickly as her pregnant state allowed.

Beatrix and the others followed her, but then hung back as she reached her husband. He put his arms around her and glowered over her head toward no one in particular.

Beatrix turned to Jane and Phoebe. "I don't suppose either of you are going to leave soon?"

"Did I miss you promenading with Lord Sandon?" Jane asked.

"No, but I think I'd prefer to go home. That despicable rumor has rather turned my stomach."

Jane's eyes sparked with anger. "Rumors are reprehensible. Those who spread them should be the ones expelled from Polite Society."

"I completely agree," Phoebe said, touching her friend's arm.

"Particularly when they could cause real damage." Beatrix gave Jane a look of apology. "I imagine you know that better than anyone."

"I do indeed." Jane's features relaxed. "Poor Rockbourne has suffered too. I can only imagine he must regret listening to a rumor five years ago. He was certainly angry about it at my sister's aborted wedding." Jane scoffed. "And I can guess the worst among us will point to that anger as 'proof' that he pushed his loathsome wife."

Blanching, Jane added, "Forgive me, I shouldn't speak ill of the dead."

How Beatrix wished she could affirm that Lady Rockbourne was indeed loathsome, and in ways that would disgust them.

"Yes, let us go," Phoebe said. "I'll go find Marcus."

"And I'll find Anthony." Jane looked to Beatrix. "Do you want to come along or wait here?"

"I'll wait here." And hope that Sandon didn't happen along.

Jane and Phoebe took themselves off, and Beatrix did her best to fade into the shrubbery behind her. Apparently, she wasn't very good at it because a woman approached her.

Tall, with a long face and a sharp chin, she wore a small but rather arrogant smile. She was dressed in an expensive walking costume—Beatrix knew because of the clothes she'd recently had made. Something about her faded blue eyes and the small dent in her chin sparked a memory. And then she spoke.

"Miss Whitford is it?" she asked sweetly. Too sweetly. God, that voice was so familiar…

"Yes." Every part of Beatrix tensed.

"Why not Miss Linley? That is your name, isn't it?" She blinked in faux innocence at Beatrix.

Words failed to come even as recognition flooded Beatrix with a horrible, prickly heat. It was *Deborah*. Awful, arrogant, malicious Deborah.

"I know that's who you really are," the woman

said loftily. "What I'd like to know is if you're still a dirty little thief."

Beatrix fought to breathe. She and Selina had wondered if they would ever encounter any of the girls they'd met at Mrs. Goodwin's. They'd hoped they wouldn't, and if they had, were optimistic that so much time had passed that no one would recognize anyone else. And since Beatrix and Selina used different surnames, no one would have made a connection that way.

They'd clearly underestimated the situation. Or just Deborah.

Beatrix wasn't even sure she could remember Deborah's last name.

Somehow, Beatrix collected herself enough to ask, "Have we been introduced?" She looked at Deborah as if she had no idea who she could be. Beatrix prayed her act was convincing.

Deborah pursed her thin lips. "Years ago at Mrs. Goodwin's. I'm now Lady Burnhope, but back then I was Deborah Mallory." Her height made it quite easy for her to look down her nose at Beatrix.

Beatrix dipped a curtsey. "I'm pleased to meet you. I am certain we haven't met. I am not Miss Linley." Not for a very long time, nor would she ever be again.

"You lie, and I'll wager you're still a thief."

Thankfully, Jane and Phoebe and their husbands were coming straight for them.

"You must excuse me. I must meet my friends." She couldn't resist adding, "Lady Ripley and Lady Colton and their husbands—the marquess and the viscount." Flashing a bright smile, Beatrix walked right past the horrid Deborah. She felt as if she were moving through paste.

They were soon ensconced in the Ripleys' coach and on their way to Cavendish Square. Beatrix clasped her hands together and hoped no one noticed her shaking.

"I'm so pleased your sister and Mr. Sheffield are living in my house," Phoebe said. "I hope they'll be very happy there."

Beatrix answered, but honestly couldn't remember what she said. Her brain was teeming with alarm and fear about what Deborah might do.

Because yes, Beatrix was still a thief. As recently as three days ago, when she'd stolen her mother's jewels from the duke's house. But that was to be the last theft.

Now, however, having the jewels made her uncomfortable. They were a reminder of all she'd been and what she wanted to leave behind. Not just stealing, but the hope that she would regain her father. The demi-parure didn't remind her of her mother. It made her think of loss and rejection. And having them made her a thief.

Didn't it?

She would return the emeralds. Her mind began to strategize as the coach drove into Cavendish Square. She departed and thanked them for their company.

Then she rushed into the house and threw her hat and gloves on a small table in the entry. The footman who was at the door didn't say a word.

"Where is my sister?" Beatrix asked without preamble.

"In the garden room, miss."

Beatrix strode partway through the hall and stopped abruptly to say, "Thank you," before continuing on. Once she reached the garden room, she closed the door.

Thankfully, Harry was not present. Selina looked up from the table where she sat reviewing correspondence. "How was the picnic?" As soon as the question left her mouth, she paled. "Something happened."

Beatrix hurried across the room and sat at the table opposite Selina. "Deborah was there. She's Lady Burnhope now."

Selina stared at her. "Tell me everything."

Beatrix described the encounter down to the last detail, including the ghastly triple-ruffled hem of Deborah's gown. When she was finished, she leaned back in her chair, suddenly exhausted. Or weary. Or both.

"Do you think she believed you?" Selina asked.

"I can't say, but my instinct says no. All she has to do is tell everyone we were at Mrs. Goodwin's. There must be records."

Selina exhaled as she put her elbow on the table and propped her hand beneath her chin. "We should have changed our first names. We were stupid to want to retain that small piece of ourselves. It won't be much of a stretch for people to believe that Miss Selina Blackwell and Miss Beatrix Linley are our real names.

"And what does that reveal about me? My maiden name before I married Sir Barnabus?"

Beatrix grimaced. "God forbid someone tries to find your nonexistent marriage certificate."

"Yes, well hopefully they won't," Selina said darkly. "As for your name, they may discover you are the bastard daughter of the Duke of Ramsgate. Would anyone blame you for changing your surname to avoid being judged or shunned?"

"That's a good explanation, actually. Too bad Society won't care. It's much more entertaining to believe I'm a thief, which I'm sure she'll tell them."

"Well then, she'll tell them I am too, because I took the blame once." Selina shrugged. "Let her try to besmirch us. We must be strong, Trix."

"Will you tell Harry?"

"Of course. I have no secrets from him. Not anymore."

Secrets. It was time for Beatrix to share hers too. "That isn't all that happened."

Selina lowered her hand to the table, her eyes rounding briefly. "Goodness, what else?"

"The Bow Street investigation into Lady Rockbourne's death has gotten out. The picnic was abuzz with the charge that Tom pushed his wife to her death."

"*Tom?*"

"That's the other part, and please don't be angry with me. I do know Rockbourne—Tom—more than I admitted to you. In fact, I met him the night his wife died. I saw the entire thing. She fell after she attacked him with a knife. Well, I didn't actually see the knife, but I apparently stole it afterward."

"You don't remember." Selina didn't ask it like a question, because she knew.

"Yes. I sold all my stolen items last Sunday, and

that's when I found it. I didn't realize what it was until the next day."

Selina gave her a dubious look. "What do you mean by all your stolen items?"

"I kept everything I'd taken over the years—most things—in a box. I decided it was time to get rid of them. Besides, I wanted to buy you a wedding present."

"That's how you did it. I was afraid you'd stolen it, but when you said you got it at the Golden Lion, I realized you'd simply gathered some funds together. But I did wonder how."

"I would never steal your wedding present!" Beatrix wasn't offended, but she wanted Selina to know that for certain. "Honestly, I don't want to steal anything ever again. The thought of it makes me ill. If I hadn't taken the knife, the constable would have found it beneath the balcony in Tom's garden, and it would have corroborated his story about Lady Rockbourne attacking him." She looked at Selina in anguish. "They don't believe him. I can't let him go to prison."

"If they convict him of murder, he won't go to prison. He'll hang. Probably."

Beatrix gasped and clapped her hand over her mouth. Tears burned her eyes.

Selina reached across the table. "You are much more than friends with Rockbourne, aren't you?"

Nodding, Beatrix wiped at the tears on her cheeks. "I love him."

Selina stood and went to hug Beatrix. "My dearest Trix."

The embrace was a bit awkward with Beatrix sitting and Selina, who was too tall anyway, standing. Beatrix rose and wrapped her arms around Selina's middle. They stood like that for a good long moment.

Beatrix stepped back and brushed at her cheeks again. "I need to tell Dearborn—the constable—what really happened that night. I should have from the start, but Tom didn't want me to jeopardize my reputation." She made a sound of disgust in her throat. "That was when I still hoped the duke would want to be my father."

Selina touched her shoulder.

"But I was also worried about you—and Harry," Beatrix said. "I don't want to cause trouble for you. I still don't."

"I understand." Selina squeezed her hand and sat back down. "Harry isn't here, but we'll ask him what to do."

Beatrix sank into her chair. "I really didn't want to involve either of you, not when you were about to be married. I never imagined Bow Street would continue their investigation. But then they got that letter from Lady Rockbourne's mother, and Tom lied to them about what happened because he was trying to keep his daughter from learning what a horrid person her mother was."

"You're going to have to explain this in a bit more detail because I'm confused," Selina said apologetically.

After she did so—leaving out the things Tom had told her about himself and his wife and their marriage—Selina gave her an encouraging smile. "Harry will know what to do. He's the very best constable at Bow Street. Dearborn is young and likely overenthusiastic. This will all turn out right."

"I hope so." Now Beatrix was certain she felt exhausted.

"What about Tom?" Selina asked softly.

Beatrix wiped her fingers over her eyelids, then focused on Selina across the table. "What do you mean?"

"Does he love you in return?"

"I don't know. He's in mourning, or at least he's supposed to be. I haven't told him how I feel. He… I'm not sure he wants to marry again." She wouldn't say more.

"Well, take my advice and tell him. I wish I had confessed my feelings to Harry sooner."

"I know." Beatrix gave her a weak smile. "But it all turned out as it should."

"So far. Hopefully, Deborah won't try to ruin things." Selina curled her lip. "Why am I not surprised she would be the one to cause us trouble?"

"Because she was the absolute worst person at Mrs. Goodwin's?"

"That is true." Selina grinned. "How lucky you and I are to have found each other there. Can you imagine if we hadn't?"

Beatrix indulged that for a moment. She envisioned a life where she took a position as a governess or perhaps a lady's companion. She might have ended up as a courtesan like her mother and ultimately as some lord's mistress. "We may have done things of which we aren't proud and which we wouldn't do again, but I am not sorry," Beatrix said with quiet certainty. "There is no one I would rather choose for my family than you."

"I feel precisely the same. And, for better or worse, we are now part of a larger family with Harry's lot."

"Plus Rafe." Beatrix had thought she'd be the one contributing members to their family, but as of now, it was just her. She felt a sudden blast of loneliness, which was silly. She would always have Selina.

Yes, but she *wanted* Tom.

"We'll sort this out with Harry," Selina said. "Then you and Rockbourne can decide what to do. I am sure he's a smart gentleman—he must be if you love him—and will realize what a wonderful woman you are."

The question was what, if anything, he planned to do about it.

~

"*P*apa, when is the nice lady coming back?"

Thomas set the puppets in the trunk that housed many of Regan's toys. He'd just regaled her with a silly show featuring Horace the Horse and Jack the Ass. She'd giggled throughout, and it had done wonders for his mood since returning from the picnic.

He closed the trunk and turned to sweep Regan into his arms. "I don't know, sweeting. You liked her?"

She nodded. "I liked her story. I want her to tell it to me again."

"I could tell it to you, if you like." Thomas was

fairly certain he could remember it. Or at least come up with something that was close enough.

"No, it has to be her."

Of course it did. Thomas agreed—he wanted Beatrix and not some substandard alternative. He realized that was him in this case.

Honestly, he didn't mind. He would be thrilled to give Regan a mother she could love and who would love her in return. Was Beatrix that woman?

"I'll ask her when she can come again," Thomas said, even as he feared he was setting his daughter up for disappointment. It was too risky for Beatrix to come at night—they agreed they couldn't continue that behavior. Which meant she'd have to visit some other time. Either she'd disguise herself, or they'd completely flout Society's rules.

He wondered if she would come dressed as a man. And if that would fool anyone in the light of day. He closed his eyes and silently chided himself. He wouldn't ask her to do that. That wasn't how he wanted their future to be.

"Soon, Papa." She fidgeted with his cravat. "Also, where's my kitten?"

"I'm working on that," Thomas said. He'd made some inquiries at the picnic, actually, and Aquilla said she was fairly certain one of the cats at Sutton Park had recently had kittens. He didn't want to get Regan's hopes up until he was certain. "You must be patient, but I know how hard that is."

Baines came into the nursery, surprising Thomas. And filling him with a sense of dread.

"What brings you all the way up here?" Thomas set Regan down.

"You've a caller. Mr. Dearborn, I'm afraid. And he is not alone."

Bloody hell. What could that mean? Dearborn and another constable had returned yesterday and searched the entire house. Thomas didn't think they'd found anything—at least they hadn't said they had. "Is Sheffield with him? Broad-shouldered fellow with dark red hair."

Baines shook his head. "That does not match the description of either of the gentlemen who accompanied him."

"There are two?" *Bloody, bloody hell.* "Will you fetch the nurse?"

Baines quickly departed.

Squatting down, Thomas crooked his finger at Regan. "I must go downstairs and meet with someone. I'll see you at dinner."

"Thank you for the puppets, Papa." She threw her hands around his neck and kissed his cheek.

Thomas held her close for a moment. He inhaled the soft, sweet scent of little girl—*his* little girl—and felt a hitch in his chest. He kissed her temple before letting her go.

Miss Addy came into the nursery and immediately took over. Reluctantly, Thomas left.

As he descended, his feet felt heavier and heavier. He realized he wasn't certain where the constables were waiting. After peering into the drawing room and finding it empty, he decided they must be in the front sitting room.

Taking a deep breath, he went down the final staircase and ran into Baines. "The sitting room?" Thomas asked.

"Yes, my lord. Do you require anything?"

"Strength? Patience?" Thomas summoned a placid smile. "Everything will be fine, Baines."

Thomas went into the sitting room. The three visitors, and Thomas assumed they were all constables, were spread about the room. One was near the door, another in front of the windows, and Dearborn stood in front of the wall where the portrait of Thomas and Thea used to hang.

"Good afternoon, my lord," Dearborn said. He inclined his head toward the wall. "What happened to the portrait of you and your wife?"

Whether it was due to irritation or a simple need to just be honest, Thomas said, "I tore it apart and burned it."

Dearborn's eyes widened, and the man near the door coughed.

"I see," Dearborn said. "Well, I suppose that answers our question about your penchant for violence."

"You came to question me about that?" Thomas asked irritably.

"Actually, no. As you know, we searched your house yesterday. We were still looking for that penknife."

"And you didn't find it."

"No. We did, however, find a substance in a container in your upstairs sitting room. It was in the cabinet where you keep the liquor. That's why we came back yesterday to search the entire house."

Thomas tried to think of what the man could be describing, but had absolutely no idea. He rarely opened that cabinet. There was always a bottle and glasses on the top—and that was all he needed to pour a drink. "What substance?"

"We weren't certain what it was, but we've since determined it to be hemlock."

Why was there poison in his bloody liquor cabinet? Oh no… Thomas felt as though the air around him had thinned. He could see precisely where this was going. "You think this is evidence," he said softly.

"It's poison."

"Lady Rockbourne wasn't poisoned. She fell."

"Hemlock can cause paralysis. Perhaps she was poisoned and that contributed to her falling."

"That's a great deal of supposition. In fact, that's all you have. She fucking *fell*. After she came after me with a knife, intent on stabbing me. She hated me, was a horrible wife and mother, and I'm relieved she's gone. If that makes me guilty of murder…" He clenched his fists. "No, it doesn't make me guilty of murder. It simply makes me guilty of despising her in return and lacking in regret at her passing." He was perhaps not as horrible as her, but he wasn't blameless. Neither was he trying to pretend he was.

"There is evidence," the constable near the door said. He was older than Dearborn, probably around forty, with gray-and-black hair and a slender frame. "The letter from Lady Rockbourne, testimony from your household as to your temperament that isn't, shall we say, completely favorable, and the hemlock. You also lied to Dearborn at the onset of the investigation. We will disinter Lady Rockbourne's body and test her for hemlock."

"You can't do that," Thomas said through his gritted teeth.

"Her mother has already requested that we do. It will be done."

What did it matter? They wouldn't find anything. Unless Thea had poisoned herself. Why the hell was there hemlock in his house anyway?

Thomas suddenly knew. *She* was going to use it on him. He thought back to how that evening had started. She'd been alarmingly pleasant, offering to pour him a brandy. Surprised and disturbed by her uncharacteristic charm, he'd declined. Now that he recalled the event, he realized she'd been disappointed. Things had escalated quickly after that, and now he knew he'd pricked her temper by frustrating her plans.

"Fine," Thomas ground out. "She wasn't poisoned, and you'll discover that soon enough."

Dearborn came away from the wall and walked to the center of the room. "Why was there hemlock in your sitting room?"

Thomas still stood just inside the doorway. "My best estimation is that Lady Rockbourne planned to poison me. She wanted a divorce. Desperately. I refused to give her one."

Frowning, Dearborn crossed his arms. "Another thing you neglected to tell us. What else are you hiding?"

"I was trying to protect the memory of a woman who didn't deserve my concern. She wanted to be free of our marriage. She was a terrible wife and mother. I didn't want my daughter to ever know that."

"She doesn't need to."

"Except that this investigation is already the latest gossip." Thomas took a modicum of pleasure from the look of surprise in Dearborn's features, followed by disappointment.

"We do not share information," Dearborn assured him.

"You also can't promise that information won't become public. Especially if I'm arrested." Thomas glanced at the other two constables. "Is that what's happening here?" He tensed.

Dearborn's face twitched. "I haven't decided yet. However, I would like it if you would come to Bow Street so we may question you formally. That way, you'll have an opportunity to provide everything you may have omitted. Including the name of the woman with whom you've been having an affair."

"I told you, I am not having an affair." At least, he hadn't been. Not when Thea had died.

But was he now? God, he hoped so.

"Will you assemble the household, my lord? We'd like to question everyone briefly," the older constable asked.

Thomas glowered at Dearborn. "Perhaps you could at least introduce me to your colleagues."

Dearborn flushed. "Of course, my apologies." He gestured to the older man, who was closest to Thomas. "This is Mr. Woodward and that is Mr. Mercer." Mercer was younger than Woodward and altogether more intimidating. He was shorter, but he was stocky, with a thick neck and a head like a block. Thomas wondered if he could be knocked down and doubted it very much.

"You want my entire household assembled?

Minus my daughter and her nurse. I won't have my daughter subjected to any of this."

"We would like to speak with the nurse as well," Dearborn said.

"Then you'll have to allow me to go up and be with my daughter while that happens."

Dearborn looked to Woodward, who gave a slight nod. "That is acceptable."

Without a word, Thomas turned and went into the entry hall, where Baines stood stiff and straight. "My lord?"

"Assemble the household. Here. I'll send Miss Addy down."

Woodward had followed Thomas into the hall. "Lord Rockbourne, perhaps this doesn't need to be said, but I would be remiss if I did not make it clear that you are not to leave the house."

"I wouldn't dream of it," Thomas said with more sarcasm than was probably smart. He was too angry to censor himself completely.

He only hoped he was able to keep his temper under control. Now was not the time for whatever parts he possessed of his father to emerge.

CHAPTER 17

*H*arry leaned against the corner of the hearth in the garden room, his face drawn in deep contemplation. Beatrix and Selina had just finished telling him everything. Mostly everything. They'd left out the part where Beatrix was quite desperately in love with Tom, instead saying that they'd "become close." Harry wasn't stupid. He knew what that meant.

"I should go to Bow Street right now," Harry said.

"Are you going to tell them there's an eyewitness to what happened?" Selina asked. She glanced over at Beatrix, who sat beside her on the settee.

"I can't, not without naming the party. For now, I think we should avoid that." He grimaced, then looked at Beatrix in sympathy. "I appreciate your reluctance to share this information in order to protect Selina—and yourself."

"If it wasn't for Selina, I'd go to Bow Street right now."

Selina gently patted Beatrix's hand.

Harry's features relaxed. "Of course you would.

Let me see what's happening, and we'll decide what to do." He rubbed his hand along his jaw. "It seems I chose a poor time to get married and take a respite from my position."

"Don't say that," Beatrix said. "This is all just an unfortunate situation. Lady Rockbourne's death was an accident, and her mother needs to accept that."

Harry nodded. "I'll be back as soon as I can."

Selina stood as he came toward her, and they exchanged a brief kiss before he left.

Beatrix rose, nervous energy making her pulse pick up speed. "I hate waiting."

"I know. It won't be long. Do you want something to eat?"

Glancing at the clock on the mantel, Beatrix saw that it was half four. And it was Thursday. Precisely the time and day her father went to the park for the fashionable hour. Which meant he wasn't home. Furthermore, it was the afternoon when several members of his household were given free time.

"I'm going upstairs," Beatrix said. "I think I just need to rest and try to get my mind off things."

Selina narrowed her eyes at Beatrix. "*You* are going to rest?"

Beatrix didn't even bother arguing—Selina knew her too well. "I can *try*. I'll probably just pace."

"I'll let you know as soon as Harry returns."

"Thank you." Beatrix would need to hurry. Which she would—all she had to do was replace the genuine demi-parure with the fake one she'd put there Monday night. She'd gotten in and out quickly then and had no reason to expect things would go differently today.

Except that had been late at night. Today, it was still light, and she would almost certainly be seen. It was a good thing she had a plan.

~

*B*eatrix managed to get away from the Spitfire house without encountering anyone. Dressed as a maid, she made her way quickly to Grosvenor Square. Instead of stealing through Tom's garden and climbing the wall into the duke's garden to gain access to his house, she would boldly enter through the servant's entrance. With her cap pulled tight about her head and a scarf tied around that, she prayed she would escape notice. She was also especially grateful for the knowledge she had of Ramsgate's house and his servants.

It was just after five when she stealthily made her way into the entrance on the lowest floor of the house. The sounds of the kitchen permeated the corridor as Beatrix hurried to the stairs that would take her straight up to the first floor, where the duke's chambers were located.

On the way, she noted an open cupboard. Inside were cleaning supplies. She grabbed a broom before continuing to the stairs.

Upon reaching the landing on the first floor, she hastened along the narrow corridor to the last door. It led directly into the duke's dressing chamber. Would his valet be present? Beatrix briefly closed her eyes and sent up a prayer that he would not.

Clutching the broom and holding her breath, she carefully opened the door. She peered inside and, upon finding it empty, exhaled.

On her last visit, she'd had to find the jewels in this very chamber. She'd known precisely what she was looking for—a purple-velvet-covered box. She'd run her small fingers over the soft velvet countless times as a child.

Today, however, she thankfully didn't need to waste time searching for the box. She went directly to its location in the bottom drawer of a narrow dresser in the corner.

She leaned the broom against the wall, taking care to be quiet in case the valet was in the bedroom. Crouching down, she eased the drawer open. The box sat where she'd found it, to the left side.

She opened the case, and the faux emeralds winked up at her. Moving quickly, she scooped up the pieces one by one and stuffed them into her left pocket.

"Thief!"

Beatrix squeezed her eyes closed. She didn't turn. Her heart thudded, and sweat broke out across her neck and brow. Trying to remain calm, she reached into her right pocket and removed the real jewels. "Here they are. There's no theft." She set the jewelry into the box, her hands shaking.

"Which maid are you? That new girl in the scullery?" The man—presumably the duke's valet—grabbed her by the arm.

She reached for the broom and jabbed him in

the stomach with the handle. Yowling with pain, he bent over. But Beatrix didn't wait to see what happened. She dropped the broom and bolted for the door to the back stairs. She didn't bother to close it behind her before racing down.

By the time she reached the kitchen level, she was panting heavily. She'd heard shouting but hadn't been able to make out what it was. If she made it out of the house, it would be a miracle.

She glanced toward the kitchen before dashing forward into the corridor—and straight into a hard chest.

Out of breath, Beatrix looked up into the dark, narrowed eyes of what was probably a footman, judging from his livery. "I was just about to run an errand," she said. "We need…salt."

The footman didn't believe her obvious lie. His gaze slitted further, and he grabbed her by the arm. "Upstairs with you."

Beatrix tried to pull away, but it was no use. The man was a bloody tree.

It seemed she was out of miracles.

He steered her back to the stairs she'd just come down, then up to the ground floor, following close behind her and keeping a tight grip on her elbow. Reaching around her, he opened the door and awkwardly pushed her into the staircase hall. They emerged from under the stairs and came face-to-face with her father's haughty butler.

Behind him stood the valet, one hand wrapped around his middle, his frame slightly stooped. "That's her, the chit who jabbed me with the broom and stole His Grace's jewels."

The butler regarded Beatrix with unveiled

contempt. "I know you. You're that insolent woman who dared visit His Grace recently."

Damn, it was too much to hope that he wouldn't recognize her. Instead of answering, she lifted her chin and gave him her own most arrogant stare.

"I've already sent for His Grace," the butler said. "We will await him in the sword room."

The what?

The footman began to pull her, but she dug her feet into the floor. "Please let go of me. I don't require your assistance."

"If you run, he will do whatever is necessary to catch you," the butler said frostily. "Do you understand?"

"Perfectly." Beatrix pursed her lips and continued to stare at him defiantly.

The footman released her, and she immediately massaged her elbow.

"Follow me," the butler directed before leading her into the round entry hall. He turned to the left and gestured for her to precede him into a room decorated with...swords.

"We'll wait here for His Grace." The butler took a position at the door, and the footman stood on the other side.

Beatrix went to the window because it was as far away as she could get from them. She could also see the front of Tom's house. What would he say when he learned she'd been arrested?

The reality of her situation made everything go fuzzy around her for a moment, as if she'd fallen into water. She gasped, taking air into her lungs.

Perhaps the duke wouldn't want to prosecute

her. She'd returned the demi-parure, after all. And she'd promise to leave him alone forever.

Of course he was going to prosecute her. There wasn't really a doubt in her mind. Would her half brother help?

Her thoughts came to a crashing halt as she saw Tom walk down the steps of his house. He was in the company of three men. One of them, a slender gentleman with black-and-gray hair, seemed very familiar. She was sure she'd seen him, but where?

At the Brown Bear across from the Bow Street Magistrates' Court where she and Selina had met Harry one day. The man was a Bow Street constable.

And Tom was leaving with them.

Beatrix spun from the window and rushed toward the doorway. Both the butler and footman stepped in her way.

"Just where do you think you're going?" the butler asked.

"Outside. Next door. I need to speak with someone. I promise I am not running away. Come with me, in fact."

"Sit down," the butler barked.

"No." She tried to remain calm despite the frenzy careening through her. "There are Bow Street constables *right next door*. I must speak with them. You can tell them anything you want. *Please.*"

The butler eyed her skeptically, but the footman reached for her arm once more. "I'll take her. You talk to the constable."

Beatrix nodded eagerly. "Yes, take me. You can hold on to me the entire time, if you like."

The butler narrowed his eyes at her. "How do you know they're constables?"

"Because my brother-in-law is a constable," she said with considerable exasperation. There was no hiding her identity now or that of her family who wasn't even really her family. Perhaps she could admit that too, and quietly skulk away without affecting Selina.

If only it were that easy.

The footman led her outside into the bright afternoon. Tom stood on the pavement with the three men.

"Tom!" Beatrix shook her head slightly. "Er, Lord Rockbourne!"

Tom looked past the men surrounding him, his brow furrowed. "Beatrix?" His gaze went to the footman clutching her arm. He stalked toward her, and the others followed, looking alarmed.

"Unhand her," Tom demanded, his eyes spitting fire at the footman.

"She's a thief," the butler said from the other side of Beatrix.

Tom's gaze softened as he turned his attention to her. "What did you do?" he whispered.

"I am not a thief. I was replacing something that I, er, borrowed."

That sounded horrible even to her. Because she *was* a thief. And she could no longer run from that fact.

She looked up at Tom, her heart breaking that she'd disappointed him like this. "I'm sorry, Tom."

Glancing toward the men behind him, she asked, "Are you going somewhere with these constables?"

"To Bow Street. They want to formally question me."

The older constable whom Beatrix recognized came forward. "Are you accusing this woman of a crime?" he asked the duke's butler.

"Yes. She was caught stealing jewelry from His Grace's house."

"I was replacing it," she said through clenched teeth. She refocused on Tom. "Are they going to arrest you?"

"It doesn't look good. They found hemlock in my liquor cabinet." His eye twitched.

It was too much. Beatrix closed her eyes and took a deep breath. Opening her eyes, she looked at the constable with the black-and-gray hair. "You probably recognize me, so you should know that I'm a credible person. I saw what happened the night Lady Rockbourne fell."

"*Beatrix.*" Tom hissed as color leached from his face.

She ignored him. "I was perched in a tree in Lord Rockbourne's garden. I saw Lady Rockbourne come toward him with a knife. He avoided her, and she fell. It was horrible, but it wasn't his fault." Now she looked back at Tom. She smiled encouragingly before murmuring, "It's going to be all right."

Another of the constables, a younger fellow with dark, wavy hair and blue eyes, came forward. "Are you Rockbourne's mistress?"

A gasp from somewhere to Beatrix's right made her turn her head. Dread crept over her as she realized a crowd of people was gathered in the square, some in the street even, and were watching her and Tom as if they were performing a spectacle for their enjoyment. She began to shake.

"No," Tom snapped. "She is not my mistress."

Beatrix was grateful for at least that.

"Why were you in his tree?" the older constable asked.

"I was spying on the duke next door." She inclined her head toward her father's house, weighing whether she ought to reveal the truth. "Why does it matter? I was there, and Lord Rockbourne is innocent."

Tom stared at her, silent, his gaze unfathomable.

"If you *are* his mistress, you could be lying to protect him," the younger man said.

Rounding on the constable, Tom curled his lip. "Say she's my mistress again, and I'll make you swallow your damn tongue."

Though the footman still held her arm, Beatrix reached out and just managed to touch Tom's sleeve. "Don't." Threatening violence wouldn't aid his cause.

"What the devil is going on here?"

Everyone's head turned toward the Duke of Ramsgate, who walked up the pavement behind Tom and the constables. The latter of whom backed up as the duke approached. Tom, however, didn't move.

"We've caught a thief, Your Grace," the odious butler said from beside Beatrix.

"You've also obtained an audience." The duke

muttered something as he continued around Tom to stop in front of Beatrix. "Look at the trouble you've caused."

Beatrix refused to waver in front of him, in front of all these people. "I didn't take anything," she said quietly. "Well, I did, but I was returning it."

"The demi-parure," he said with certainty.

Her jaw dropped. "You knew?"

"I checked it every night after your visit. Don't forget that I know who you are. Who you've *been*."

"We can take her to Bow Street for prosecution, Your Grace," the older constable offered.

The duke turned toward him. "No, I won't be prosecuting."

The footman instantly let go of Beatrix's arm, and again she massaged her abused appendage. The butler squeaked.

"Well?" The duke eyed the constables. "Go on your way."

"We weren't here for her," the younger man, whom Beatrix realized must be the Dearborn Harry had mentioned, explained. "We are investigating the death of Lady Rockbourne."

"But you're finished," Beatrix insisted. "Because I already told you what happened, what I *saw*."

"Can we bloody take this inside, out of view and hearing of the spectators?" the duke demanded.

At that moment, a man rode up on horseback, causing several people to move back. He stopped in front of the houses and dismounted.

"What's going on here?" Harry asked, his gaze

going from Beatrix to the constables to Tom and back to Beatrix.

"It's a terribly long story." Beatrix suddenly had an urge to laugh.

"Inside. Now." The duke stalked toward his house. Apparently, they were all to follow him.

And that was precisely what they did.

They did not, however, return to the sword room. He led them up the stairs to the drawing room where Beatrix had met with him.

Beatrix stood near Harry. The duke took a position near the hearth, while his butler and footman lingered just inside the doorway. Tom and the three constables moved to stand in front of the windows.

The duke glowered at the constables. "I can't begin to imagine why you're investigating Rockbourne about the death of his wife. Didn't she fall off the balcony?"

"Yes, Your Grace," Dearborn answered, looking a bit pale. "However, evidence and information has come to light that require investigation."

Beatrix took a step forward. "Such as the fact that I saw the entire thing, and she *fell*. He didn't push her!"

Harry briefly put his hand on her arm. "Let me." He addressed his colleagues. "I just came from Bow Street, where I went to speak with you, Dearborn. My sister-in-law did see what happened. She did not come forward sooner because she didn't realize there was a need. And, as you can imagine, to do so would have jeopardized her reputation."

The duke made a noise in his throat. "Her reputation... How did you manage to see this, girl?"

Just when Beatrix thought she'd controlled her shaking, she started to quiver once more. "I was in Lord Rockbourne's tree. I, ah, I was watching you until I was distracted by Lady Rockbourne yelling."

The duke glanced toward Tom. "The viscountess could be a bloody banshee." He cocked his head at Beatrix. "Why were you watching me? That's very odd."

"Because I wanted to see you. I wanted to feel...close to you. It was odd. And foolish." She almost said she regretted it, but she couldn't, for that would mean she would never have met Tom. And that she would *never* regret.

Shockingly, the duke's features softened. But just for a moment. He hardened back up, like ice forming, before he spoke. "It was extremely foolish. You should have come to see me when you arrived in town. We could have come to an... arrangement." He looked at the constables again, using the same haughty stare he'd used with Beatrix at their prior meeting.

"Miss Whitford is my... Well, she's a close friend's daughter. She can be rather silly, as evidenced, but if she says she saw the viscountess fall, then the viscountess fell. I wouldn't doubt it, in any case. Lady Rockbourne was so often intoxicated, I daresay it's a wonder she didn't fall from the balcony, or somewhere else, long before now."

Beatrix stared at him. He hadn't admitted he was her father, but he'd provided a reason for them to be friendly at least. And he'd instructed the constables to believe her.

Harry cleared his throat. "Since that's two of us vouching for Miss Whitford, I think you must accept her testimony and conclude your investigation." He looked toward the older constable. "Don't you agree, Woodward?"

He nodded. "I do."

"Excellent. That should take care of things," Harry said firmly.

"No."

Every head in the room swung toward Tom.

"No?" the duke asked, sounding irritated.

"That does not take care of things. Beatrix—Miss Whitford—went to great lengths to protect me." Moving to stand before her, Tom sank to one knee and took her hand. For the dozenth time that hour, Beatrix's breath caught, but for a far better reason this time.

He looked up at her, and her chest swelled with joy. "She is not my mistress, but I desperately hope she will be my wife."

"Absolutely not," the duke thundered. He looked to the constables and pointed to the door. "Out." Then he glared at Harry. "You too."

Harry didn't leave Beatrix's side. "Miss Whitford is my sister-in-law. I am not leaving."

Tom turned his head toward the duke as the constables—as well as the footman and butler—filed out of the room. "You can't mean for me to leave too."

"No. I mean for you to gain some sense."

CHAPTER 18

Thomas rose and moved to stand on the other side of Beatrix. He took her hand, which felt cold even through the thin glove she wore. The urge to pull her into his arms and never let her go was nearly overwhelming. Instead, he would endure whatever nonsense her father wanted to spout.

"I have sense enough to recognize this woman's strength and loyalty," Thomas said. "Pity you don't have the same."

Ramsgate's nostrils flared as he looked to Beatrix. "He knows?"

She nodded. "As does Harry." She inclined her head toward Sheffield. "They are the only ones, however." Lifting a shoulder, she added. "As well as my sister and brother, of which you are already aware."

"They are not your sister and brother."

"Careful, Ramsgate," Harry said in a low voice.

Beatrix wished Selina was here to see how wonderful her husband was. But of course she already knew that.

"Worth is also aware," Beatrix said. "But then, you know that. I *had* to say something because he wanted to court me. Even you can agree that could not happen." She enjoyed the look of horror that flashed across her father's features.

"Beatrix has done an excellent job keeping the reality of her parentage a secret," Thomas said, squeezing her hand. "You should be grateful. You should also be regretful. What kind of father abandons his daughter after her mother dies?"

"I didn't abandon her," the duke said defensively. "I sent her to school. I could have turned her out into the street."

"That school was awful," Thomas continued, eager to slay the dragon who would hurt his beloved. "Did you ever once write to her? Visit?"

Ramsgate waved his hand. "Bah. Fathers don't do that."

"I would have." No, Thomas would never have sent Regan in the first place.

"She ran away before her education was finished. That was hardly my fault."

Thomas's anger boiled. "She was miserable. The other girls knew she was unwanted and took every opportunity to remind her."

Ramsgate's eyes narrowed. "She was also a thief."

"I couldn't help it," Beatrix snapped, drawing both Thomas and Harry to look at her. "I can't always…control myself. I never stole anything until I went to that bloody school."

"Are you saying you couldn't help stealing your mother's demi-parure?" the duke asked snidely.

"Oh no, that I took on purpose." There was a

pride in her voice that nearly made Thomas smile, but he thought better of it. "Those emeralds are *mine*. She said they would be. How did you know the ones I left were fake?"

"The bracelet had a very small inscription—the date Lottie and I met."

Thomas felt a tremor pass through Beatrix and pulled her closer to him.

"You left fake jewels in place of the real ones?" Harry looked at Beatrix with a mix of incredulity and admiration.

"It seemed wise since I assumed he would know I stole them if they just went missing. He'd already accused me of being a thief."

"Very wise," Thomas murmured, and this time, he did smile.

Beatrix took a small step toward Ramsgate. "If you knew they were fake, why didn't you report the theft?"

The duke looked away and coughed. Clasping his hands behind his back, he returned his cool attention to Beatrix. "If you were going to go to that much trouble to have them, I decided you deserved them."

Her jaw dropped. Then she snapped it closed.

"Very kind of you, Ramsgate," Harry said. "What is unkind, however, is your interference in Beatrix's life. If Rockbourne wishes to marry her, why would you try to stop it?"

"He ought to know what he's getting into—who she really is."

Thomas let go of her hand and put his arm around her shoulders. He drew her tight against his side. "I know precisely who she is and what I'm getting into. And I go willingly, *joyfully*, my eyes—and my arms—wide open." He glanced over at Beatrix and saw a tear sliding down her cheek as she looked up at him.

He smiled at her and wiped the tear away. "Don't cry, my love."

She smiled back, her face lighting with happiness.

"Even knowing she is a thief and illegitimate, you don't care?" Ramsgate looked utterly befuddled.

"Not in the slightest. Actually, that's not true. I care about every part of her. As should you."

Ramsgate sniffed.

Beatrix took a deep breath. "I should tell you, Your Grace, that our secret may not remain secret much longer. One of the girls I attended school with recognized me earlier today. I acted as if I didn't know her, but she knew a Beatrix Linley and that I was your daughter."

Ramsgate's face flushed. "You told them?"

She flinched against Thomas. "I didn't have to. They all knew."

"Those idiots." The duke sneered. "Only one of the teachers at that school could have told them. Unless you did."

"I would just as soon no one know the truth." Beatrix looked her father in the eye. "I prefer to remain with my real family—Selina, Rafe, and now Harry and his family."

Thomas had never been prouder of anyone. He leaned down and said, "I've never loved you more than this moment."

Her eyes glowed as she looked up at him. "I

love you too." She turned her head back toward the duke. "So, if you wouldn't mind, let's just pretend what you said outside is the truth—I'm the daughter of an old friend. But it can't be my mother since I share her with my siblings."

The duke frowned in distaste. "Rest assured, I will say as little as possible."

"I must confess, I'm rather confused by you, Ramsgate," Harry said. "You were willing to let Beatrix keep her mother's jewels, and yet you want nothing to do with her."

"Actually, it makes perfect sense," Beatrix said. "It's much easier for him to make a transaction. He gives me the jewels in exchange for my leaving him alone."

Harry gave his head a shake. "How…sad."

Beatrix straightened, and Thomas dropped his hand to her back. She pulled a fistful of emeralds out of her pocket and held them out in her palm. "If you'd like to fetch my mother's jewels, I can give you these in exchange."

"Keep them." He went to the door and called for his butler. They spoke quietly in the doorway for a moment.

Ramsgate returned. "They'll be down in a moment. I will hope our business is now concluded."

"Completely," Beatrix said. "Thank you. Without you, I never would have met Tom." She slid her arm around his waist.

"And I never would have met Beatrix. Yes, thank you. From the bottom of my heart." Thomas bowed.

"To be clear, I do not want to attend your wedding."

"Nor will you be invited," Thomas said with glee.

Ramsgate took a long look at Beatrix, appraising her quite intently. "You do look like your mother. She'd be happy to know you are to be a viscountess." He straightened, running his hand down his coat, over his paunch. "I wish you both well."

Then he left.

A moment later, the butler entered. He handed Beatrix the purple velvet box. She clasped it reverently, her gaze soft as she regarded the treasure.

"May I see you out?" the butler asked with more than a touch of hostility.

Beatrix gave him a sickly sweet smile. *"Please."*

Thomas escorted her downstairs, and Harry followed. Outside, Thomas was glad to see the crowd had dissipated. A few people stood in the square watching. He quickly ushered Beatrix toward his house.

"Ah, my horse," Harry said, drawing Thomas to stop and turn. "I see one of your grooms has him." He nodded toward where one of Thomas's stable lads was tending him.

"I should probably go," Beatrix said, taking her arm from Thomas.

Thomas didn't want that, but for those still watching, they would see her going into his house unchaperoned. "I've never hated rules more than right now."

She laughed. "Before I go, my answer is yes."

He hadn't realized that she didn't give him an answer. So much had happened in the last half hour. He was free. No, not free. He was tangled hopelessly and helplessly with this woman before him, and he didn't want to be any other way.

"I could kiss you."

"But you won't because you're far too proper." She grinned. "Why don't you come for dinner?"

"Ah, Beatrix?" Harry interrupted. "It's Thursday."

They typically had dinner at Aylesbury House with Harry's family on Thursdays. She turned her head toward him. "Are we going tonight? I thought you were on a honeymoon."

Harry shrugged. "Selina and I decided this morning that we would go. She likes my family, what can I say?" He inclined his head toward Thomas. "Why don't you come too? Since you're going to be part of the family soon."

"Thank you, I will."

"See you later," Beatrix started to go, but Thomas stopped her.

He snagged her hand and brought it to his lips. "Regan will be delighted to know you will be her mother. She's been asking when you will return."

"Oh, Tom." Her eyes flashed first with apprehension, and then with hope. "Can I really be her mother?"

"I have no doubt you will be wonderful." Thomas knew in that moment that he'd made the right decision—the best decision of his life. "I meant what I said to the duke," he said softly. "I know precisely who you are, and I want every part of you."

"Good, because you're stuck with me." She blew him a kiss and then joined Harry as he walked his horse toward Cavendish Square.

Thomas watched them until they were gone from sight. Then he turned and strode inside, wondering how difficult it would be to obtain a special license.

~

Following dinner at Aylesbury house, the extended family gathered in the library. Everyone was present, including Rafe and Harry's brother, the Viscount Northwood. But Beatrix scarcely noticed anyone but Tom. They'd been seated side by side at dinner, of course, and had spent the course of the meal furtively touching each other under the table.

Now, in the drawing room, Thomas addressed everyone with Beatrix by his side. "Thank you for inviting me to dinner this evening. While you are no doubt already aware, I wanted to formally announce the betrothal of myself and Miss Beatrix Whitford. She has made me the happiest man alive."

"Not possible," Harry said, grinning from across the room, his arm around Selina, who elbowed him gently.

Thomas laughed. "Very well. I know this betrothal will spur a tidal wave of gossip given the abbreviated length of my mourning period, but as my Aunt Charity has assured me—I will be forgiven since I'm a man with a small child." He glanced toward his aunt, who'd also joined them for dinner.

"Because you are clearly in desperate need of a wife," North cracked.

"As it happens, I am." Thomas looked down at Beatrix. "I'm desperately in need of *this* wife."

Beatrix felt her heart would burst. She could not *wait* to get him alone and hoped that might be possible later.

"Because of that," Thomas said, addressing the room once more, "I will be obtaining a special license tomorrow so that we may be wed on Saturday. Perhaps that will give the gossips something else to talk about." He winked at Beatrix, and she couldn't help but laugh.

"Let them talk about anything they wish," she said.

"My goodness, that is quick," Lady Aylesbury said. "How can we plan a proper wedding breakfast?"

"I would prefer something small—just those who are present, in fact. And my daughter, of course. The wedding will take place at my house as well," he said.

He and Beatrix had discussed this on the way to dinner. She'd ridden to Tom's house with Selina and Harry. They'd all then walked the short distance to Aylesbury House on Mount Street.

"That sounds lovely," Harry's sister Rachel said. "So many weddings." She looked at their brother North, her brow arched. "I think it must be your turn."

North's eyes rounded in horror. "Not me. Him." He jabbed his thumb toward Rafe, who stood to his left.

Rafe simply shook his head, then sipped his port.

At Selina's suggestion, Beatrix wanted to ask

Rafe if he would give her away. She was a bit nervous about it, but Selina had assured her he would be delighted. Even so, Selina had agreed to support her when she asked.

As conversation started around the room, she decided now was as good a time as any. She exchanged a look with Selina who nodded. Beatrix then turned to Tom. "Will you excuse me a moment? I need to speak with Rafe."

"Of course." Tom knew what she meant to ask, for they'd discussed that as well.

Beatrix met Selina near Rafe, then they pulled him into the corner.

"This looks serious," Rafe quipped.

"Not terribly," Beatrix said. "I have a request, and I hope you won't think it too forward since we haven't known each other very long. It's just that, well, I find myself without a father or a brother."

"Not true," Selina said. "You have a brother. He's standing right there." She looked at Rafe expectantly.

"Yes, you do," he assured her. "What do you need?"

"Someone to give me away at the wedding. Would you mind?"

Rafe was silent a moment, his vivid blue eyes settling on her and that orange mark in the right one giving him an added intensity. "It would be my honor," he said softly.

Beatrix relaxed. "Oh, thank you."

He arched a brow at her. "You didn't really think I'd say no?"

"I told her you wouldn't," Selina said.

"I take nothing for granted," Beatrix said in her defense.

"That is an excellent outlook." Rafe pulled a folded piece of parchment from his coat. "I'm glad to have a moment to speak with both of you. I haven't been able to stop thinking about that folly I remembered the other day. I drew a picture of it." He opened the parchment one-handed and showed it to them.

Selina took the drawing and held it for Beatrix to study it along with her.

The illustration was incredibly detailed. It showed a small, templelike building with a statue of a woman in the middle. There were fish and other water creatures around the base.

"This is astonishing," Beatrix said. "I'd no idea you were a skilled artist."

Rafe snorted softly. "I wouldn't say that I'm skilled."

Selina's brow creased as she studied the drawing. "Is that Aphrodite in the center?"

"I think so," Rafe said. "Because she came from the sea."

"You remembered quite a bit of detail," Selina remarked.

"Some of it is my imagination filling things in, but I recall the statue of a woman—a goddess, I am almost certain—and that dolphin in particular. I also recall other fish, but not what they were specifically." He folded the paper and replaced it into his coat. "I'd like to find it."

"I can't imagine it will be difficult given the specifics you remember." Beatrix hoped it would be possible. "Do you think you could discover who your parents were?"

Rafe's eyes took on an even darker intensity. "That is my objective."

Selina touched his arm. "Even if we find the folly, we may not find our parents. What if this is just one place they visited?"

"Presumably, they would have known the owner, and I have to believe that person would know of a couple with small children who visited. Especially since those people died in a fire. That isn't something one forgets, even after twenty-seven years."

"How will you go about finding it?" Beatrix asked.

"I plan to show this drawing to people and ask if they've ever seen a folly like it and that I plan to build one at Spring Hollow." That was the pleasure garden Rafe owned in Clerkenwell.

Selina smiled at him. "A brilliant plan."

Rafe tipped his head and lifted his glass of port. "I hope so."

They spent the rest of the evening as a family should—in conversation and camaraderie. By the time Beatrix left with Tom, Harry, and Selina, her face hurt from laughing.

The walk back to Tom's house took only a few minutes. Harry and Selina's coach was ready, as they'd sent a footman to the Grosvenor Square mews in advance.

"I'm not even going to pretend you're coming with us," Selina said. She kissed Beatrix's cheek. "Just be discreet. Like we were." She sent a sly smile toward Harry.

Harry helped her into the coach and waved at them before they left.

Beatrix took Thomas's hand and led him back down the square.

"Where are we going?" he asked.

"We're being discreet."

"We're going in through the garden, aren't we?"

She narrowed her eyes at him playfully. "Walking in the front door *isn't* discreet."

He laughed. As soon as they were out of the square and in the alley that led to the mews and his back gate, he took her in his arms and kissed her.

Beatrix pressed her body to his and held him tightly. She reluctantly pulled back and tugged him toward the garden. "Come on or we'll never get inside."

"Sorry, I've been waiting an eternity to do that."

Giggling, Beatrix led him into the garden. They walked, hand in hand, to the balcony where Beatrix stopped short. "Is it all right that we will live here?"

"Because of her?" he asked quietly.

Beatrix nodded.

He faced her, taking her other hand too. "When I look at that balcony, I see you climbing over the side and almost-waltzing with me. I don't see sadness. I feel happy. For the first time in ages, I feel *happy*."

"Oh good. I really don't want to move. There's something delicious about living next door to the duke and waving at him as good neighbors do."

Thomas let out a belly laugh. He pulled her toward him and kissed her again. "How I adore you."

"I hope you won't mind if I refurbish her room, however." She didn't think she needed to clarify who "her" was. "I was thinking we could make it into a family sitting room that's less formal than the drawing room and larger than your sitting room—something with toys and maybe a small bed where Regan can sleep if she wanders downstairs. Not that I mind her sleeping with us," she added. "I just thought there might be times when, well, when we..."

Tom clasped her waist and drew her against him. "There will be plenty of those times, including tonight. You, my love, are brilliant."

Waggling her brows at him, she turned and went to the trellis.

"Wait, you aren't going to climb that in your gown, are you?" he asked.

She put her hand on her hip. "Do you have a better suggestion?"

"Perhaps we should go inside and take the stairs."

"I can do it," she said. "Or do you think I can't?" She fluttered her lashes at him.

"You can do anything—of that I'm certain. Let me go first and help you." Tom quickly ascended the trellis and leapt onto the balcony. He held out his hand.

Beatrix grasped the iron and started to climb. "My dress isn't the problem. It's these damned slippers." And she'd even worn her sturdiest pair since they'd planned to walk from Tom's to Aylesbury House. "Useless accessories."

Tom helped her onto the balcony and into his arms. "But they look lovely on your feet."

She lowered her voice to a seductive tone. "Wouldn't they look better off them?"

He swept her into an impromptu waltz straight into the house and onward into his—their—bedchamber. "Most definitely."

EPILOGUE

*T*he afternoon was bright and warm, more like August than June. Thomas swung the picnic basket as he walked beside his cousin-in-law, the Earl of Sutton. Ahead of them were their wives and children—his son and Thomas's daughter.

Wife.

Thomas could scarcely believe he'd married Beatrix two days ago. He *was* the luckiest man alive, regardless of what Harry believed.

Beatrix walked beside Aquilla, and in front of them, the children chased the four kittens, two of whom would be coming home with Regan, much to her delight.

"Look, Bebe, they're chasing a butterfly!" Regan took Beatrix's hand and pulled her forward.

They crested the small hill, and the lake came into view. "Beautiful," Thomas said.

Sutton briefly shielded his eyes. "Thank you. This is a nice spot, especially at this time of year."

They walked down the hill to a flat area in the shade of a tall oak tree. Sutton laid out the blanket he'd carried, and Thomas set the basket down on the edge.

"Regan, don't get too close to the water," Thomas said.

"Yes, Papa." She stopped and looked toward him. "Do kittens like water?"

He smiled at her. "I don't think so, sweeting."

"Oh good." Regan skipped after the largest of the kittens, a fluffy gray one.

Beatrix stood just outside the shade and looked to the other side of the lake, which was long and narrow. "Lord Sutton, does that folly belong to Sutton Park?" She turned her head toward the blanket.

"No. That's Ivy Grove. The lake divides our properties."

"Who owns it?" Beatrix asked.

"The Earl of Stone."

Thomas went and joined Beatrix, snaking his arm around her waist and pulling her against his side. "Devereaux House doesn't have a folly, I'm afraid." He could hardly wait to show her his estate later in the summer.

"I'm interested in *that* folly," she said, her gaze fixed on the small temple. "That's a dolphin at the base, isn't it?"

Thomas looked more closely. "It is indeed. And a whale beside it. I think that must be Aphrodite in the middle, don't you?"

"Yes." Beatrix turned and went back to the blanket.

Aquilla was in the process of laying out the food, but the children were already eating. "I'm afraid I couldn't stop them," she said with a laugh.

"Have you been to that folly?" Beatrix asked, sitting down next to Regan, who was nibbling a strawberry that was turning her fingers red.

"Yes, but not in some time," Sutton said. He looked toward his wife. "I don't think you've ever been there, have you, dear?"

Aquilla shook her head. "I haven't. But I admit I find it fascinating. The sea creatures are splendid."

"The Earl of Stone, you say?" Beatrix asked, sparking Thomas's curiosity. What was this about?

Before he could ask, Beatrix looked at him and barely shook her head. She mouthed, *Later.*

And so it was much later—after they'd returned to London—before Thomas could ask about the folly. He lay in bed as Beatrix emerged from the dressing chamber in a night rail so transparent that it may as well have been nonexistent.

"I like your nightgown very much. But is there really a point to it?" He held the covers back for her.

She glanced down and shrugged. "I suppose not." Then she whipped it over her head and cast it aside before climbing into the bed.

Thomas laughed as he gathered her against him, pulling the bedclothes around her. She snuggled against his chest as he rested against the headboard.

"I've been waiting to hear about your interest in that folly today. What was that about?"

She put her palm on his chest. "It's extraordinary, but I think it may hold the key to finding Selina and Rafe's parents. I told you they died in a fire, and Selina and Rafe were taken in by a man who claimed to be their uncle, but who turned out to be no relation whatsoever."

Thomas wasn't sure he understood. "A folly is the key to finding them?"

"That folly in particular," Beatrix said. "Rafe drew a picture of it from memory—right down to the statue of Aphrodite in the center and the dolphin on the base. He recalls sitting on his mother's lap at the edge of a lake and looking up at that folly. It has to be the same one. He was there as a child."

"He's certain?"

"Quite. He'd forgotten about it until I gave Selina her wedding present—that coral necklace. It's similar to one their mother wore. When Rafe saw it, he recalled the folly."

"Does he think he visited there?"

"He doesn't remember, but perhaps the Earl of Stone can help him. Perhaps the earl knew their parents." She looked up at him, her eyes glowing. "Wouldn't that be wonderful?"

"It would. However, that was a long time ago, wasn't it?"

"Yes, but surely he would remember a couple who died not long after that in a fire."

"Did no one look for the couple's children?" Thomas asked.

"*That* is a mystery. Rafe doesn't know what happened, just that their parents died in the fire and he and Selina were rescued."

"By a man who claimed to be their uncle. That's suspicious, isn't it?"

"He didn't do the actual rescuing. That was their nurse." Beatrix laid her head back against his shoulder. "Rafe remembers the smoke and heat and the nurse taking him and Selina to safety. And telling him that their parents were gone," she said sadly.

Thomas stroked her shoulder. "How tragic. I hope this helps them discover who their parents were." He took a deep breath. "And yet, I worry how that will affect you. If they suddenly have parents—who would be known to the Earl of Stone—where does that leave you, their supposed sister?"

She turned her head and looked up at him, her lips curling into a smile. "You are sweet to think of me, but I don't care where that leaves me. Deborah is still out there and may yet decide to call me a bastard." Beatrix had told him all about Deborah.

"And I don't care if she does," Beatrix continued. "I don't care if people learn I'm illegitimate or that I am not actually related by blood to Rafe or Selina. I have everything I want and need right here." She leaned up and kissed him. "And upstairs." Regan.

Beatrix's love for his daughter was a gift he would cherish for all his days.

"I feel precisely the same way." He kissed her again, his tongue finding hers in a gentle exploration. It wasn't, however, enough. He scooted down and rolled her to her back.

She stroked his face with her fingertips. "You don't mind being married to a thief and a bastard?"

"It's a vast improvement over my last wife." He grimaced. "Sorry, I don't ever mean to compare you. I'm just so damned grateful to have you in my life."

She gave him a soft smile. "I know. We're both lucky. What started as a scandalous bargain between two strangers became something much more."

"It became everything." He lowered his head and kissed her thoroughly—first her mouth, then her neck, then lower still.

She twined her fingers in his hair. "I love you, Tom."

"And I love you, Beatrix." He looked up at her from her navel and gave her a wicked grin. "Let me show you how much."

And so he did.

Want to discover who Rafe and Selina's parents were? Can a disillusioned Society miss heal the heart of a former criminal or will he succumb to the darkness of his past? Find out in the exciting next book in The Pretenders series, A ROGUE TO RUIN!

Thank you so much for reading A Scandalous Bargain! It's the second book in The Pretenders trilogy. I hope you enjoyed it!

Would you like to know when my next book is available and to hear about sales and deals? Sign up for my VIP newsletter at https://www.darcyburke. com/readergroup, follow me on social media: Facebook: https://facebook.com/DarcyBurkeFans

Twitter at @darcyburke
Instagram at darcyburkeauthor
Pinterest at darcyburkewrite
And follow me on Bookbub to receive updates on
pre-orders, new releases, and deals!

**Need more Regency romance? Check out my
other historical series:**

The Untouchables
Swoon over twelve of Society's most eligible and
elusive bachelor peers and the bluestockings,
wallflowers, and outcasts who bring them to their
knees!

The Untouchables: The Spitfire Society
Meet the smart, independent women who've
decided they don't need Society's rules, their
families' expectations, or, most importantly, a
husband. But just because they don't need a man
doesn't mean they might not *want* one…

Wicked Dukes Club
Six books written by me and my BFF, NYT
Bestselling Author Erica Ridley. Meet the
unforgettable men of London's most notorious
tavern, The Wicked Duke. Seductively handsome,
with charm and wit to spare, one night with these
rakes and rogues will never be enough…

Love is All Around
Heartwarming Regency-set retellings of classic
Christmas stories (written after the Regency!)

featuring a cozy village, three siblings, and the best
gift of all: love.

Secrets and Scandals
Six epic stories set in London's glittering
ballrooms and England's lush countryside.

Legendary Rogues
Five intrepid heroines and adventurous heroes
embark on exciting quests across the Georgian
Highlands and Regency England and Wales!

If you like contemporary romance, I hope you'll
check out my **Ribbon Ridge** series available from
Avon Impulse, and the continuation of Ribbon
Ridge in **So Hot**.

I hope you'll consider leaving a review at your
favorite online vendor or networking site!

I appreciate my readers so much. Thank you,
thank you, *thank you*.

ALSO BY DARCY BURKE

Historical Romance

The Untouchables: The Pretenders

A Secret Surrender

A Scandalous Bargain

A Rogue to Ruin

The Untouchables

The Bachelor Earl

The Forbidden Duke

The Duke of Daring

The Duke of Deception

The Duke of Desire

The Duke of Defiance

The Duke of Danger

The Duke of Ice

The Duke of Ruin

The Duke of Lies

The Duke of Seduction

The Duke of Kisses

The Duke of Distraction

The Untouchables: Spitfire Society

Never Have I Ever with a Duke

A Duke is Never Enough

A Duke Will Never Do

Love is All Around

(A Regency Holiday Trilogy)

The Red Hot Earl

The Gift of the Marquess

Joy to the Duke

Wicked Dukes Club

One Night for Seduction by Erica Ridley

One Night of Surrender by Darcy Burke

One Night of Passion by Erica Ridley

One Night of Scandal by Darcy Burke

One Night to Remember by Erica Ridley

One Night of Temptation by Darcy Burke

Legendary Rogues

The Legend of a Rogue

Lady of Desire

Romancing the Earl

Lord of Fortune

Captivating the Scoundrel

Secrets and Scandals

Her Wicked Ways

His Wicked Heart

To Seduce a Scoundrel

To Love a Thief (a novella)

Never Love a Scoundrel

Scoundrel Ever After

Contemporary Romance

Ribbon Ridge

Where the Heart Is (a prequel novella)

Only in My Dreams

Yours to Hold

When Love Happens

The Idea of You

When We Kiss

You're Still the One

Ribbon Ridge: So Hot

So Good

So Right

So Wrong

THE UNTOUCHABLES: THE SPITFIRE SOCIETY SERIES
NEVER HAVE I EVER WITH A DUKE

"Never have I ever given my heart so fast . . . an enticing addiction that stays on your mind and in your heart long after the story is through."

– Hopeless Romantic

'There was such a fabulous build-up to Arabella and Graham's first kiss that when they finally give in to it I wanted to high five somebody.'

– DragonRose Books Galore Reviews

A DUKE IS NEVER ENOUGH

"I loved Phoebe and Marcus! Whether as individuals or together, they are just wonderful on the page. Their banter was delightful, and watching two people who are determined not to start a relationship do exactly that was a whole lot of fun."

– Becky on Books....and Quilts

"I love the passion between Marcus and Phoebe and not just the steamy bedroom scenes they had, but the passionate nature of their relationship. Their feelings for each other went far past that of just the physical even if they didn't re-alize it."

A DUKE WILL NEVER DO

THE UNTOUCHABLES SERIES

THE FORBIDDEN DUKE

THE DUKE of DARING

"You will not be able to put it down once you start. Such a good read."

-Books Need TLC

"An unconventional beauty set on life as a spinster meets the one man who might change her mind, only to find his painful past makes it impossible to love. A wonderfully emotional journey from attraction, to friendship, to a love that conquers all."

-Bronwen Evans, *USA Today* Bestselling Author

THE DUKE of DECEPTION

"...an enjoyable, well-paced story ... Ned and Aquilla are an engaging, well-matched couple – strong, caring and compassionate; and ...it's easy to believe that they will continue to be happy together long after the book is ended."

-All About Romance

"This is my favorite so far in the series! They had chemistry from the moment they met...their passion leaps off the pages."

-Sassy Book Lover

THE DUKE of DESIRE

"Masterfully written with great characterization...with a flourish toward characters, secrets, and romance... Must read addition to "The Untouchables" series!"

"If you are looking for a truly endearing story about two people who take the path least travelled to find the other, with a side of 'YAH THAT'S HOT!' then this book is absolutely for you!"

THE DUKE of DEFIANCE

"This story was so beautifully written, and it hooked me from page one. I couldn't put the book down and just had to read it in one sitting even though it meant reading into the wee hours of the morning."

"I loved the Duke of Defiance! This is the kind of book you hate when it is over and I had to make myself stop reading just so I wouldn't have to leave the fun of Knighton's (aka Bran) and Joanna's story!"

THE DUKE of DANGER

"The sparks fly between them right from the start... the HEA is certainly very hard-won, and well-deserved."

-All About Romance

"Another book hangover by Darcy! Every time I pick a favorite in this series, she tops it. The ending was perfect and made me want more."

-Sassy Book Lover

THE DUKE of ICE

"Each book gets better and better, and this novel was no exception. I think this one may be my fave yet! 5 out 5 for this reader!"

-Front Porch Romance

"An incredibly emotional story...I dare anyone to stop reading once the second half gets under way because this is intense!"

-Buried Under Romance

THE DUKE of RUIN

"This is a fast paced novel that held me until the last page."

-Guilty Pleasures Book Reviews

" ...everything I could ask for in a historical romance... impossible to stop reading."

-The Bookish Sisters

THE DUKE of LIES

"THE DUKE OF LIES is a work of genius! The characters are wonderfully complex, engaging; there is much mystery, and so many, many lies from so many people; I couldn't wait to see it all uncovered."

-Buried Under Romance

"..the epitome of romantic [with]...a bit of danger/action. The main characters are mature, fierce, passionate, and full of surprises. If you are a hopeless romantic and you love reading stories that'll leave you feeling like you're walking on clouds then you need to read this book or maybe even this entire series."

-The Bookish Sisters

THE DUKE of SEDUCTION

"There were tears in my eyes for much of the last 10% of this book. So good!"

-Becky on Books...and Quilts

"An absolute joy to read... I always recommend Darcy!"

THE DUKE of KISSES

"Don't miss this magnificent read. It has some comedic fun, heartfelt relationships, heart-breaking moments, and horrifying danger."

-The Reading Café

"...my favorite story in the series. Fans of Regency romances will definitely enjoy this book."

-Two Ends of the Pen

THE DUKE of DISTRACTION

"Count on Burke to break a heart as only she can. This couple will get under the skin before they steal your heart."

-Hopeless Romantic

"Darcy Burke never disappoints. Her storytelling is just so magical and filled with passion. You will fall in love with the characters and the world she creates!"

-Teatime and Books

LOVE IS ALL AROUND SERIES

THE RED HOT EARL

"Ash and Bianca were such absolutely loveable characters who were perfect for one another and so deserving of love… an un-put-downable, sensitive, and beautiful romance with the perfect combination of heart and heat."

– Love at 1st Read

"Everyone loves a good underdog story and . . . Burke sets out to inspire the soul with a powerful tale of heartwarming proportions. Words fail me but emotions drown me in the most delightful way."

– Hopeless Romantic

THE GIFT OF THE MARQUESS
"This is a truly heartwarming and emotional story from beginning to end!"

– Sassy Booklover

"You could see how much they loved each other and watching them realizing their dreams was joyful to watch!!"

– Romance Junkie

JOY TO THE DUKE

"…I had to wonder how this author could possibly redeem and reform Calder. Never fear – his story was wonderfully written and his redemption was heartwarming."

ONE NIGHT OF TEMPTATION

"One Night of Temptation is a reminder of why I continue to be a Darcy Burke fan. Burke doesn't write damsels in distress."

– Hopeless Romantic

"Darcy has done something I've not seen before and made the hero a rector and she now has me wanting more! Hugh is nothing like you expect him to be and you will love him the minute he winks."

– Sassy Booklover

SECRETS & SCANDALS SERIES

HER WICKED WAYS

"A bad girl heroine steals both the show and a highwayman's heart in Darcy Burke's deliciously wicked debut."

–Courtney Milan, *NYT* Bestselling Author

"…fast paced, very sexy, with engaging characters."

–Smexybooks

HIS WICKED HEART

"Intense and intriguing. Cinderella meets *Fight Club* in a historical romance packed with passion, action and secrets."

–Anna Campbell, *Seven Nights in a Rogue's Bed*

"A romance...to make you smile and sigh...a wonderful read!"

–*Rogues Under the Covers*

TO SEDUCE a SCOUNDREL

"Darcy Burke pulls no punches with this sexy, romantic page-turner. Sevrin and Philippa's story grabs you from the first scene and doesn't let go. *To Seduce a Scoundrel* is simply delicious!"

–Tessa Dare, *NYT* Bestselling Author

"I was captivated on the first page and didn't let go until this glorious book was finished!"

–*Romancing the Book*

TO LOVE a THIEF

"With refreshing circumstances surrounding both the hero and the heroine, a nice little mystery, and a touch of heat, this novella was a perfect way to pass the day."

–*The Romanceaholic*

"A refreshing read with a dash of danger and a little heat. For fans of honorable heroes and fun heroines who know what they want and take it."

-The Luv NV

NEVER LOVE a SCOUNDREL

"I loved the story of these two misfits thumbing their noses at society and finding love." Five stars.

–A Lust for Reading

"A nice mix of intrigue and passion...wonderfully complex characters, with flaws and quirks that will draw you in and steal your heart."

–BookTrib

SCOUNDREL EVER AFTER

"There is something so delicious about a bad boy, no matter what era he is from, and Ethan was definitely delicious."

-A Lust for Reading

"I loved the chemistry between the two main characters...Jagger/Ethan is not what he seems at all and neither is sweet society Miss Audrey. They are believably compatible."

-Confessions of a College Angel

scribe this book! It is wonderfully, magically delicious. It sucked me in from the very first sentence and didn't turn me loose—not even at the end ..."

"If you love a deep, passionate romance with a bit of mystery, then this is the book for you!"
  -Teatime and Books

CAPTIVATING the SCOUNDREL

"I am in absolute awe of this story. Gideon and Daphne stole all of my heart and then some. This book was such a delight to read."

"Darcy knows how to end a series with a bang! Daphne and Gideon are a mix of enemies and allies turned lovers that will have you on the edge of your seat at every turn."

Contemporary Romance

RIBBON RIDGE SERIES

A contemporary family saga featuring the Archer family of sextuplets who return to their small Oregon wine country town to confront tragedy and find love...

The "multilayered plot keeps readers invested in the story line, and the explicit sensuality adds to the excitement that will have readers craving the next Ribbon Ridge offering."

-Library Journal Starred Review on YOURS TO HOLD

"Darcy Burke writes a uniquely touching and heart-warming series about the love, pain, and joys of family as well as the love that feeds your soul when you meet "the one."

-The Many Faces of Romance

I can't tell you how much I love this series. Each book gets better and better.

-Romancing the Readers

"Darcy Burke's Ribbon Ridge series is one of my all-time favorites. Fall in love with the Archer family, I know I did."

-Forever Book Lover

RIBBON RIDGE: SO HOT

SO GOOD

" ...worth the read with its well-written words, beautiful descriptions, and likeable characters...they are flirty, sexy and a match made in wine heaven."

SO RIGHT

SO WRONG

taking your heart and ripping it right out of your chest one second and then the next you are laughing at something the characters are doing."

-Romancing the Readers

Darcy Burke is the USA Today Bestselling Author of sexy, emotional historical and contemporary romance. Darcy wrote her first book at age 11, a happily ever after about a swan addicted to magic and the female swan who loved him, with exceedingly poor illustrations. Join her Reader Club newsletter at https://www. darcyburke.com/readerclub.

A native Oregonian, Darcy lives on the edge of wine country with her guitar-strumming husband, incredibly talented artist daughter, and imaginative son who will almost certainly out-write her one day (that may be tomorrow). They're a crazy cat family with two Bengal cats, a small, fame-seeking cat named after a fruit, an older rescue Maine Coon with attitude to spare, and a collection of neighbor cats who hang out on the deck and occasionally venture inside. You can find Darcy at a winery, in her comfy writing chair balancing her laptop and a cat or three, folding laundry (which she loves), or binge-watching TV with the family. Her happy places are Disneyland, Labor Day weekend at the Gorge, Denmark, and anywhere in the UK—so long as her family is there too. Visit Darcy online at https://www.darcyburke.com and follow her on social media.

facebook.com/DarcyBurkeFans
twitter.com/darcyburke
instagram.com/darcyburkeauthor
pinterest.com/darcyburkewrites
goodreads.com/darcyburke
bookbub.com/authors/darcy-burke

Printed in Great Britain
by Amazon